Graham Travers

Fellow Travellers

Graham Travers

Fellow Travellers

ISBN/EAN: 9783337208776

Printed in Europe, USA, Canada, Australia, Japan

Cover: Foto ©Andreas Hilbeck / pixelio.de

More available books at **www.hansebooks.com**

FELLOW TRAVELLERS

BY

GRAHAM TRAVERS

AUTHOR OF MONA MACLEAN, MEDICAL STUDENT

NEW YORK
D. APPLETON AND COMPANY
1896

CONTENTS.

AFTER MANY DAYS.

I've heard of hearts unkind, kind deeds
With coldness still returning.—WORDSWORTH.

I.

"THIRD-CLASS, if you please," he said brusquely. "A working-man with a family can afford no kick-shaws."

"No," said the young widow, looking up in the rugged face with a tearful smile; "and that is why he can afford to come all these miles without a fee, to visit a sick child!"

"Tut, tut!" he answered shortly. "Will corbies pick oot corbies' een? That wasn't much to do for poor Tom's boy—and yours. Now, don't fret. The child's all right. Keep up his strength, and don't be afraid of fresh air. Good-bye."

"Good-bye," she said, scarcely lowering her voice as much as he could have wished. "God bless you! You are—the shadow of a great rock in a weary land!"

The train was moving slowly out of the station, and the doctor hastily clapped the pockets of his baggy old ulster in search of his daily paper. Its columns had already received much closer attention

1

than he could, as a rule, afford to the claims of poli-
tics; but a newspaper, like most good things, serves
many purposes.

What a fuss that girl did make about nothing to
be sure! She always was a neurotic, fusionless,
anæmic thing. He had told Tom so before the marriage, and he remembered still how indignantly his
old chum had replied, "All right, old boy, many
thanks; but I leave it to you to choose your wife by
the number of her red blood corpuscles!" Tom
was a fool, of course. Next to a meek and quiet
spirit, what did a woman want more than plenty of
red blood corpuscles? Latin and Greek and piano-
playing were a poor business in comparison. Ah,
well! with all her faults, and with all his ill-luck,
poor Tom had at least had a devoted wife. What
was it she had said as the train was moving off?
"The shadow of a great rock in a weary land."
Stuff and nonsense! And yet, perhaps, it was only
fair that someone here and there should look at a
man through rose-coloured spectacles. That didn't
happen too often now that one was growing grumpy
and middle-aged, with no gift for making pretty
speeches, and no belief in the universal divine mission of women!

The doctor folded his paper with a grunt, and
looked almost defiantly at the other occupants of
the carriage.

There were only two. An old lady was nodding
comfortably in the other corner on his own side;
and opposite her sat a young girl gazing intently
out of the window.

"Another neurotic specimen!" thought the doctor almost indignantly, "white lips, and muscles all on the strain! What is the race coming to? And no doubt, if one only knew it, some young fool is daft about her, and declines to concern himself with the number of her red corpuscles!"

As if·in response to his gaze, the girl turned her head, and an unconscious, shuddering sigh revealed yet more clearly the tension of her nerves.

"Or is she in love with him?" went on the merciless critic. "If so, it looks as if he *had* been wise in time,—and this is the result. Rough on her, poor little goose! Would Ethel have looked like that, I wonder, if Tom had taken my advice? Poor Ethel! When all is said, she is a plucky little soul,—considering that Nature never meant her to face the world alone,—and least of all with a delicate child on her hands."

The train drew up at a station, and the old lady, awaking with a start, proceeded hastily to collect her chattels.

The young girl rose with automatic courtesy. "If you will get out first," she said, "I will hand you the things."

But the step was a very high one, and the old lady hesitated.

"Wait a bit," said the doctor gruffly, "I'll go first."

He helped her out carefully, landed the parcels, and then returned to his corner.

"Well, she can't say we're not polite," he remarked with grim humour, as if half ashamed of the trouble he had taken.

The girl smiled in the same absent, preoccupied way. It seemed as if outward things could not penetrate beyond the extreme surface of her mind.

The doctor began to be interested in his companion from a professional point of view. Hers was a striking face, now that he got a good view of it,—not so pretty as Ethel's, but intellectual, cultured; and the pose of the dainty head on its slender neck reminded him irresistibly of one of his own Scotch bluebells.

But surely there was something more amiss even than the want of red corpuscles! Either the girl was on the eve of an illness, or she was in a state of almost unbearable nerve strain. Instinctively the doctor laid his hand on the pocket that contained his clinical thermometer.

For she was not an ordinary hysterical subject by any means. He noted with quiet appreciation how she controlled every muscle when the express whizzed shrieking past; such perfect inhibition was not acquired in a day; and he waited expectantly till he saw the pale face turn a few shades paler when the noise was over.

"Perfectly ridiculous that she should be knocking about the country by herself!" he thought. "I'd like to know what her people are thinking of."

The girl let down the window at this point, and leaned forward to get the full benefit of the sharp air.

"Much better lie down, if you are afraid of fainting," continued the doctor, still to himself. "If I had any voice in the matter, I'd pack you off to do light work on a dairy farm for the next six months. Little goose!—overwrought and underfed to such an extent that she is scarcely responsible for her actions."

He began to wish that she was not so supremely unconscious of his existence. He would have liked to enter into conversation, and to give her the benefit of the wholesome advice that was drifting about in his mind. Overworked country doctors are not often guilty of such weakness, and our friend was far from being an exception to the rule; but the consciousness of his own generosity in making this journey at all, and the pathetic gratitude of the poor little widow, had kindled his mood into an unusually mellow glow.

"The shadow of a great rock in a weary land." The words reminded him of the dreams of his youth, of the hopes and aspirations that had floated through his mind when the great man spoke such thrilling words on Graduation day. Heigho! Life was a great disillusioner—as no doubt the great man knew—but speeches had to be made!

"The shadow of a great rock." Not many of his patients would be disposed to apply those words to him nowadays. They thought him rough and unsympathetic, and rather keen about his hard-earned fees. But then, on the other hand, women had ceased to care about shadow in these times. They preferred the glaring, merciless, all-revealing sunlight. Not Ethel! Ethel was never one of that sort, bless her! Perhaps poor old Tom had not made such a bad choice after all. Heigho! When all was said, they were a poor lot, women, a poor lot,—always excepting, of course, his own little sonsie-faced lassie, who had hated the country, and hated his work, and who lay now asleep in the dreary, unbeautiful kirkyard.

"The shadow of a great rock." Involuntarily he glanced again at his companion, and to his amazement he saw that a complete change had come over her mood. No longer unconscious of his existence, she was gazing at him with such a hungry, searching look that his own glance fell before it. Her eyes were like those of a hunted animal. "Is this a haven," they seemed to say, "or only another snare?"

His curiosity was thoroughly aroused now, and in another moment he turned to her with a preliminary cough.

But she saved him the trouble of breaking the ice.

"You are a doctor, are you not?" she said, controlling her voice with a painful effort, and coming nearer to where he sat.

"I am."

"I wanted to ask you," she went on, struggling to speak dispassionately, "what you would do with me if—if anything should happen to me before I get to my journey's end?"

"What should happen to you?" he asked abruptly.

She did not answer.

"Do you feel ill?"

"No. I don't think so—not exactly ill. I feel"

—she seemed to be gathering her forces for a desperate effort—"as if—as if I were going mad."

Well, this was a plunge into the depths! Fortunately the doctor was an experienced hand, so he held his breath and waited quietly till he came to the surface again.

"In the first place, let me set your mind at rest," he said gruffly; "you are not going mad—this time. In the second place, do you mind telling me why you did not eat a proper breakfast this morning?"

He half expected that she would be angry, but she was obviously too much in earnest for that. A faint smile strove vainly to relax the tension of her face.

"I can't eat," she said shortly.

"That's what fools say. When a wise woman can't eat, she rings the bell and asks for a glass of milk. Did you do that?"

"No." He had succeeded at least in arresting her attention.

"So I thought. And you have given up beef and mutton, haven't you?—such gross, brutal diet! All very well for mere *men!* But a cup of tea fits one so much better for work, doesn't it? That is one of the great economical discoveries that we owe to your sex?"

She was almost laughing now, though rather resentfully.

"I suppose I have given you the right to assume that I am a silly girl; but it is scarcely the case. I am a working woman."

He bowed. "I am not surprised. It seems to my old-fashioned eyes that the one class shades imperceptibly into the other nowadays. My friends in town tell me that every ballroom *coryphée* is either absorbed in some East End mission, or is working up for what she is pleased to call the 'Higher Locals.' Let me own up at once! If you begin to quote Greek, I am lost: and, as for Latin, I don't believe I could write a prescription without abbreviations. Be merciful! I am only a very dull, very humdrum, stupid old country doctor."

"Oh *don't* mock me!" she cried, a rich colour rising into her delicate cheek. "I don't know any Latin and Greek. I thought once I could paint—and—and other people thought so too; but it is all gone. I am a drone—a drone!"

So this was all, was it? She couldn't paint. Was the moon really out of reach, pretty dear? What a shame!—Well, well! He had patients in the workhouse asylum who had gone off their heads for less assignable reason than that. Patience! Let her quiet down a bit and then hear her out.

"I suppose," he said abruptly, "you would think me a boor, if I asked your leave to smoke?"

"I wish you would!"

He produced a well-seasoned old meerschaum, looked at it caressingly, and then held it out to her.

"Isn't that a beauty?" he said.

She smiled. "It's a fine bit of colour."

"So I think." He nodded approvingly, filled the bowl, lighted it deliberately, and drew a few appreciative whiffs.

"Yes," he said, arranging himself more comfortably in his corner, "it's an old friend, and one of the best I've got. It has helped me over many a fret, and at times—not too often—it has shared a bit of honest pleasure. It was given me by a college chum —he's dead now, poor fellow!—the husband of that lady who was with me."

"I know," she cried involuntarily,—"the lady who said you were——"

"Ay," he interrupted grimly. "Her child has been ill, poor thing! She'd have said anything just then. And that reminds me, I am bound in honour to eat the sandwiches she gave me. You'll help me, won't you?"

The very thought of eating made her throat feel like redhot iron, and the sandwiches—produced from a battered, professional bag—smelt strongly, she fancied, of antiseptic bandages; but, conscious as she was beginning to be of how completely she had given herself away, if he had asked her to eat the bandages themselves, she must needs have attemped it.

"Take a mouthful of sherry," he said kindly. "That'll help it down. Feel better now?"

Her answer was an indirect one.

"Oh," she said, rising and walking to the opposite window, "what an utter, *utter* fool you must think me!"

He knocked the ashes from the bowl of his pipe.

"It never does to be in a hurry," he said slowly, "when you're judging which of your fellow-creatures are fools. So much depends on how you look at them. I *don't think*—I have quite made up my mind yet whether you are a fool or no."

She smiled—a wan wintry little smile.

"Oh, I *am* a fool!" she said. "It is past hiding so far as you are concerned. And yet—you are a doctor—you ought to understand. For days past I have been so horribly afraid of going mad. Whenever people looked at me, I fancied they noticed something odd about my actions. Only yesterday —I had gone into a field to gather some coloured berries—not that I cared to have them!—and two men were carting brushwood, and they stopped and watched me—oh——" she pushed away the foot-warmer with a force of which he would not have believed her capable, "it is too ridiculous!"

"Ay," he responded gravely, "it is ridiculous; but I've no doubt it was real enough at the time."

There was silence between them for some moments.

"What put it into your head that you could paint?" he asked suddenly.

She smiled again. A man like this was an entirely new fact in her experience.

"I don't know," she said, "except that I always was painting from the time I could hold a pencil. They all opposed me, my people at home. I mean, they thought I should be content to paint watery landscapes and Christmas cards and useless terra cotta plaques. 'So nice to be able to give pleasure to your friends!' they said. As if at my time of life—I was only a girl then," she interposed naïvely, with a seriousness which tried his gravity almost

beyond endurance—"as if at my time of life I had
any right to be content with work that led nowhere,
that was an end (God forgive the word!) in itself!
As if, indeed, anyone short of an idiot would rest
content with producing rubbish like that!"

He nodded with real appreciation. From widely
different starting-points they had arrived at what
was probably their one foothold of common ground
in the domain of Art.

"However," she continued more brightly, little
guessing how narrow the foothold was, "I got my
way in the end." And she told him a story of
earnest effort, of eager delight in work for work's
sake, of divers small successes, culminating in a
definite result which even his unskilled ears could
roughly appreciate.

"I hope you don't think," she said with sudden
shyness, "that I am giving you the opinion only of
admiring friends. I was never afraid of criticism.
I used to think—then—that there was no delight on
earth like standing by, while some one not only told
me, but *made me see*, where I had failed. And I
think people knew that, more or less, and were
honest with me. They told me, of course, that my
work was crude; but they thought I had ideas, and
an eye for colour, and even some force in my own
small way."

She paused in some confusion.

He nodded gravely. No doubt there was an
undercurrent of profound amusement in his mind;
she took herself and her Art so seriously, this over-
strung child—as if, forsooth, there were not pictures

2

enough in the world! But, as a case, she was interesting; and there was a curious charm about every movement of the harebell head; and—a pathetic little woman had told him only an hour before that he was "the shadow of a great rock in a weary land."

So he nodded gravely, and the girl felt herself lifted, like a stranded boat, on the wave of his strong personality.

"And so," she said, "I seemed all at once to find myself in the running, don't you know? And they told me if I would only undertake a serious bit of work, I should make my mark. I really began to believe myself that I should, and that was a new experience for me! I had never before realized that anything I did was good till one or two people had assured me of it, and I had come to look at it with their eyes. But now I was full of hope and confidence. I chose my subject—I believe I flattered myself that it 'came to me'!—and, after I had made a lot of studies, I ordered a big canvas and began."

She broke off with a sigh that was almost a sob.

"Oh, I can't talk of it!" she said. "I worked hard—tremendously hard, and at first everything seemed to go on as usual. Then I began to feel that there was something inherently wrong; but I had felt that so often before—and just when I was doing what proved to be my best work—that I thrust the idea aside, and worked harder than ever. I knew I was applying myself too constantly, but I could not rest. I felt I must have my fate decided one way or the other. And all the time the feeling that something was wrong kept haunting me, as it had never done before.

"I saw very little of my friends in those days. When they came to the studio, I either did not show them the picture, or I did not encourage anything more than conventional comments.

"But at last one day a friend came in, with whom I had a sort of tradition of mutual honesty. He was a good deal my senior, and he had helped me often, and—I knew he would not find it easy to lie to me. I can't tell you how I felt, how I longed to escape, or hide the picture or anything; but it was too late. There I was, stripped of my defences, and my day of wrath had come!"

The doctor's eyes had been fixed for some moments on the hurrying line of trees above the railway bank, but now he turned and looked sharply at his companion.

Yes, she was thoroughly in earnest. The eager, quivering face bore ample evidence to that; but, apart from the pathological aspect of the case, how supremely ridiculous the whole thing was! What if he should begin to talk about his *Dies Iræ* when a fracture failed to unite, or a patient complained of the effect of a prescription? Nay, he might suggest the expression to his little Polly as a relief to her feelings when her doll's gaudy millinery turned out less satisfactory than usual!

Fortunately the rugged face was but a poor index to the passing thoughts that came and went behind it, so the girl went on—

" He stood behind my stool without speaking for what seemed to me an eternity. Not that there was anything new in that. It was always his way before he criticized anything. The strange thing was that this time he seemed to be struck by his own silence, and he began to praise the pose of this, the drapery of that—any detail that pleased him. I missed the genuine ring in a moment, and I pushed back my seat from the easel, and threw aside my palette. ' In other words,' I said quietly, ' the thing is a failure!' It was hard on him, I know; but I was past caring for him. It was life and death to me. I don't know what he would have said if I had given him time. As it was, he hesitated, and—at least he knew me well enough to see that after that no half-hearted assurances would be of the smallest use. ' The fact is,' he said, ' you're done up. You have been sticking at it too closely. Go off home for a bit and take a rest. You'll make a success of this yet some day.' "

" Excellent advice!" said the doctor, glad to be able to approve of something at last.

" Excellent advice!" she repeated bitterly, " and, like most excellent advice, utterly useless. Rest! How can I rest when I am haunted by the conviction that I have begun to—*decay?* Don't you see— I have staked everything on this? If it fails, I have nothing left. Rest! Oh, how I *could* rest, if I could only do one little bit of good work first!—Just enough to give me one little ray of hope for the future! But, try as I will, I can't; and, if I can't do it to-day, what reason have I to hope that I shall be able to do it to-morrow, or next day, or any day?"

Her companion did not answer. Inured as he was by long discipline, to the constant involuntary self-sacrifice of a country doctor's life, he was almost appalled by the supreme naïve self-absorption of the spoilt child before him. Fortunately her next words struck a chord that vibrated in his being too.

"But the last few days," she went on in a lowered voice, "even that fear has been lost in the other awful fear I told you of. You may guess what it must have been before I let myself be driven to speak of it—even to you!"

There was a long silence. The neuroses of modern life did not bulk very largely in the good doctor's practice; and, when cases did occur, he was apt to classify them under rather unflattering names. If any one else had consulted him about this girl—her mother, for instance—he would have made very short work of the case; a few rough sentences and a brief prescription would have been, in his estimation, amply sufficient to meet its exigencies; and, assuredly no notice of it would have appeared among the meagre and occasional jottings in his case-book. But she was so obviously ill, as she sat in front of him there; her misery was so real to her; her faith in him so pathetic; and, above all, she had so much spirit and pluck in her own odd way,—that, in spite of his utter want of sympathy with her aims, he found himself making a clumsy effort to approach her plane of life and thought.

The train rushed shrieking into a tunnel, and he waited till they emerged into daylight again.

"I suppose you can still draw a straight line?" he asked abruptly.

Her reply was a quivering laugh.

"I don't know," she said. "I don't like to be too sure. Straighter than most people, I suppose."

"Well, then, give a hand to the folks behind you! There's a village school in your parts, I suppose? Why not go and teach the bairns to draw? I don't care much about pictures, but many's the time I have felt the want of not being able to make a bit of a diagram. Why, there are times when a few straight lines save a world of words, and that's a good job, if nothing else is. Depend upon it," he went on, warming to his work as he felt the ground firmer beneath his feet, "you'll never be so badly placed but what you'll find some bit of work at hand that you can *do well*. That's enough to keep any man sane, I take it. If you probe your trouble to the bottom, you'll find you are fretting yourself to death because you can't do the thing you want to. Well, you must just make up your mind to that. Neither I nor anybody else can help you there. The work you want to do won't go undone, never fear. Somebody else is sure to do it for you. Your business is to come down a step, and do the thing you can. God bless my soul, child!" he broke forth impetuously, "who are you that you should pick and choose? Don't you suppose we've all had our dreams?"

There was no answer, and he did not seem to expect one.

"For the rest," he went on, drawing down his brows more grimly, as if a disagreeable duty had to be got over, the sooner the better,—"for the rest, your artist friend was quite right. You've got the glass of your telescope all smudged and begrimed, and here you are (yes, in that respect you *are* a fool, no doubt!) straining your weary eyes to see through it! You'd be better employed if you'd rub up your lenses a bit, and let the stars take care of themselves!"

She looked up half-puzzled, but with a dawning smile of appreciation; and he smiled too, in spite of himself, well pleased that she understood.

Then he put away his pipe, and, frowning, shut the shabby bag with a snap.

"Quite beneath the dignity of a great astronomer, I admit," he said, "to see that his glass is kept clean, but his work won't be good for much if he doesn't! Well, here I am! Do you go much farther? Hallo, what's up?"

The quiet wayside station was a scene of unwonted excitement, and almost before the train had stopped, the station-master opened the carriage-door.

"There's been a terrible accident at the pit, sir," he said, "and everybody is crying out for you. Your man has the gig at the gate."

Without even lifting his hat, the doctor was gone; and so it came to pass that the little girl with the head like a Scotch bluebell passed out of his mind almost as completely as if they had never met.

II.

THE rain had almost ceased now, but a drenching white mist enshrouded everything, making its way into many an unsuspected crevice. The day was darkening fast, and the wheels of the doctor's gig splashed heavily along the muddy road.

"Shoe loose, sir!" exclaimed the young groom.

"Well," growled the doctor, "I suppose I have ears as well as you!"

Poor old doctor! You will see that his temper had not improved in the last ten or twelve years.

The lad looked injured. *He* was wet and hungry too.

"We're so near the smithy, sir," he said, with the air of a man whose wisdom and foresight are not adequately acknowledged by his contemporaries.

"Confound the smithy!" was the surly reply. "That's the man who lamed Darby a month ago. I said then I'd never go back to him, and I won't. Darby will get home all right. I'll take Joan out to-morrow."

But, even as he said it, the horse began to limp unmistakably.

"Just get down and look at his foot, will you? It's the off hind. What like's the shoe?"

The lad dismounted as quickly as his stiff cold limbs would allow.

"There's a nail come loose, that's pricking him, sir; and I can't get it out without the pinchers."

"And where the deuce are the pinchers, I'd like to know? Bless my soul! I might as well bring a

tame cat out with me for all the good you are! Pull
off the shoe, and look sharp! He'll go well enough
without it for all the distance."

The lad stared in amazement.

"Hall right, sir," he said; and a moment later
he added cheerfully, "There's a lot of metal on the
road, sir."

"Light the lamps," said the doctor, pretending
not to hear the last remark. "We'll be having an
accident next."

In another minute they came in sight of the
smithy, which stood some distance back from the
road. The blacksmith's quick ear had caught the
false ring of the loose shoe in the distance, and he
stood now, expectant in the doorway, his figure
forming a fine silhouette, with the ruddy glow of the
furnace behind it.

When the gig had rattled past, he returned to his
forge, with a scowl that gave way to a smile.

"Anybody else 'd 'a bin glad to warm hisself at
the smithy fire on a night like this,—were't nought
else," said he; "but the doctor's the doctor. Well,
he'll find that two can play at that game! My
missis must just make shift wi' the new man when
her time comes round. They say he's clever, for all
he's so young."

Meanwhile the doctor tossed the reins to his
companion, and resigned himself, as he had so often
done before, to passive, hopeless endurance of his
discomfort. There were worse troubles after all
than rain and wind and cold, and—and Ethel had
been more ailing and fretful than usual that morn-

ing. Polly would be at home, to be sure,—bless her sonsie face! If only she and he could have a quiet hour together by the study fire! But what would Ethel say to that?

Poor thing, poor thing! It was a shame to find fault with her. What wonder, with her ill health, that she was jealous and peevish? If she could only get to Bournemouth for a month or two, with that spoilt boy of hers, it would do her all the good in the world. But, alas, the moon itself was not less attainable than Bournemouth just now, when there seemed to be no prospect· of paying the butcher's bill, let alone the school and college fees that were rapidly becoming due!

The doctor leaned forward with a groan, and, as he did so, a stream of water from his shabby umbrella made its icy way inside his soaked woollen comforter; but he did not flinch. What mattered one small discomfort the more? Darby was dead lame now, but at least they were at home.

"Let him stand with his foot in a pail of cold water," said the doctor. "He'll not be much the worse."

"Yes, sir," and the lad shrugged his shoulders in the darkness.

"Oh, dad, darling!" cried Polly's eager voice. "Come in quick! There's a lovely fire in the study, and all sorts of things warming for you. I'll go and see about dinner while you change. Nonsense! I shall kiss you if I choose." There was just the least suggestion of pathos in her laugh as she added, "My poor old frock won't hurt."

The doctor paused for a moment outside the sitting-room door. He knew he ought to look in, and say just a word to his wife, but he *could not do it*, so he tramped on to his own room.

The warmth and glow cheered him in spite of himself, and a quarter of an hour later, when he went in to dinner, he stopped to kiss the pale woman on the sofa.

"Well, old lady," he said with gruff kindness, "how do you feel now?"

Poor Ethel! She had thought of him so much all day, when she heard the rain pattering against the window-panes; but now that she had listened to Polly's eager greeting in the hall, her own kind words froze on her lips.

"It matters little how I feel," she said.

The doctor was sorely tempted to say that it mattered a good deal to *him* how she felt, when he came in at night worn out and longing for rest; but, with a mighty effort, he held his peace. He knew her well enough to be quite sure that she would have given a good deal not to speak those chilling words; but he knew too that the remorse she felt would not prevent her from doing the same thing again and again and again, though all the time she was acutely conscious that such words were daily widening the breach between her husband and herself.

Fortunately Polly came in at this moment. When she was at home she never allowed the slatternly maid-of-all-work to wait on her father. As soon as she had left the room with the empty soup-plate,

Ethel tried to say something kind. It would not have been possible for her to say it in Polly's hearing. It was always so easy for the bright attractive idolized girl to trump her stepmother's ace.

"You must be very tired," she remarked gently. "I hope you won't be called out again to-night."

"I'm sure I hope not. Has anybody been? Somebody said Mrs. Steele's boy was ill."

His tone did not respond to her advance, and she answered coldly.

"Yes, Jane saw Dr. Maxwell's carriage at the Steeles' door."

"Nonsense! Not Mrs. Steele's!"

"Yes."

"She must have known I was away, and got frightened——"

"No," continued Ethel firmly. "Jane spoke to the coachman, and he said Mrs. Steele had mentioned in her message that she wanted Dr. Maxwell to attend them for the future."

"Shows what a confounded cad the man must be to undertake it without a word to me. I'll see myself far enough before I help him out of a——"

The doctor stopped short. With all his faults and misfortunes, he had not sunk so low as that. So he changed the line of attack.

"I wish to goodness," he exclaimed, "that you would forbid your servants to chatter all over the place. The wonder is that I have any patients at all, with all this backstairs gossip going on."

"Pray ring the bell, and give any orders you choose. It is two months now since you asked me

to put a stop to Susan's gossiping—or was it Mary
Ann then? I did my poor best, with the result that
each tit-bit was flavoured with, 'Now mind you don't
let on as I told you. They'd be that mad if it got
talked about.'"

To show an angry man that he is wrong is rarely
the way to pacify him; but Ethel had not finished
her say.

"As to Mrs. Steele," she continued, with a bitter
little smile, "I have been expecting it all along.
There are not many eligible men in this place, and
her two eldest daughters are getting on!"

He might have said the same thing himself in a
cynical moment, but he could not stand it from her.

"Well, of all the women who belittle their own
sex," he exclaimed angrily, pushing his chair back
from the table, "you are about the worst! I
don't wonder Polly calls herself a 'woman's rights
woman'!"

"Nor do I," was the quick rejoinder, "when her
father gives in to every whim she has. If it were
poor little Algy now——"

"I am *so* sorry you have had to wait, father
dear!" said Polly, entering the room with a tray,
her bright face flushed with her unwonted culinary
experiments. "I was showing Jane how a steak
ought to be cooked, and she says my way takes
'longer than hers!"

She set down the tray, and looked up with a
smile at her own expense; but the smile vanished in
a moment when she saw the faces of the other two.
Things had never been so bad as this when she had

been at home before; and now, of course, it was not
to be expected of human nature that she should see
both sides of the question.

"Oh, *poor* Father!" she said, leaning her head
wearily against the wall when she had left the room,
"and there will be no end to it—no end—no end!"

"Well," said the doctor, when the door had closed
behind her, "you were saying something, I think.
If it were Algernon——?"

"*There!*" exclaimed Ethel indignantly. "It all
lies in that one word—*Algernon.* You have your own
Jack and Polly. Would you speak of a son of your
own as *Algernon?*"

"God forbid," said he devoutly, "that any son
of mine should come by such a name! But "—he
attacked the steak vigorously—" I'm blest if I know
what you would have! I'm rough enough with my
tongue at times, God knows! But I've never said a
rough word to him."

"Precisely!" she answered bitterly. "You have
said plenty of rough words to Polly."

"Look here, Ethel," he said, forcing himself to
speak calmly. "We've been over this ground a
hundred times; but, if it will give you any satisfaction, we'll go over it for the hundred and first. My
bairns have faults of their own, and, as you say, I've
been down on them sharply enough; but at least I
have some idea *what they would be at.* Your son I
simply cannot understand. His mother thinks and
plans for his welfare night and day, but he never
gives her a thought in return: with infinite trouble
we get him on the foundation at Charterhouse, and

—after being warned—he gets himself expelled. No doubt I'm old-fashioned and out of date, but I frankly confess that a lad of that kind has no place in my reckoning. I ventured once or twice to say a word, a word meant in all kindness; but you know what the result of that was. I don't want to be hard on any one whose nature is a complete enigma to me, so I simply give him a wide berth."

"Poor little Algy!" she sobbed. "I sometimes think it would have been better for him—if—if—you had never made that journey twelve years ago, and saved his life!"

The doctor smiled grimly. So he and his wife had one thought in common after all.

"And no doubt you think the next journey I made in the same direction might also have been omitted with advantage?"

She sobbed outright. "Oh, I know you only did it out of pity! and I have been a terrible drag on you ever since! If it were not for Algy, I should pray God——"

"Oh, drop that!" he cried savagely; and then he was ashamed of himself.

"Look here, Ethel," he said, rising and sitting on the sofa beside her. "Can't you see that I am dead-tired, and sick at heart? Don't hit a fellow when he's down!"

She was genuinely sorry for him, and strove to forgive the bitter words. "Well, dear," she said, stroking his rough hand, "you know you have brought a double day's work upon yourself, because Polly plagued you to take her to town to-morrow.

And then—if you *will* give your son and daughter
an expensive education—why do you stay on here?
You are only losing one patient after another.
What chance can you possibly have against an un-
married man with £300 a-year of his own? The
butcher has been here again to-day——"

He sprang to his feet with an oath on his lips,
and just then Jane opened the door.

"If you please, sir," she said, "that's Jim to
know if there's any more orders."

"No," said the doctor shortly. "You said no
one wanted me?" he added, turning to his wife.

"No," she answered, "Mrs. Napier sent to ask if
you would look in to-morrow or next day."

The doctor sighed. "Good soul!" he said
wearily.

"No doubt," said Ethel quietly; "but I think it
would puzzle you to name her complaint. If I had
a face like a winter apple I'd be ashamed to have
a doctor dangling about me continually. Talk of
fancies!"

"Ay," he said sternly, splitting a large coal with
a neat thrust of the poker. "She's given to fancies,
and she's taken a mighty queer one at present. She
thinks she sees the wolf approaching the door of an
old friend, and she's minded to ward it off if she
can. The simplest thing would be to send him a
cheque for £20 or so—upon my soul, I don't know
that I'd refuse it!—but she thinks I'd be insulted, so
she puts herself to infinite trouble and invents no
end of imaginary ailments. She must know that I
see through it all; I don't think she ever took me

exactly for a fool; but she knows too (God help me!) that I can't afford to charge her with it."

He shook himself like a great dog, and strode out of the room.

" Polly," he shouted recklessly. " Come and have a chat in the study!"

Polly needed no second call. In another moment she was seated on the rug, with her head on her father's knee—in one of those easy unconstrained attitudes that bespeak long habit.

He lighted his precious old meerschaum, and, for a time, they sat in silence.

" Heigho, Polly," he said at last. " It's a weary world!"

She drew a long breath of relief. She had wanted so much to speak.

" I've been horribly selfish, Dad darling," she said, " but indeed it was sheer stupidity. I did honestly think that a day in town would be a sort of a holiday for you too!"

" And so it will, my bird," he said, striving to speak cheerfully; " you won't ask me to look at pictures *all* day, will you."

" Poor bullied old Dad! I'll tell you my plan. We'll go straight to the Academy, so as to see the pictures in some peace before the crowd comes; and you and I will trot round for about an hour. Then the Trelawneys are to meet me,—I shall be so proud to show them my noble old Dad, with his 'crown of glory'!—and in due season they will carry me off to lunch. You will be under oath to get a good lunch too, and then you shall spend the whole afternoon

3

with your cronies. You always have so much to say
to them."

He winced. The main thing he had to say to
them next day was that he must borrow money
somewhere! But there was no need to tell Polly
that.

"Then," she continued, "the Trelawneys will
conduct me to the station in the evening to meet
you——"

"Ay," he said, "in a carriage and pair, with a
footman to wait on my Polly. Poor little Cinder-
ella! and it has all got to turn into a pumpkin
again!"

"Now that is exactly what I want to speak to you
about. It ought never to be anything but a pumpkin. I hate to drive in state while my grand old
dad goes on the top of the bus. I only come by my
smart friends because you insist on sending me to a
first-class school. My honours are earned by the
sweat of your brow, and they're too dear,—a world
too dear! I won't have it. No, no, Dad! My
education is finished. Once for all I am on strike.
I won't go back!"

He did not speak immediately.

"Polly, lass," he said at length, "you know it's
an old-fashioned fad of mine that my bairns should
do as they're bid; but I'll give you my reasons for
this. I have often told you that your grandfather
and grandmother were quite common folk—as this
world reckons commonness; but they were proud
and Scotch, and they made up their minds that their
son should go to college. So they stinted and well-

nigh starved, and in due time I took my degree.
My Mother was never given to wearing her heart on
her sleeve, but when she saw me capped, she sobbed
out loud, so that all the people round could hear—
'That's him noo! That's oor Jock!' As if it was
me all the folk had come to see!"

He stopped and bit his lip.

"They've both been in the kirkyard this many a
year," he said; "but I can't bear to think that my
Mother's saving and starving should all have been
for nought." He paused and broke in eagerly upon
his own thoughts. "It wasn't for nought, Polly,
lass," he cried. "It wasn't for nought! No doubt
I'd have done better at the plough, but I can at
least give a lift to my bairns; and it was for them
she saved, Polly, not for me. Don't you see?"

But Polly saw nothing—with her bodily eye at
least—save a blazing blur of flame through a blinding mist of tears.

"I once made sure you'd marry," he went on
after a pause; "but it's astonishing how a man's
notions change; and at least I won't have you
driven to do it. You are just the sort of lass who
could make her own way, if you were so minded;
and your education isn't going to prevent your taking the right man if you find him."

There was another long silence before he continued—

"You're so nearly through, now, both you and
Jack, that I'd be loath to give it up. I may be
driven to it, but I'll live on oatcake and brose first!
Such a little would do it! I only want a lift for the

next year or two. I don't deny that there's some difficulty just now, but I can't think but what we'll get past it somehow. I'll be honest with you, Polly, because I know you won't make a fuss when you see it's for your father's sake as well as for your own;—when you know that the education of his bairns is your poor old dad's main stake in life nowadays. I lost some hundreds this winter in an investment. I've aye been over canny with my money, so Dame Fortune turned her back on me when I lippened to her for once. And then—although this new man hasn't taken many of my patients, he has taken some of the ones that pay best. You see he lives in style compared with me; and it's something worth paying for to have a carriage like that stop at one's door!"

This was the first time the subject of the new doctor had been broached between father and daughter.

"I can't think how they can be such *fools!*" cried Polly indignantly. "A whipper-snapper like that! And, Father, if you only *saw* how he bandaged Joe Simpson's leg! I am sure *Darby* could have done it better."

"Ay," said he. "He's one of the kind they turn out in plenty nowadays; all theory and no grit. I am told he laughs at what he is pleased to call my 'exploded idees'; but give us an epidemic or a pit accident, and I'd like to know where he'd be! I can't think that it'll last. I've taken his measure pretty well, and surely other folks will do the same in time. They may want to marry their daughters,

as Ethel says; but they can't want to *bury* them.
The fact is, he's the fashion just now, and it's mainly
my own fault. I have been so crabbed and cross-
grained at times, and folk couldn't know all I had
to worry me."

Polly did not answer. Her father had never
taken her into his confidence like this before, and
her words would not come.

"But you mustn't blame Ethel," he continued
presently. "God knows it's more my fault than
hers! The truth is, we've seen too much of each
other lately. If she could only get away for a
change, we might both make a fresh start; but of
course that is out of the question. Well, good
night, little woman! You should have been asleep
an hour ago."

She rose and kissed him. "Oh, if only everybody knew what a hero my daddy is!"

"There, there!" said he smiling. "He's a poor
grumpy old fellow; but you can tell the folks he
wants no pity as long as he's got his lass!"

III.

TRULY a fickle goddess is this weather of ours!
After days of rain and wintry cold, the sun rose into
an unclouded sky, and the gay toilettes on the steps
of Burlington House were a wonder and delight to
happy Polly.

"Don't get a catalogue, Dad," she whispered.
"We don't need it a bit."

The next moment she could scarcely believe in her own tactlessness; but her father was in no mood to take offence.

"All right, my bairn," he said kindly. "It isn't a shilling catalogue that will make me or break me."

So they got the catalogue, and made their way into the great galleries, feeling lost and bewildered, as well they might; but, before they had gone far, a friend of the doctor's came up to them with outstretched hand.

"Well," he said quietly, when the conversation came to a natural pause, "did you sit for the portrait?"

"What on earth do you mean?"

His friend looked at him in musing scrutiny.

"It was not taken yesterday," he said, "nor yet last year. Now that I see you the resemblance strikes me less; but it is certainly *there*. One of the pictures of the year, too, by Jove! But there! Go and see it for yourself—241."

Polly hastily turned up the number in her catalogue.

"The Shadow of a great Rock," she read out.

"*What!*" exclaimed the doctor. He had not forgotten the day when Ethel spoke those memorable words.

Polly repeated the name; and, without another word, they made their way up to the picture.

It was well hung; and the pleasant balancing of light and shade, together with the warm broad harmony of colour, would have struck an art critic who saw it from the other end of the room; but it was not such things as these that interested the doctor. Unless the anatomy of a figure, or the general perspective, was gravely at fault, he saw little in a painting beyond its subject, and a certain ill-defined quality which he called "life-likeness." In other words, so far as his criticism went, it was good.

And certainly there was nothing to jar on him here.

The picture represented a garret, with a poor bed, on which a sick girl lay apparently asleep. The doctor stood by her side, in a stream of light from above, his whole being absorbed in observation and profound thought, one hand resting on the patient's wrist so gently that she did not stir, the other held up quietly to prevent the eager mother, who had just rushed into the room, from awakening her.

A number of artists were discussing the technical value of the picture; but, from the point of view of the public, its great merit lay in the doctor's face.

It was not that of the ideal Christ, as painters have loved to picture it under all conditions: there were too many hard lines in it for that. It was rather—if one may be allowed the comparison—the face of Jehovah, as He might have appeared to a devout Jew in the days of Isaiah,—all-seeing, resolute, self-contained, yet with strangely tender lines about the mouth. One felt that the brain behind that face had grasped the situation down to its minutest details, though not a ripple of emotion was allowed to appear on the surface; and, on gazing,

one became conscious of a sensation of infinite rest;
one ceased to ask what was the matter, or whether
the girl would live or die. It was enough that a
man with a face like that had taken the burden on
his shoulders.

"It is an inspiration," said one gazer, with tears
in her eyes. "She can never have seen a face like
that!" and, though the speaker unconsciously turned
to the doctor as she spoke, it never occurred·to her
to think, "She saw it here!"

And yet it was like him, though the difference
was greater far than the resemblance. It was his
face etherealized, with the querulous lines of irritation wiped ont, and something kindled behind it
purer, nobler, truer, than the poor old doctor's dim
ideals.

"I am free to confess," said their cicerone after a
long silence, "that it is somewhat idealized, but you
see the resemblance, don't you?"-

"It's not a bit idealized!" said Polly indignantly.
"Of course he doesn't look like that when Jane lights
the fire with the *British Medical*, but if *you* sat on the
rug at his feet as I do in the evening——"

"He would doubtless say, 'Get out, you beast!'
but I daren't even picture to myself how he would
look!"

The doctor had not been listening to them. "I
can't see an atom of resemblance," he said quietly.
"Who painted it?"

"Miss Beauchamp. She has been coming steadily
to the front for some time, but there is no doubt this
is her *chef d'œuvre*. She told a friend of mine she

had had it in her mind for years. If you don't mind waiting, I may be able to point her out to you! She's not above the pretty weakness of listening to the criticisms of outsiders. She has had a number of good pictures in the Academy, and my friend says the success of her studio is astonishing. She has a perfect genius for teaching,—or perhaps an 'infinite capacity for taking pains'! I believe she can't take half the pupils who want to come to her. There's a fine tocher awaiting the happy man when he comes along, but they say she's quite content as she is. She's not young, either,—not so young as she looks. Here she comes,—watch!"

They did watch, with the result that the approaching lady's attention was attracted in a moment. She glanced at all three, but she only *looked* at the doctor, and—as the look deepened into a gaze—a wonderful, spontaneous smile and blush swept over her sweet, frank face.

"Oh," she cried impulsively, holding out both hands, "how I have longed to meet you again!"

The doctor was no society man at the best of times, and now he was more completely taken aback than he had ever been in his life before. He was profoundly conscious of the faintly perfumed presence of a beautifully dressed woman, in whom the lithe slimness of girlhood was giving place to the matronly curves of middle life; but his amazement and perplexity were so great as scarcely to leave room even for regret that so charming a greeting could not possibly be meant for him.

"I am sure I beg your pardon, madam," he stam-

mered out with an awkward bow, "but I'm afraid
you have made a mistake."

"Oh, no, that is impossible! But if I had not
been taken so completely by surprise, I should not
have forgotten that you could not possibly remember me. Shall we go over to that settee—people
will stare so if we talk in front of my own picture—
and I will tell you all about it?"

She leaned back with the air of a woman accustomed to luxurious surroundings, while the doctor
sat bolt upright, prepared to take himself off at a
moment's notice, so certain was he that this curious
interview must come to a speedy end.

"Do you happen to remember," she began slowly,
wondering how she could best open the subject, "a
journey you made from Longhurst to Eastdean some
eleven or twelve years ago? A lady in mourning
came with you to the station——"

"Yes," he said; and he added gravely, "The lady
is now my wife."

"Ah!" she answered brightly, "then you are sure
to remember it. And—do you think you can recall a
sickly nervous girl who happened to be in the same
compartment, and to whom you were surely kinder
than ever stranger was to stranger since the days of
the Good Samaritan?"

He looked at her hard for a minute or so.

"God bless my soul!" he began, almost inaudibly.
"You were never her?"

She smiled.

"It seems to come back to me that I have seen
you somewhere," he went on with characteristic

honesty, forgetting to remove his trying gaze.
Years had taken from her something of the dainty,
harebell effect by which he could best have recalled
her. "But I'd never have recognized you. And
yet I don't know how I could forget a face like
yours. I remember all about it now——" He
laughed softly, as he might have laughed with Polly
at the remembrance of some childish folly she had
long outgrown. "——You were vexed because you
couldn't paint!"

The words were out before they struck him as
having any connection with the present circumstances; and now, as the idea rushed tardily into his
mind, the hot blood rushed into his face.

"I haven't the least recollection what I said to
you," he stammered, "but of course I had no notion
that you were capable of the like of that."

"I suppose that is why you did me so much
good," she answered quietly. "You see I had been
frightfully spoilt by my artist friends. I cared for
nothing but pictures and music. I hadn't even read
Carlyle! You seemed to me so *big* in your scorn of
my gods. You took me out of myself as I had
never been taken before; and then you reminded
me that each of us is responsible first of all for being
a human being. If in addition to that we chance to
be poets or musicians or painters, the added responsibility is entirely a secondary one, and may never
for a moment justly usurp the place of the first."

"It seems to me," said the doctor, "that you are
still mistaking me for someone else. I have no
doubt that what you say is true; but I never thought

it, much less said it, and indeed I'm not quite sure
that I even understand it!"

She laughed pleasantly. "We won't argue about
it," she said.

> "'As long as my life endures,
> I feel I shall owe you a debt,
> That I never can hope to pay.'

If you have forgotten all your good deeds, as you
have this one—what a pleasant surprise you will get
when you follow after them to judgment! I suppose," she added, half wistfully, after a pause, "you
are engaged to lunch?"

"No," he said, turning to Polly for the first time.
"My daughter is, but I am not."

Miss Beauchamp's soft laugh had a curious
break in it, that might almost have been a sob, but
for her beaming eyes. "My lucky star must indeed
be in the ascendant to-day! Is this your daughter?
I hope we shall be good friends some day, and I
hope you will let me make the acquaintance of your
wife too."

Polly had been waiting for an opportunity to
introduce her father to Mrs. Trelawney; and now,
after a few friendly words, the two parties separated.

"I had no idea you knew Miss Beauchamp," said
the great lady to Polly. "I wonder if your father
would say a word to her for Alice? Miss Beauchamp
refused her as a pupil on the ground that her number was made up; but your father's influence might
make a difference,—he seems to know her well."

And Polly, who had been wondering greatly what might be the meaning of the morning's proceedings, answered discreetly—
"I will speak to him about it this evening."

Scarcely a word passed between the artist and the doctor, as they made their way to her home, a fine roomy house in a green unfashionable square. Fortunately the doctor was quite unaware of the effect of the spring sunshine on his shabby Sunday coat; and he could scarcely have believed that it wellnigh brought the tears to his companion's eyes.

"These are the two studios," she said brightly; "one for my pupils and one for myself. I pay them a visit more or less often, according as Jekyll or Hyde gets the upper hand. No, no! You didn't think I meant to take you round! I am sure you have seen pictures enough for one day. Come to my den!"

"And now," he said, when lunch was over, and they were comfortably installed in the most beautiful room he had ever seen, "I want to hear all about it. Did you get safe home that day?"

"Oh yes! Fortunately I got a touch of pleurisy on the way down, and, as soon as the doctor could give it a *name*, of course I didn't care what befel me. It was a long time before my strength really came back to me, though I 'rubbed up my lenses' to the best of my ability. But it was the other part of your advice that came to me like a tonic when I was getting stronger. I could not paint, of course; but it was perfectly true that there was always some

simple thing at hand that I *could do well;* and indeed I soon learned that, if you do a thing just
tolerably, people are only too ready to recognise it
and to say 'Go up higher!'

"Do you remember telling me to teach in the
village school? It was a long time before they
would let me, but I got my way at last." She
laughed at the recollection. "Poor little chaps, I
am afraid it was sore drudgery for most of them. I
hadn't many Raphaels or Angelos, but a number
learned enough to be useful, and I think one or two
may 'live to be hung'!"

She rose from her low easy-chair, and, kneeling
on the soft white rug, began absently to brush up
the hearth.

"By the way," she said, trying to speak lightly
in spite of the colour that rose to her face, "you
must meet all sorts of people in your practice. If
you come across a struggling genius, it would be a
real kindness to let me know. I am simply rolling in
money." Her voice shook slightly, and the move-
ments of the hearthbrush became more aimless and
uncertain. "It is not only my pictures; they bring
in a windfall from time to time; but my studio is
the fashion just now, and—with my quiet ways—I
don't know what to do with all that comes in. Comfort, and even beauty, cost so much less than
show!"

The colour had been rising steadily in his rugged
face too. Was this his chance? No, no! Not her!
Not her! Think of presuming on a fanciful claim
like that, when he had not even recognized her!

It was a minute before he spoke, and then it was only to say very gruffly,

" Well, I'm sure it is time I was going! "

" No, no! " she said desperately, and, as she spoke, a vivid mental picture rose before her of Polly's faded frock. " I have more to say to you first."

With a mighty effort she threw her nervousness to the winds. " Listen," she said, turning to him with a pretty, girlish smile that became her well. " I owe you so much, that I have a right to ask a favour. Twelve years ago, when you were a total stranger, I took you into my confidence, as I never took man or woman before or since. God knows I have had no cause to regret it; but I don't need to tell you that there have been depressed and cynical moments when I have called myself a fool, and have wished with all my heart that I had given myself away less completely. So you see you have it in your power to be very generous now. You can take away such thoughts for ever. *Give me back what I gave you then!* Tell me about your life! It is not for nothing that your face is so worn and your hair so white."

There was silence for a moment, and then he opened his lips to speak, but a great sob broke from him unawares. He made haste to cover it with a cough, but the attempt was a failure. The sob remained a fact; it seemed to go echoing on in the room long after the actual sound must have ceased.

So, as soon as he could regain control of his voice, he told her—with such reservations as a husband or wife must make—the story of his life since they met, of his worries and frets and disappointments and trials.

She listened with breathless interest. "And do you mean to say," she said at last, "that *you* want money?—only money!"

"Mainly," he said grimly. "Money is a good deal to some of us."

"Oh," she cried, "what a pity I did not give you my name that day! Perhaps you would have seen —that I was getting on; and it might have occurred to you that the mouse's turn had come!"

"No doubt I should have seen your name," he said, smiling in spite of himself, "but I am at a loss even now to know what the poor old beast did for the mouse! I wonder what it was I really said? —Some platitude, no doubt, out of which you have been weaving all sorts of pretty things."

"Perhaps it was a platitude," she said musing. "Most things are till the right moment comes, and the right lips speak them."

"And the right ears hear them."

"And the right ears hear them!" she admitted. "To me what you said was simply the key of the universe. It came just at the right moment—at the turning-point of my life, when I was just beginning to be wise enough to take it in."

"I am afraid I can't take credit to myself for that."

She smiled.

"Your credit is your affair: my debt is mine. I can never repay it, you know. I shall wear my shackles proudly and thankfully all my life. And yet——" She sprang to her feet and clasped her hands behind her, unconscious of the tears that were raining down her cheeks. "——do you know, I can scarcely believe in my own happiness? I didn't deserve it a bit. Are you sure it isn't a day-dream?—a castle in the air?"

She dropped her hands again, with a long sigh; and it seemed to him that the soft, sweet curves of childhood had taken possession of her face as she went on, "I shall never even ask to paint a good picture again! I have had my share of happiness for this life,—'full measure, pressed down, shaken together, and running over'!"

THE EXAMINER'S CONSCIENCE.

If there's a hole in a' your coats,
I rede you tent it.—BURNS.

I.

PERHAPS I ought to say quite definitely at once that the examiner had a conscience.

I wish to make this clear at the outset, not because I have any doubt of the reader's discernment; but because—titles are such misleading things nowadays! and besides, even when philosophers have had their say, conscience remains for most of us a relative thing, and we are almost tempted to think at times that, in the special walks of life, one would require a technical education before pronouncing wisely and fairly on the morality of any given act.

Of course we all number divers examiners among our acquaintance, and excellent cronies they often make, with their booty of entertaining anecdotes snatched from the quivering minds of their tortured victims. Very frank and communicative they sometimes are; but their world of conscience, their standard of morality, remains for the most part a *hortus inclusus ;* they don't talk much about that.

44

And this is why I say at once that the examiner
had a conscience.

A cynic might seek to explain the persistence of
this "appendage" by the fact that the examiner
had been only recently appointed,—but the cynical aspect of the case has nothing to do with the
story.

The day was grim and cloudy and bitterly cold.
A frostwork tracery of curling fronds and stately
firs and leafless branches obscured the windows of
the railway carriage, and the examiner was fain to
turn up the collar of his fur coat and to draw his cap
over his eyes as he ensconced himself in a comfortable corner.

Truly it was no joke travelling across country to
examine fellows in such weather as this; and indeed
the January examination was on the whole an un-
satisfactory one in any weather. Capable men who
knew their work went in at the end of term in April
or July. January was the innings of the fellows who
had failed or "funked."

The examiner was young and enthusiastic, and he
knew his work, so he was not nervous about his own
share of the programme; moreover he possessed the
gift—so useful to examiners—of keeping a firm hand
on the helm of a *Vivâ voce* examination, instead of
weakly delivering it over to the wily candidate; and
yet, when the occasion tempted him to experiment,
he could cede it gracefully enough (is it not here
indeed that the very essence of the humour of an
examination comes in—from the examiner's point of
view ?), and watch with amusement or admiration, as

the case might be, the use the poor devil would make of it.

Thus it is evident that, in addition to a conscience, the examiner was possessed of real ability, and that, if he sinned, it cannot be said of him—what unsuccessful candidates are so generously ready to say of their examiners—that he sinned in ignorance.

The train drew up at a provincial station, and a blast of biting wind came in at the opening door.

The examiner shivered and scowled, but withdrew his tacit remonstrance as his eye fell on a peach-blossom face framed in soft brown hair and cheap but becoming fur.

"Jump in, Dick!" said a girl's pleasant voice.

Dick had a peach-blossom complexion too, but it failed to convey any impression of beauty. Indeed his whole appearance was commonplace and underbred. Obviously Nature had tried her 'prentice hand on him before she made his sister.

"Jump in!" he repeated derisively, showing a row of faulty teeth as he spoke. "First-class!"

"Yes, certainly First-class," she urged with pretty motherly solicitude. "I've taken your ticket now, so you must. It is bad enough to have to travel at all in this weather with your cough, you poor boy!"

She coughed herself as she spoke, and drew him gently towards the carriage. Neither of them took any notice of the passenger in the corner, and indeed he was so wrapped up in furs that he looked more like a mighty chrysalis than a human being.

"You know," the girl continued softly, "we shall

be all right once you get on the register; and I am quite quite sure you are going to pass this time—you have worked so splendidly!"

"Yes," he said, with a feeble, flattered, anxious smile; "I don't see how I can miss it,—if I get an examiner who knows his work."

"Oh, but I am sure you will—this time! Only don't mix up aconite and atropine, as you did last night. Do you know what I found, Dick,—just outside the booking-office? Look!" She held up a battered threepenny-bit with a hole in it. "Isn't that lucky? Do you think it would be better for me to wear it round my neck or for you?"

"I think you had better."

"Very well, I will; and I'll think of you every single minute till you come back. I *know* you'll pass, but—" she hesitated, "—you won't fret, dear, will you—whatever happens? You are off now. Take my shawl to put over your knees."

"A woman's shawl!" he said, with a somewhat fatuous laugh.

She lowered her voice. "It is very warm," she said coaxingly, "and no one will notice that it isn't a plaid. Take it quick. Good-bye! God bless you!"

The train moved off, but only to stop a moment later, and then the bright face appeared at the window again.

"What do you think has come by the train? A turkey from Uncle Jack! So the fatted calf is all ready for you. Isn't that a good omen? Uncle Jack is beginning to see that you are a person of

some importance after all. Won't we make a night
of it when you come back ?"

The train was really off now, and the examiner
looked out from the small space between his cap and
his collar at the other occupant of the carriage.

So this was one of the candidates, was it ?—this
poor little chap who "mixed up aconite and atropine"! and, even if he got his diploma, what use did
he suppose it was going to be to him in the teeth of
such obvious physical disqualifications ? Why, his
course of study had almost finished him. There was
no stamina left to begin practice with. Experience
proved that a doctor could get along without super-
fluous strength—or breeding—or ability—or learning; but even the great gullible public scarcely
liked to dispense with all four !

The examiner sighed. He was used to candidates
who ought to be at the plough; but it was ridiculous
to think of the plough in connection with this poor
lad. It was a little difficult to say where his niche
was to be found in the economy of Nature.

The young man had taken a well-worn book
from his pocket, and was poring over the contents,
muttering to himself the while, and turning over
the leaves with moistened thumb. The examiner
recognized the volume in question. It was a cram
book to which he had a particular dislike. From
time to time the reader stopped and hastily turned
back a few pages, with an expression of intense anxiety, having evidently forgotten some fact he had
just read.

It was all the examiner could do to help hold his

peace. "Put that away, you fool!" he longed to
say. "Isn't that poor weak brain of yours quite
muddled enough already?"

At the next stoppage an elderly lady entered the
carriage. She looked at the student with pitying
motherly interest, and took an early opportunity of
offering him a cough-lozenge.

He seemed grateful for a little human sympathy.

"Beastly nuisance going up for an exam.!" he
said.

"Is that what you are doing? Poor thing! But
it will be a comfort to get it over, won't it?"

He nodded doubtfully. "If I do get it over!"
Then the kindness of her face moved his facile nature to unnecessary confession. "I have been
ploughed four times," he said.

"Poor boy! How dreadful! But I am sure you
know your work this time. You look as if you had
been reading very hard."

He shook his head. "I don't know it any better
than I did last time," he said doggedly. "I can't
think how I failed. It's all luck. You see some
of the examiners have written books, and they all
have theories of their own; and, if you don't happen
to have read the book, or heard the theory, it's all
up with you! There are such a lot of them, too—
examiners, I mean—and you never know beforehand
who you are going to get. And, with the best will
in the world, one can't read everything!"

The lady looked horrified, as well she might.
"How very unfair," she said. "How—how *small-
minded!*"

The examiner glowed inwardly with a sense of injustice, but he did not fight with foemen unworthy of his steel, and—the situation had a humour of its own. Besides, if he revealed himself now, he would only shake the little chap's nerve at the eleventh hour, and give his poor petty mind reason to believe for evermore that these indiscreet disclosures was the cause of a failure which seemed to the examiner almost a foregone conclusion.

"Well, when you do pass," continued the friendly lady, "I hope you will get rid of that troublesome cough. Can't you get away to the south for a bit?"

"Oh, bless me, no! I'm as fit as a fiddle. We've been a bit hard up the last few months,"—he glanced at the shabby wisp of crape on his sleeve—"but we'll be all right when the fees begin to come in."

Her kind eyes yearned over him.

"But I am told they don't always begin to come in very fast—just at once, you know."

He laughed and rubbed his hands. "Oh, I'm not afraid. Quite a lot of people have consulted me about odds and ends lately,—of course they couldn't offer me fees before I was qualified. The fact is, I have a sort of knack of getting on with people. There is a great deal in manner!"

Her face fell. Poor boy! So there was—a great deal in manner!

"I wish you would give me your name and address," she said at last, rather doubtfully. "I might be able to be of use to you sometime."

"Flattered, I'm sure." He tore a leaf out of his

notebook, and handed it to her with a bow that was meant to be gallant.

Just then the train drew up at the terminus, and the young fellow jumped out to join some companions on the platform. The examiner saw him make a motion with his head in the direction of the motherly lady.

"Odious little brute!" he ejaculated, as he exchanged his fur cap for a professional-looking hat. "I suppose you are telling them that 'the old girl was awfully smitten with you.' I should like to knock you down—if Nature had not done that already!"

II.

IT was growing late, and the examiners were very tired. What they really wanted was a brilliant candidate to wake them up, but the brilliant candidate was not forthcoming.

"Bless my soul!" said an elderly man, stretching himself with a yawn. "They are always talking of the extent to which we have raised the standard of the examinations. I wish they would raise the standard of the men a bit. We ask stiffer questions than our fathers did, but we don't get half such good answers. The thing's as broad as it's long—or broader."

The speaker was a specialist, and much dreaded by the students as a merciless examiner.

"Well," he continued in a tone of resignation, "let us have the next man in! Have you got his paper? Richard Allison? How does he stand so far?"

Our friend glanced at the paper with furrowed brows.

"Written—rather feeble," he said. He mentioned the figures, of course; but the reader need not be troubled with *minutiæ*. "Clinical—somewhat better. He will have to do a pretty fair *Vivâ*, if he means to get through."

"That is precisely the position most of them are in," said the elder man with a grunt. "Lucky for him that your marking leans to mercy's side!"

"I am afraid that benefit is somewhat neutralized by your questions," retorted the other, smiling.

The door opened and the candidate was ushered in. Poor Dick! It was well for his quivering nerves that he failed to recognise in the tall well-groomed examiner the amorphous chrysalis of the railway-carriage.

I know of few things more remarkable than the variety of views which obtain among candidates as to the bearing, conduct, and mode of speech which are most likely to propitiate the bloodthirsty examiner. A whole volume of folklore might be written on the subject by anyone who took the trouble to investigate it; but for the present it is sufficient to say that Dick's idea of ingratiation was to walk in with a jaunty air of confidence and self-satisfaction.

Three well-planted questions from the elder man, uttered very slowly, and with a manner absolutely unsympathetic and non-committal, were sufficient to destroy these flimsy outworks; and, at the

end of five minutes, poor Dick had forgotten that
he had a manner. He sat there with crimson cheeks,
with parched mouth, with beads of perspiration on
his brow,—his whole *physique* the exponent of simple
mental anguish.

Not that he was altogether a fraud by any means.
It was easy to see that he had read much, and, in a
sense, carefully. But he possessed the cast of mind,
so irritating to some examiners, and so difficult at
all times to appraise fairly, which seems to nibble
indefinitely round a subject, without ever being able
to take a good bite. It may be that he was in no
way responsible for this,—that he simply belonged by
nature to the great psychological class of *Rodentia*.

The younger examiner raised his eyebrows as he
bent over the paper before him, and reflected—not
for the first time that day—that his *confrère* was a
trifle severe.

At this moment a tall urbane-looking individual
in broadcloth entered the room and bent over the
elder man. " One word, doctor," he said, and whispered in his ear.

The communication seemed to be of some importance, for the examiner laid down the "specimen " he was holding, and rose from his chair with
a frown. Then, as an afterthought, he turned to his
colleague.

" Just get on—get done," he said in an undertone. " This is the last candidate, I believe ; " and
he drew his friend over to the fire.

The younger examiner raised his eyes to the tortured face beside him.

"Keep cool," he said roughly but kindly. "Don't lose your head. I've no doubt you can answer the questions I am going to ask."

But the friendly words seemed to come too late. Dick felt himself sinking into a bottomless abyss. He lost all sense of time and place, and there was a great surging in his ears. The questions still seemed to reach him, however, from somewhere, in a queer far-away voice; and, with a last instinct of self-preservation, he tried to shout back the reply.

"That will do," said the examiner at last.

The words seemed to break a spell, but still Dick sat in his chair without moving.

"That will do," repeated the examiner. "You may go."

Could it really be over? It seemed to have lasted an eternity, and yet he could not believe that it had come to an end. He had ceased somehow to believe that it ever would come to an end; and now, following quick on the heels of his relief, came an awful sense of despair.

He had failed again, of course; he never, never would pass now; and Kate had worn her poor little threepenny-bit in vain!

The tears rushed into his eyes, and he turned to the examiner a face from which all the vulgarity seemed to have melted away. It might almost have been his sister's face, and there flashed across the examiner's mind the thought of the "fatted calf"!

The candidate had left the room, and the senior examiner still stood by the fire with his friend.

Slowly the younger man added up the figures. They fell short without doubt, though not so very far short, and indeed he knew quite well that the man was *not* up to the mark. And yet—the poor fellow had done his best; it was morally certain that he never would do better, if indeed——

The examiner thought of the lad's cough, and again he saw the sweet, flower-like face at the window. " No one will notice that it isn't a plaid," he heard the girl say, with a queer little throb in her anxious, motherly voice; and then—he took up his pen.

" By Jove ! " said the elder man a minute later. " Do you mean to say that fellow has passed ? I am afraid, sir, you haven't sufficient regard for the standard of a noble profession ! "

" He picked up a bit after you were gone," said the other indifferently—and with doubtful veracity. " He obviously isn't in a state of health to do himself justice."

Some half-dozen men were assembled in the waiting-room when Dick came out.

" Hallo ! " they said, when they read the report in his altered face.

" I tell you what it is, you fellows," he said, sitting down, "I'll just go and cut my throat. I can't face it. It's the fifth time, and I really did know my work. Upon my soul and conscience, I did. I daren't go home. I——" He stopped.

" My governor will be awfully down on me too," said another man grimly.

"*Governor!*" repeated Dick. "If it were my *governor!*" But again he pulled up short. Even he could not talk of his sister here.

"We all seem to be in the same boat this time," remarked a man with a turn for philosophy. "My opinion is they are asking deuced unfair questions. What do you think the fellow said to me? 'How does the psoas get out of the pelvis?' As if anybody ever thought of that! *I've* never seen it in any of the books. Well, what's the odds? It's all in the day's work. They give back part of the fees, don't they? Let's go and have a jolly good spree!"

"Galbraith!" said the porter

"Oh, Lor'!" exclaimed the men, for the moment had come now when they must go in one by one to learn their fate.

The extra assessors had arrived, and a formidable circle was assembled in the council-room. Dick never knew how he commanded himself sufficiently to walk in when his turn came.

"I have to tell you, Mr. Allison," said the chairman without effusion, "that you have satisfied the examiners."

Dick staggered, and caught hold of the back of a chair. "Beg pardon," he gasped with quivering face, "did you say—I'd *passed?*"

The chairman nodded, and pointed in the direction of the roll-books. "Sign your name," he said shortly.

"And now that you are likely to have a little spare time, you might take a few lessons in hand-

writing," said the custodian of the first book severely, as he surveyed the shaky sprawling sig-
nature.

" You seemed surprised at the result," murmured
another member of the *Vehmgericht.*

But Dick's jaunty manner had returned in full
force.

" Oh, no," he said, " I wasn't really afraid, but it's
always a relief."

" Humph ! Very great relief, I should think.
I should advise you to call for your marks to-
morrow."

Dick entered the waiting-room with a bound.
" Passed ! " he cried, with his arms in the air.
" Passed ! passed ! " and seizing his cap, he rushed
out into the street.

There he stopped and looked at his watch. In
another moment he was tearing along in the direction of the railway station as fast as his exhausted
limbs could carry him.

III.

I HAVE said quite truly that the cynical aspect
of the case has nothing to do with the story; and
yet it seems necessary to remind the reader at this
point that the examiner had been only recently appointed. In this connection it may be well to add
that—although he did not yet see his way to pay the
rent of the house he had taken—he was rapidly getting into busy practice, and that he was still young

enough to be deeply interested in the behaviour of
his favourite microbe.

So what with one thing and another, I suppose
he began to get overworked; and although to all
appearance as robust as ever, gradually fell into the
state of health in which a man is no fair match for
his conscience.

"Examinations are not a true test!" he exclaimed,
as he lay with sleepless eyes in the small hours of the
morning.

"Then why be an examiner?" said Conscience
placidly.

"And, indeed, what does school and hospital
work amount to at the best?" he continued, striving to shut her words out of his consciousness.
"Good doctors get their education from their first
year's patients; bad doctors never get it at all."

"Hitherto," said Conscience, "you have invari-
ably argued on the other side of the question.
If you have changed your views, why be an
examiner?"

"Why not I as well as another? Public opinion
demands that someone shall do the work."

"And does public opinion demand that someone
shall turn it into a farce?"

"I didn't turn it into a farce," retorted the examiner hotly. "The fellow had worked well."

"Perhaps public opinion would have preferred
that he had worked wisely. In any case the fact
remains that better men were ploughed."

"The poor chap was run down and out of
health."

" No doubt in after years it would be a consolation to his patients to know that he was allowed to pass, because the Board of Examiners considered him physically as well as intellectually incompetent."

" Bless my soul !" cried the examiner, unconsciously falling back into the words of Mephistopheles. " He is not the first ! "

" True," said Conscience, " but he is the first for whom *you* are responsible."

Conscience knew her man,—as she usually does. The shaft struck home.

The examiner became more indignant.

" I am not paid," he said, " to be a mere reckoning-machine. You can't express everything in figures. Even in an examination the vital spark must come in somewhere."

" No doubt. But there wasn't much vital spark about this man, was there ? From the point of view of the public, he could have been very well expressed in figures—with a *minus* sign before them perhaps ? "

" Unfortunately we can't provide all humanity with perfect doctors."

" True," said Conscience. " Is that any reason for not providing them with the best we can ? "

" And if I had ploughed the fellow and sent him off in despair, you would have worried me about that."

" I might have worried the *man*," said Conscience candidly ; " certainly not the examiner."

5

There was no reply, but Conscience is never content with the mere triumph of getting the last word.

"Most of this argument is quite beside the point," she pursued remorselessly. "The case lies in a nut-shell. You were appointed to a position of public trust, and you have failed in carrying it out—not some wild high-flown ideal of your own—but the ordinary, decent, commonplace expectations of your fellow-men."

And so on *da capo*. It is extraordinary of how much reiteration the human mind is capable, in the small hours of the morning.

"I wish to goodness I had waylaid the fellow on his way out of the council-room," he said wearily, "and advised him to take some post-graduate classes."

But even as he spoke, he knew that the wish was perfectly futile. In the face of such obvious poverty, what hope was there of post-graduate classes?

The examiner sat for a long time before the dressing-table with his face buried in his hands.

"It would be ridiculous to go and look the fellow up, and see what he is doing," he said at last; "and besides it would imply that I wasn't easy in my mind at having passed him."

This, of course, was obviously ridiculous.

The weeks went on. With the yielding of the frost, there came a violent outbreak of influenza, and, as doctor after doctor succumbed to the prevailing malady, the popular practitioners among the residue were hard pressed to fit in their daily quota of visits.

For some time the weather was mild, damp, relaxing, and in every way favourable to the persecutions of conscience; but, suddenly in the middle of March, a sharp frost set in, working havoc among all the young green things, which had been tempted into a deceitful world under false pretences.

"Thank heaven!" ejaculated the examiner, as he awoke from a good night's sleep to feel a sharp, stimulating bite in the morning air.

Among his letters that morning was one from an old college chum.

"—I wish you could spare time to run down and see a case with me. You might be able to suggest something I haven't thought of. It is just the sort of thing you used to be strong on. . . . I don't think it is a matter of life and death, but it hangs fire in a way I don't like; and I've had a run of ill-luck lately. What a hydra-headed brute this influenza is!"

The examiner took out his pocket time-table, and glanced again at the address on the paper. Surely he had some special association with that place? Ah, yes, to be sure! It was there that fellow had got into the train,—"Dick"—Dick—what was his name? Richard Allison. It would be interesting to hear what he was doing, poor chap—he, and that "airy fairy" sister of his. Assuredly it would be

•

worth while to go and see the case. It would be killing two birds with one stone.

A few hours later the consultation was satisfactorily over and the two medical men stood together on the doorstep.

"I think I'll walk to the station if you don't mind," said the examiner, buttoning his overcoat across his broad chest. "I see I have time."

"Ah, you miss your comfortable brougham. All right. I'll send the trap home, and walk with you. It will suit me just as well. You have taken a load off my mind. I never believed in luck till a few weeks ago."

"And you are not going to believe in it now," said his companion, reassuringly. "By the way, do you happen to know a young fellow—a doctor, Richard Allison?"

The other started. "Did you know him?"

"Slightly." The examiner refused to notice the past tense. "He wasn't very fit, poor chap. Is his home hereabout?"

"Under the mools," said the other with dismal stoicism. "He died last week. It was awfully hard on me; I lost two cases in one house; but the truth was they gave neither themselves nor me a chance. I believe they were half-starved."

"Good Lord! Is the sister dead too?"

The other nodded.

"This way," he said. "There's a short cut through the churchyard. It's an awfully pathetic story all round. You know Allison had failed over and over again in his Final."

" Yes ? "

" He ought to have given up long ago, but the family were all sanguine—and phthisical. Dick's passing always represented the coming in of their ship. Everything was to be *couleur de rose* when that consummation was achieved. It was perfectly amazing how they never seemed to doubt that the guineas would begin to roll in as soon as his plate was on the door. He lost two sisters during his course of study, and last autumn the father died, leaving him and one sister alone. The father never appeared to do much, but his death seems to have made a difference to them, poor things !

" Well, I can't think how it was managed, but in January Dick did contrive to squeeze through ; and if he had been senior wrangler or—or prime minister, his sister could not have made more fuss about it. She——" The speaker paused and broke a twig from a frost-bound willow-tree. ——" She was an awfully lovable girl ! I never could make out what she saw in the little chap, till—till the end came.

" I believe they had a royal feast the night he came home. A turkey had been sent them from somewhere, and—the poor girl went to the inn for half a bottle of champagne. Awful trash it must have been ; but neither of them would know that. The next day a plate appeared miraculously on the gate,—' Dr. Richard Allison.' I confess I was annoyed, for of course he had no right to the title. I wish to heaven I had let it alone, but I spoke to him about it, and he—well, he wasn't very civil. That afternoon the sister called and told me they had ordered the plate years and years ago, when he went up for his University Final. They were all so sure he would pass! 'But he is a doctor, isn't he?' she asked naïvely.

"Certainly," I replied; 'legally he is as much a doctor as I am.'

" Poor thing, she was looking so bonny that day, but the excitement and strain and privation had been too much for her. The family malady came down like a wolf on the fold,—you know how it can come!—and then I found out what she saw in her brother."

" But had they no friends to help them?"

" Well, you see, they were proud, and the poor fellow hadn't the knack of making himself very popular. He had a great notion that professional men should take their position in society (God help us!), and society didn't see it. Anybody might have taken up his sister, but he was one of the people who always seem to take liberties when one shows them a little attention. Of course everything was changed as soon as folks realized how ill his sister was. One lady alone, whom he had only met incidentally in the train, sent enough soup and jelly and fruit to stock a small hospital, but it was all too late."

" And the lad?"

"I gave him some work to do for me, partly to help the exchequer, and partly to give her the impression that Dick was making a practice. There was a lot of influenza about, and he took it. I sent him to bed; but it was no use; he was in his sister's room the moment my back was turned. There was no deliberate self-sacrifice about it. He had just picked up that she was really going to die, and from that moment he simply did not *know* that he had a life of his own. He stayed with her night and day till the end, and then—he went down like a stone. I don't wonder,—she was an awfully lovable girl!"

The speaker cleared his throat noisily, and there was a pause before he proceeded with studied indifference,—

" So then of course folks discovered that he was a hero—look!"

The sun had shone forth brightly about noon, melting the snow that had fallen in the night, and kindling into something of a glow the marble whiteness of that great bank of flowers.

"How pleased he would be, poor chap! I hope he sees it. It can't do anyone else any good."

"It does me a little, I confess," said the examiner quietly. "When you come to think of it, what more can the best of us do than go to our death in absolute self-forgetfulness? I am glad folks saw it."

The other did not answer immediately. "Oh, there is nothing to regret," he said coldly. "When a family gets into that state there is nothing for it but——"

" The short cut through the churchyard ? "

" Ay. Shall we go ? "

The examiner nodded; but he did not follow his friend at once. A whole flood of thought was surging through his mind. He noticed absently now that the flowers were too transparent, and that a faint breath of decay was mingled with their fragrance.

Poor boy, poor little girl! Youth ought to be so full of roses and sunshine and vitality; and their share of the beauty of life had surely been but melting snow and tainted lilies. Poor boy! Poor little girl!

It was very irrational, of course. The examiner knew as well as you or I could tell him that the morality of his action was in no way affected by the mound of fading blossoms at his feet; and yet, as he turned away, in the teeth of a cutting wind, the remembrance of that one fatted calf rushed across his mind again with a glow of real thanksgiving, and, in some odd illogical way, his conscience was appeased.

A GREAT GULF.

Oh Galuppi, Baldasarro, this is very sad to find !
I can hardly misconceive you ; it would prove me deaf and blind;
But although I take your meaning, 'tis with such a heavy mind.
                                           ROBERT BROWNING.

I.

IT was Thursday afternoon, and they were standing on the platform at Victoria, awaiting the depart-
ure of the Club train. The beautiful girl was ac-
companied by her maid, and the plain young woman
by a friend.

"Fine eyes," observed the plain young woman
quietly.

Her companion nodded. "Pretty gown," she
added indifferently.

"Actress ? "

"American, I should think."

Their friendly interest was not reciprocated.
Under ordinary circumstances plain young women
had no existence for the beautiful girl.

"Well, keep your spirits up ! " she was saying
with easy familiarity to her maid. "And you will
get those sleeves brought up to date a bit, won't
you ? I shall be back very soon, and next time I
will take you with me."

Ten minutes later the train was well on its way, and the girl was absorbed in a Society journal. The plain young woman had extracted Morley's "Compromise" from an unpretentious travelling-bag, but her eye wandered incessantly from the page to rest with keen physical satisfaction on the exquisite profile in front of her. "I wish I could alter the contour of the hat a little," she said to herself critically, "but the face is perfect."

The train rattled on, the voices of the other passengers rose and fell: a lad, hawking swallow-bedecked post-cards, stopped expectantly in front of the two girls; but his diagnosis was at fault; the symbolism was too obvious for the one, too far-fetched for the other. The waiter with afternoon tea found a better market, and, as the two travellers simultaneously raised their cups, their eyes met, and, quite involuntarily, they exchanged a smile. The car rocked from side to side. With a frown of impatience the beautiful girl rose, and laid her cup on the table at which the other was sitting.

"It is getting dark," she said tentatively.

"Very." The tone was encouraging on the whole.

"Do you cross to-night?"

"Yes."

"Do you think it will be rough?"

"I hope not."

"Are you a good sailor?"

"Not very. Are you?"

"Oh yes. I am an old hand."

The plain young woman smiled, and withdrew

into the shelter of her Morley. When they arrived at Dover she rose, and, with that quiet unselfconscious independence which characterizes the plain young woman of the present day, she handed her bag to the first porter who entered the car, and followed him out into the night. She was obliged to follow him rather rapidly, for, regarded simply as a " fare," the plain young woman is not very promising, and the porter was anxious to get back to the train in time to secure another. So they hurried along the platform and down the quay; and then, timidly groping her way down the dark steps, the young woman found herself on deck.

The December evening was mild as May; the water plashed softly against the vessel and the quay. A delicious sense of holiday, of escape from all restraint, came upon her. Her figure grew lithe and agile under the severe folds of the shabby travelling-cloak, and with a step as light and elastic as that of a child, she sprang up and down companion-ways, reconnòitring the vessel from stem to stern. In the course of her exploration she came upon her acquaintance of the teacups, and, in the fulness of her heart at the moment, would have stopped to speak; but the beautiful girl was engaged in conversation with a man. Even in that dim light the plain young woman was struck by his military bearing and quiet air of distinction.

" I wonder," she mused, as she seated herself in a dark exposed corner of the deck, and allowed herself to be wrapped up to the ears in tarpaulin,—" I wonder whether he is a total stranger, a chance ac-

quaintance, or an old friend. Given a girl like that,
it is impossible to say. Nature seems to mix some
people without throwing in so much as a suggestion
of immortality."

A wholly unconscious smile of superiority played
on her lip, but it vanished in an instant, giving place
to her wonted expression of quiet thought.

The wind blew hard; the Channel steamer rose
and fell on the dancing waves; the lights of land
died away in the distance, and came to view again;
and then, with a heavy sigh, as of one roused from
a pleasant dream, the young woman went below to
wash the brine from her lips, and smooth her rebel-
lious locks.

To her surprise the beautiful girl rose limp and
bedraggled from a couch in the saloon.

" I've been deadly sick," she said, turning feebly
to the mirror,—" for the first time in my life too!
And I do believe," she added resentfully, " you have
been enjoying it ! "

The plain young woman tried in vain to conceal
the physical exhilaration that radiated from her
whole being. " I am a most disreputable object,"
she said, laughing, as she carelessly straightened her
hat. " I hope you will feel all right now that the
pitching is over. Good evening."

Without giving another thought to her companion, she turned to leave the saloon ; but a few
minutes later, when she entered the dining-car
on the train, the beautiful girl motioned to her
eagerly.

" Do come and sit at my table ! " she said

"These men stare so if a woman chances to be alone."

The plain young woman smiled. *She* had never been inconvenienced by the staring of the men. As she sat down, her eye fell for the first time on a pair of long white hands, blazing with diamonds and emeralds. To her inexperienced eyes the jewels seemed priceless, and a pang of something like fear shot through her. " Emancipated " as she was, she could still be afraid of her own sex ; but another look at the girl's face reassured her.

" I hope you feel better," she said pleasantly.

" Thanks. I shall be all right when I have had a pint of champagne. There is nothing like it, is there ? "

" I suppose not, but I am not an authority. Champagne hasn't come much in my way."

" Are you going far ? "

" To Cannes."

" I never heard of that place. How do you spell it ? "

" C-a-n-n-e-s."

" I should call that cans," said the girl placidly. " Where is it ? Anywhere near Monte Carlo ? "

" Yes ; some thirty miles away, I should think— on this side the frontier."

" I mean to go to Monte Carlo later in the season —not this time. I am just running over to Paris to get a few gowns from Worth. I often do that. They can't make gowns in England at all. You'll see, of course, that this is a Redfern I have on. I got it in a hurry, and it does to knock about in."

The plain young woman looked down at her own home-made serge with keen appreciation of the humour of the situation. "I think even that gown will pass muster," she said, smiling.

"Oh, I know I am looking a fright this evening," said the girl discontentedly, turning to the mirror, and trying to arrange her fringe. Then a new thought struck her. "How old do you think I am?" she asked suddenly.

"I can't guess ages."

"Never mind. You won't offend me. Guess!"

"Twenty——five," said the young woman slowly, subtracting a year or two from her mental estimate.

"I thought you would say twenty-seven. Everybody says so, but I am only twenty-three. It's my manner, I suppose. You see I have knocked about so much. I believe I have travelled over the whole world! Usually I take my maid with me, but I couldn't afford it this time. Poor girl, she was awfully disappointed!"

She sighed, and then took up an evening paper that lay on the table beside her. "Do you know anything about gold shares?" she said.

"I am told they are an amusing thing to play with if you have a few hundreds to lose."

The girl looked up anxiously. "But I haven't a few hundreds to lose," she exclaimed hastily. "I hate losing money. Do you really know anything against them?"

She seemed so genuinely distressed that the young woman hastened to reassure her,

" Don't mind me," she said. " I am shamefully
ignorant about these things. If your man of business advised the investment, no doubt it is all
right."

" He didn't advise it. I was determined to have
them. A friend of mine made heaps of money in
gold mines, and I don't see why I shouldn't make a
little. It takes such a lot of money to live nowadays," she added pathetically. "Just look at this
bill !—seventeen francs—that is nearly a pound—for
a single dinner ! And what can one do ? One must
have a little wine !"

In another moment her whole face lighted up. A
man was walking up the car with a lady on his arm,
and she raised her eyes to bow to him. The jewels
flashed more brilliantly than ever ; the picturesque
hat was pushed back ; the wine had lent a more sen-
suous charm to the beautiful face ; but one man at
least was guiltless of the indiscretion of "staring" :
the man who had spoken to her on the steamer
passed her now without a glance.

A cloud like the sudden chill of sunset came over
her face. "Come," she said sharply, "let us go."
When they reached the corridor she added, " The
man will be making up your berth, so you can come
to my den for a bit. I told them I should not lie
down, as I leave the train at Paris."

They entered the tiny half-compartment, and the
girl lifted a sealskin coat from the seat. "It got
wet on the steamer," she said, "and I spread it out
to dry. If you don't mind, we'll put it over our
knees."

"Great honour for me to be clad in such raiment for once!"

The owner of the coat stroked it caressingly.

"You see the line where it was joined, though, don't you?" she said, with serious, childlike simplicity. "They said it wouldn't show, but it does. It was so awfully unlucky! I bought it *just* before long coats came in, and there it was, useless! But you should see my *new* sealskin! Such a beauty—nearly down to my feet!"

"Do you know," said the plain young woman deliberately, but with a very pleasant smile, "that you are a most extravagant young woman?"

"I know," was the eager, self-satisfied response. "In dress I am. You see, dress is my hobby. I have got some lovely gowns I wish I could show them to you!"

"I wish you could. I love pretty gowns."

A cloud came over the beautiful face again, and the girl sighed. "But it's all no use," she said pathetically. "I have no chance to wear them. They are simply thrown away. That is why I am going to Monte Carlo. They do dress there, don't they?"

The young woman looked up with a feeling of something like reverence for such utter frankness. "I don't know," she said quietly. "I have never been on the Riviera. I am only going now for my health—or I should not be travelling in state like this."

The girl frowned slightly, as if a disagreeable subject had been broached. "How horrid for you!" she said, rather coldly.

A silence fell on them after that. The train rattled on through the night. The lamp was reflected in each window, but nothing else was visible. It seemed to the plain young woman as if two oddly assorted human souls were adrift on a raft in the midst of eternity. Perhaps some such thought was vaguely present also in the mind of the other, for what little conventionality they both possessed dropped from them like a garment. It was the girl who broke the silence.

"I am feeling awfully low," she said suddenly.

A luminous sympathetic smile brightened the young woman's face. "Are you?" she said. "Am I to ask questions?"

"I don't fancy I could answer them if you did. Do you know what it is to feel as if you were always just within reach of something, and yet never could quite get hold of it?"

"I do indeed." The young woman began to modify her original estimate of her companion on the raft.

"It is so queer," continued the girl. "All we have got, people can take from us; but the one thing that is really our own is the power to think our own thoughts. Nobody can get hold of that. They think they have us in their power, but that one thing they never can get. We are under their very eyes, but they can't see us a bit."

She paused. "And yet," she added suddenly, with a revulsion of feeling that was almost dramatic in its expression, "the very thing we dread most is to sit and think our own thoughts. We knock about

6

and talk and travel, and do anything rather than think. That is why I like my maid so much. She chatters away, and never lets me think. I wish I had brought her with me! I wish I had her to-night!"

The young woman could scarcely find words. This was indeed a turning of the tables. A moment before she had prided herself innocently on being able to sympathize with an enthusiasm for dress; and now, behold, without any flourish of trumpets, an incursion had been made into her own particular realm of philosophy! And this was such genuine philosophy, too, of its kind! No second-hand *ré-chauffé* of modern essays and magazine articles, but a bit of pure, crude, untutored reflection, freshly secreted from a human heart and brain. Her reply, when it came, was not philosophical—scarcely even relevant.

"I suppose you know," she said slowly, leaning her head on her hand, and looking up into her companion's face, "that it is a little unusual for a pretty girl of twenty-three to be rattling about the world in Worth toilettes, with—or without—a maid as young as herself; investing in gold shares on her own account, and dropping into casinos as if they were picture-galleries?"

The other laughed rather unpleasantly.

"It is just that pretty girl of twenty-three," she said, "who knows life. Men? I believe no woman living knows men as I do. If I were to tell you things that have happened, things that I have seen——" She paused.

" I should listen with deference, but say that your view was necessarily a one-sided one."

" Why ? " The word was a challenge.

" Because "—the young woman was surprised at her own boldness—" going about as you do, you don't meet the best men, nor see the best side of those you do meet."

" You believe there is a best side, do you ? "

" I don't. I know it."

The beautiful lips curled contemptuously. " If I were to write a book, and tell my experiences——"

" Do. I should read it, for one."

" Would you ? Bah ! They're not worth it." She snapped her fingers. " I don't care that for the whole sex—except one, of course !—and he is horrid : I believe that is why I am feeling so low to-night."

The friendly interest which had brightened the plain woman's face died out. As an outcome of the previous conversation, this was disappointing.

" In that case I should be horrid too," she said coldly. " I would not break my heart for him."

The girl looked as if an insult had been offered to her intelligence. " Do you think I am such a fool," she said, " as to cut off my nose to spite my face ? No, no. I don't need anybody to tell me what to do. I shall wait quite quietly—quite quietly—till he is nice again,—and then I will show him how horrid *I* can be ! "

The young woman laughed. " Is that the correct treatment under the circumstances ? " she said. " It never would have occurred to me."

" I suppose you don't care about men ? "

"I do—extremely. I have one or two friends,
who——"

"Oh, *friends!*" exclaimed the girl wearily.

"By the way, you had a friend with you on the
steamer, had not you?" The young woman despised herself the more for the direct question when
she saw the colour rise to the fair face.

"Yes—no—that is, yes, he is a sort of a friend.
I hope you don't think," she exclaimed suddenly,
"that is the man I was talking about! The one on
the steamer is—well, no matter! He is a cut above
me, anyhow; and besides, he is married already. It
is a duty to be kind to him, poor fellow! His wife's
a brute."

The little woman laughed—a fresh young laugh.
"I am not an authority on men, like you," she said;
"but I should have thought you must have discovered that it js rather delicate work for a pretty girl
to be kind to a man 'whose wife is a brute.' Matri-
monial duties and responsibilities can scarcely be
safely delegated."

"Do you really think me so pretty?" was the
eager, irrelevant response.

The plain face hardened,—then broke again into
a smile. "I do. I suppose it is needless to add
that 'favour is deceitful and beauty is vain.' Your
retort would be too obvious. But I don't grudge
you your quarter of an hour's start of me."

"You mean you don't care to be good-looking?"

"Would you believe me if I said so?"

The girl hesitated. "I never believed any woman
yet who said so; but you——" she broke off sudden-

ly, with a slight blush. "You know I did not mean to say you were plain," she said nervously; "you are——"

"Thank you; that will do." The plain young woman rose into quiet dignity at once. "I suppose you are not actually a Venus; and my friends, no doubt, would tell you that I am not irredeemably ugly; but we are speaking broadly, and, broadly speaking, there is no doubt that we are fair representatives of the two classes. You are a beautiful woman, and I am—what, by a euphemism, we call plain. Naturally you think the advantage is all on your side. If you had thought of me at all when we met at Victoria, you would have said, 'Poor devil! but why at least doesn't she wear a decent gown?'"

The beautiful girl glanced at the dark serge folds, and tried in vain to find a redeeming feature in their quiet severity.

"And yet," continued the speaker, "if by any chance you and I were to travel again to-morrow night with all these men, they would say, when you entered the dining-car, 'Here is that handsome girl again!' When I came in, it would never occur to any of them that they had seen me before. Don't you see? I am invisible. I have got the ring of Gyges. Nobody is on his guard with me—I see people as they are."

The young girl did not answer. She was perplexed, but one thing was clear to her mind. It was obviously possible to pay too high a price even for the ring of Gyges.

"It must be such a responsibility to carry about a work of art in your own person," went on the other. "You must inherit yourself to such an extent that you cease to inherit the earth."

The unintentional rudeness of this remark was fortunately lost on its hearer.

"I expect," she said a little nervously, "that you are very learned."

"Oh no!" The young woman laughed pleasantly. "Well, we are talking more or less honestly, so I will confess that I am learned enough to know when somebody else writes a good poem, or paints a good picture, or composes a good—waltz."

"And that contents you?"

"Sometimes. It leaves room for other things. At the present moment it contents me just to look at your face."

"I thought you despised beauty?"

"Then you are a fool," was the young woman's mental comment, but she only said, "I don't think you can have thought that. I don't despise the Koh-i-noor because I should not care to wear it in Regent Street."

"Do you write books yourself?"

"No."

"Nor paint pictures?"

"No."

"Nor compose?"

"No."

"Are you engaged to be married?"

"No."

There was a half minute's silence, and then the next question came suddenly—

"Do you believe in the immortality of the soul?"

Accustomed though the young woman was to the intense talk of the youth of the present day, the abruptness of this attack took her breath away. "I don't know" she said, surprised out of all caution. "I agree with a great teacher of mine who says that it is no concern of ours. We have enough light to live by without that. It is surely a want of faith to ask for more."

The girl tapped her foot impatiently on the floor of the carriage. These were not the lines on which her mind had worked.

"What I always say is," she said, "that nobody ever has come back. Why should we ever have taken it into our heads that there was another life? We had no reason to think so. One after another goes, but nobody ever comes back to tell us."

"'Why should we ever have taken it into our heads that there was another life?'" repeated the young woman meditatively. "I suppose—if we are to think of the matter at all—that is the one great argument for its existence."

"*Billets, s'il vous plaît!*"

The smart young conductor stood in the doorway.

"Oh, bother our tickets!" exclaimed the girl, looking up with a charming smile. "If you plague me, you shall get no tip—do you understand?"

The man bowed with very evident admiration for the lovely speaker.

"Tell me," she went on, "do you go all the way with this train?"

"Yes, madame."

"To Monte Carlo?"

"Yes, madame."

"Pretty place, eh?"

"Oh, but beautiful, madame!"

"Lots of pretty gowns, I suppose?"

"Very pretty, but none perhaps so pretty as madame's."

The girl laughed gaily. "You do mean to have a heavy tip," she said. "Shall you still be on this train in a month or two?"

"Probably, madame."

"Perhaps I shall be going to Monte Carlo then. No such luck this time. Tell us about the casino. What is it like?"

"Will you allow me to pass, please?" said the plain young woman coldly to the conductor. In the corridor she paused and looked over her shoulder. "I am going to see if my berth is ready," she said. "I shall see you again. *Au revoir!*"

But half an hour later, when she returned to say good-night, her place was occupied by the man "whose wife was a brute."

"A curious acquaintance!" said the young woman to herself as she slipped away unobserved,— "cuts her pointedly in the dining-car, and, an hour later, settles down for a comfortable chat in her compartment. Save me from such friends!"

And with this reflection she betook herself to bed.

II.

THE darkness of an autumn night was settling over Llandudno, but a rich mellow afterglow still shone back from the placid bosom of the sea. Away out on the radiant streak a boat moved imperceptibly along, and the soft plash of the oars could be heard now and then from the shore. The band had ceased playing, and most of. the promenaders had gone home for the night; but down on the beach a little crowd was gathered still, listening to the eager thrilling voice of a mission preacher.

"Let us take a turn along the parade, if you are not too tired," said a young man to his companion. "It is a glorious evening, and, now that the world, the flesh, and the devil have retired, the place is almost bearable."

He spoke with a pleasant air of *camaraderie*, and the plain young woman looked up with a smile. "It *is* lovely," she said, "and I am not a bit tired; but I am afraid I am Philistine enough to enjoy the world, the flesh, and the devil too."

"I must apologize, then, for taking you up to the solitude of the Great Orme."

"I have enjoyed it so much," she said simply. "It has been one of those walks that stand out in one's memory after long years. It is very good to see you again, Fred."

Her companion did not answer immediately.

"And I am so glad you mean to devote yourself to figure-painting," she went on. "I have always felt sure that was your line. I am certain you will get on now."

" It is certainly a line that lends itself to the production of pot-boilers ! " he said moodily.

" That's an advantage I had not thought of," she answered, laughing. " And yet I don't know. One ' sees plenty of pot-boiler landscapes. You know the kind of thing—finikin foliage, and a boat with reflections in the water."

" Yes, I know ; like the picture I was so proud of getting into the New ! "

" I absolutely decline to rise to that, Fred ; but I am very glad you mean to stick to figures. I shall look for a great success in May."

" And will you provide the subject ? "

" I might, if I had one brilliant idea for your twenty." She paused, and then laughed softly. " Such an odd recollection comes back to me through the years, of a picture I planned when I was a girl and thought I could paint ! It was to be called ' The Shadow of the Cross.' "

" Your acquaintance with contemporary art must have been limited. How long was it before you exclaimed, ' *Pereant qui ante nos nostra dixerunt!* ' ? "

" I never said that in my life," she answered proudly ; " and on that occasion even my baser nature was in no way tempted to say it, for Holman Hunt's idea was not ' nostra ' at all. The cross did not come into my picture—it was supposed to be on the left—but the great shadow threw its whole length across ; and into the shadow I put—all my ideals. I was wonderfully catholic even then. Of course a young priest was the prominent figure; but I had soldiers, and—I forget now who they all were. Some of them accepted the shadow with rapture; some were crowding into it; and some were trying, oh, so hard! to get out of it. There was one woman of society—in whose jewels I revelled in prospect—stretching out her arms to the brightness. Most of her figure was in brilliant light, but the shadow fell right across. Crude, was not it?"

"Very," he replied. "Why didn't you stick to art?"

"I did; but I found it more profitable to stick to other people's."

"Mine, for instance," he observed cynically.

"Yours, for instance."

They walked on for some time in silence, till, gradually rising in intensity as they approached, the voice of the preacher fell, full, mellow, and deliberate, on their ears—

"'He was wounded for our transgressions, He was bruised for our iniquities: the chastisement of our peace was upon Him; and with His stripes we are healed.'"

The two companions stopped short in something like awe. Only dimly in the distance could they see the outline of the motionless little throng; the wonderful voice came straight out of the darkness of the night.

"Don't go, Fred!" said the young woman under her breath. "This is magnificent."

"Pity to spoil the illusion," he said. "It *is* a fine

voice. More suited to the music of Isaiah than to the meeting-house rant you will hear presently. Come !"

" For an artist and a philosopher, Fred," she said a moment later, " not to add, a man of the world, you are curiously bigoted. Do you expect an abstract statement of the Absolute Right to convert the world? You are like a scientist who wants to feed himself and his fellows in strict accordance with a physiological table of diet, quite regardless of the fact that they *won't eat* the food he provides."

" Am I ? " he said reflectively. " I don't think so. But I prefer to choose my own sauce."

" And to scoff at other people's ? "

" No ; but I don't see why I should pretend to share their tastes."

The young woman sighed. " It really is the great problem of life," she said, " how to reconcile absolute intellectual honesty with intense emotional appreciation of every striving after right."

They had turned back in their walk, and now came again within hearing of the preacher's voice—

" ' We elder children grope our way
From dark behind to dark before ;
And only when our hands we lay,
Dear Lord, in Thine, the night is day,
And there is darkness nevermore.' "

" Is that meeting-house rant ? " she asked.

" It will be directly. He can't stick to quotations for ever. Come ! "

" No; I am going to join in the service." She

sprang lightly down on the beach, and then turned to look up. "You are tired to-night, Fred, and no wonder. Go home."

"You don't want me to come with you?" he asked doubtfully.

"Certainly not."

"Will you come for a walk again to-morrow?"

"With all my heart."

"Then I'll call about ten. Good-night."

Very softly the young woman made her way over the shingle till she stood on the outskirts of the little gathering. Then, ascending the steps of a stranded bathing-machine, she seated herself to listen and watch.

A lamp by the preacher's side cast an uncertain light on the eager, upturned faces: one might have thought that here was a missionary in a heathen land, preaching a new gospel of salvation. For, whatever doctrine this man might teach, there was no doubt about his power to influence his fellows. That smartly dressed lad in the front row had clearly forgotten where he was; those tears were evidently unusual visitors on the painted cheeks over which they flowed; that beautiful girl—— Why, where in the world had she seen that beautiful face before?

Gradually it all came back to her,—the night journey through France, the swaying carriage, the lamp reflected in the window-panes. In this dim light the girl looked lovelier, almost younger, than ever; and yet it must be two?—three?—years ago.

The sermon was over, and a parting hymn rang

out plaintively over the water. The young woman descended from her seat, and was about to make her way homewards, when, to her great surprise, the beautiful girl came up to her with outstretched hand. The great eyes were strangely bright, and the muscles of the lovely face quivered in pathetic self-revelation.

"I thought it was you," she said eagerly, as though they had only parted the day before. "I saw you come, and during the last hymn it flashed on me who you were. You will let me walk home with you, won't you?" Her voice was almost imploring.

"Better let me come with you," said the young woman gently, glancing at the flushed cheeks and ruffled hair. "You look—tired."

"Tired?" The girl laughed excitedly. "I never was less tired in my life!" She slipped her hand in her companion's arm. "Wasn't it *wonderful?*"

"It was extremely fine."

The words, though spoken cordially, struck chill on the girl's overstrained mood, and she turned on her companion with a quick, suspicious glance; but the plain face was very grave, very sympathetic, nothing more.

They walked on in silence for a time. "These are my diggings," said the girl at last, her voice still shaken by strong feeling. "Won't you come in? Do! I am all alone."

"Not to-night, I think, thank you."

"Oh, but you must! I want to talk to you. I

must have some one. Do come in! I won't be left alone to-night!"

The full lips pouted like those of a spoilt child, and an expression of terror came into the great eyes, as, with an almost caressing gesture, she drew her companion into the house.

A bright little fire burned in the grate of a pretty sitting-room, and a dainty supper was spread on the table. The window stood open, but the air was heavy with the fragrance of flowers.

"If you please, ma'am," said the maid, "Colonel Whyte called while you were out. He said he would come again."

The girl looked at the speaker for a moment with dazed, uncomprehending eyes; but gradually a deep flush spread over her face. "I quite forgot," she said. Then turning to her companion, she drew her hand across her brow as if trying to collect her thoughts.

"It is so odd," she said dreamily, with a nervous shiver, "to find everything going on just precisely as it did before,—supper and callers and flowers— and a jolly fire! Sit down. I feel as if I were just beginning to wake from an extraordinary dream —the sunset and the sea and the darkness—and that man's voice! I felt almost as if the last day had come, as they used to tell us it would, and it seemed quite natural that you should be there. Do you know, I have often thought of you? And you see I did know you again in spite of—what was it?—your magic ring." She laughed more naturally now; she was regaining her self-control.

" Your memory is marvellous."

" Oh no; it isn't that.   I have no memory at all.
But you were so queer, you know.   I never met anybody in the least like you."

The words gave the plain young woman an un-
pleasant sense of responsibility.   " Are you quite
sure," she said, a little awkwardly, "that this is not
the dream ?—the flowers I mean, and the callers, and
the fire—and the other the reality ? "

" Do *you* think it is ? "

" I am inclined to think that the other is at least
nearer the reality than this."

" But you don't really believe all he was saying ? "

" I didn't hear it all."

" I know.   I saw you come.   Are you engaged to
that man ? "

The young woman found it difficult to follow
these conversational gymnastics.   " No," she said
shortly.

" Nor going to be ? "

" Nor going to be."

" I never feel quite sure that you haven't a trump
card up your sleeve all the time."

There was no answer.

" Are you still as contented as ever ? '

" I think so.   Life seems sadder than it did ; but
when all is said, it is very beautiful."

The girl sighed impatiently.   " I wish I could see
where the beauty comes in ! "

" Well, in that scene on the beach, for instance—
the intense earnestness, the magnetic human influence, the longing for better things."

"And yet you don't believe what the man said?"

"At least he made me wish myself a better woman."

The girl sprang to her feet, and paced up and down the room.

"I believe," she said with intense vehemence, "you could save my soul if you would tell me what it is you do believe!"

A look of genuine distress came over the little woman's face. "Believe, believe!" she said. "Why do you talk so much about belief? I believe it is worth while trying to be good."

"Why? Is there another life after this? Is there a heaven?"

"Here at least—yes."

"And a hell?"

"Yes."

"Where we shall burn?—really burn"—she put her pretty finger close to the bar of the grate—"to hurt?"

"It would be a poor look-out for us if it did not hurt; but some people never seem to feel it."

The girl laughed. "I know what you mean," she said. "I once heard a clergyman say that. You mean that I am in hell now."

"God forbid! I don't need to go beyond my own experience. But I never cared to *stay* in hell long."

"I don't know. One might be in a worse place. I am afraid," she went on, with a weird laugh, "I am one of the people who are not sensitive enough to feel it!"

7

The little woman shuddered. "Don't!" she said.

"Why not?" The splendid figure drew itself up defiantly. "Why should I talk gammon to you? What do you in your grey little world know of life, of temptation?"

"More, perhaps, than you think."

"Bah! It is easy for you to talk of 'trying to be good'! Were you ever in love? Were you ever married? Were you ever——" she hesitated, looked straight into the honest eyes, and then continued boldly, "Were you ever married and *then* in love?"

For the first time the young woman's eye fell on the plain gold circlet which had replaced some of the flashing gems. "I did not know," she said, weakly, "that you were married. I remember— that night—you told me there was a difference between you and the man you cared for."

"If only it had lasted! God! if only the difference had lasted! His coldness piqued me, don't you know?—he had been so much at my feet; and I was so determined to win him back that I don't think I realized how much I had begun to think of somebody else. But somebody else wasn't —wasn't 'free,' as the library books say; and—and it was time I was getting settled. I had lost money in gold shares, and my life was all in a muddle, and I hadn't the society I was entitled to at all. So I married—and then I knew that I loathed him—and somebody else's wife died. If there is a God at all, it just seemed as if he was laughing at me! What was the use of making me pretty, and giving me money to buy nice clothes, if I am never to be happy—never, never to have what I want? And my youth is slipping away, and nobody seems able to tell me whether there is another world or not. I meet people—clever *men* who ought to know!— who say it is all moonshine; and you would have me grow old and ugly, '*trying to be good*'! Do you know"—she fell on her knees, and threw her arms across her companion in magnificent abandonment —"I almost wish you would tell me there is no other life, for then I could have what I want in this!"

"Colonel Whyte, ma'am," said the maid.

With a bound the girl sprang to her feet, and raised her hands to her dishevelled hair. "I have kept you an unconscionable time," she said, with a nervous laugh, "and no doubt you are longing to get home. It was awfully good of you to come in!"

The young woman had flushed as though some one had struck her. "Yes," she said quietly, "it is time I was at home. Good-night."

Before she had reached the threshold, however, the uncomfortable sense of her own responsibility came back upon her.

"Where is your husband?" she said earnestly, laying her hand on her companion's arm. "Who is this man?"

But the tide had turned.

The girl looked annoyed and nonplussed for a moment, then broke into a laugh.

"Come in, Colonel!" she cried. "Here is a

young lady who is anxious to make your acquaintance."

Without another word or glance the little woman
slipped past the waiting figure in the hall, and made
her way out into the night.

III.

" WELL, this is a change from smoky London
lodgings ! "

The plain young woman stood with a friend at
the open window of the hotel. A heavy shower had
fallen in the afternoon, but now the sun was shining
genially, and the subtle, invigorating fragrance of
the heather was borne in from the Yorkshire moors.

" We have earned our holiday honestly, haven't
we ? and we mean to make the most of it. *Three
whole weeks !* For three weeks we are going to bask
on the heather, and read Heine, and look up at the
blue sky : we will forget that we ever attended a
woman's suffrage meeting, or interviewed a celebrity, or described what royalty wore. We have left
our moral responsibilities behind, too. It is a duty,
a positive duty, to cultivate the sentiments and the
emotions. I hope there will be some pretty gowns at
dinner. I hope there will be lots of courses—lots—
daintily served ! We are grand ladies, Rita, you and
I—for three weeks !—and we know how things ought
to be done. Do you think we can afford half a bottle of Médoc ? "

The plain face looked older than at Llandudno ;

but the lines that took from its fresh youthfulness were genial, friendly lines, such as endear a face to those who know it.

"Change your gown, dear girl, and don't chatter. The gong will sound in ten minutes."

"Sadly beneath the dignity of a grand lady, isn't it, to dress in ten minutes? Heigho!"

She slipped on an old-fashioned black silk, and went to explore the possibilities of the reading-room before going down-stairs.

Two ladies were sitting there in earnest conversation. They lowered their voices slightly when the plain young woman entered; but, as she stood by the window, newspaper in hand, she could hear every word.

"—all her life men have treated her better than she deserves. Her husband actually offered to take her back; but when she refused, of course he instituted proceedings for divorce. The action was quite undefended, and, as soon as it was over, Colonel Whyte married her."

The plain young woman grasped her newspaper more tightly, and turned her back upon the speaker.

"It was a great surprise to every one, for socially she was very much beneath him, and of course they were cut by all the *nice* people. I am told she was a mere adventuress!"

"American, was not she?"

"Yes, but I believe she left America when quite a girl. She prides herself on being cosmopolitan. Cosmopolitan, forsooth!"

"And is she still as fascinating as ever?"

"When I saw her drive up to the door on Saturday afternoon, I thought she was handsomer than at the time of her marriage. She has a better colour— I don't think it is rouge—and I never saw such eyes —simply lustrous! But when she comes near——" the speaker nodded significantly. "Her age will soon begin to show, I can assure you!"

Very eagerly the plain young woman scanned the faces assembled at *table d'hôte*, but without finding the one she sought. Five years must have made a change, no doubt; but even when all allowance was made for that, there was no woman present who could by any possibility be the *cidevant* beautiful girl.

Dinner was more than half over when the door opened, and a lady and gentleman were ushered up to a small table in the window. Ah, there was no doubt about it now! The plain young woman would have known that face again anywhere.

And it *was* more beautiful than ever!—transparent, pensive, etherealized. Poor soul, she must have suffered——!

Was it more beautiful? A sudden turn of the head had brought into startling relief the hollow in the oval of the cheek; and was it not too transparent? was the flush—deepening as the evening went on—not almost that of hectic?

Scarcely a word was passing between the two in the window. The gentleman's manner was uniformly courteous; but it would have been hard to say which face bore more evident marks of ennui, of disillusion.

The plain young woman gazed as if fascinated, only responding absently now and then to the remarks of her companion. At last the beautiful head turned, the wonderful eyes looked straight across to where she sat. It was a mere glance at first, then a puzzled look, and then a showy lorgnette was raised for a deliberate stare. It dropped again presently, and its owner made no sign of recognition.

"It would have been strange if she had known me again—or cared to know me!" mused the young woman, as she rose to leave the table. "Is this the curtain at last, I wonder,—or only another drop?"

Some minutes later the chamber-maid knocked at her door with a visiting-card. A few lines were scrawled on the back—

"Do come to my room for a few minutes. My husband has just gone out. No. 8, 1st floor."

No. 8 was a fine room, and its occupant lay stretched on a *chaise longue* in the oriel window.

"Come along!" she said rather wearily, but with the old charming smile. "How odd that we should meet again! I can't think how I recognized you. Sit down. That is rather a comfortable chair."

"I am afraid you are not very well."

"Who could be well in this hateful place? The sharp air makes me cough incessantly. What ever induced *you* to come? And yet I don't know. These cold, grey moors are admirably in keeping with your philosophy. I wonder,"—she looked up

with an arch smile—"I wonder if you are still ' trying to be good ' ? "

The young woman walked to the window and
looked out on the daffodil sky and rich purple
heather.

" Cold,—grey ! " she said. " Why, it is all blazing with colour ! "

" And you know the Riviera ! It seems to me
you carry your own world about with you, and see
things that are invisible to ordinary mortals. What
was it Jack was quoting last night ?—

' Oh, the dreary, dreary moorland ! '

And these long evenings depress me unspeakably.
If you had only heard the church bells yesterday !
I thought they would drive me mad before they
stopped. I want sunshine—real sunshine—and roses
and blue water ! I am making my husband take me
away the first thing to-morrow ; and he has gone out
now to see if there is nothing going on that would
pass away the time for an hour or two."

She was silent for a few moments, and then resumed with a light sneer that only half concealed
her nervousness. " You know all about me, I pre-
sume ? I have become quite a celebrity since we
met."

" Yes, I heard that you had married Colonel
Whyte."

" Saintly of him, wasn't it ? All the good women
said so. Ugh, how I hate good women ! "

" Do you know," said the plain young woman
almost tenderly, "I don't think you should go out

to-night. If your husband goes I will come and read you—something amusing. You are wearing yourself out."

A curious look of fear came into the beautiful eyes—a look that was only made the more pathetic by the laugh which hastened to hide it.

"You think I am a gone case, do you? How long do you give me? Two years? One? Six months?"

"Don't talk nonsense!" said the other sharply. "You are knocking yourself to pieces at present. Take a little ordinary care, and you will be all right."

A fit of coughing was the only answer. Hastily the beautiful woman lifted her handkerchief to her lips, and in another moment its snowy folds were stained with a crimson drop.

"Do you see that?" she said quickly.

"Yes, and I have often seen it before in people who are well and strong now. It means that you must rest, and take care of yourself, and get strong."

"No, no, no!" The answer came like the clang of a passing-bell. "No need to tell me what it means! I have seen it all in my mother. I am getting thin"—she slipped the rings from her long white fingers—"and my neck—— But you never saw my neck in the old days!" she interposed regretfully. "I had a dark velvet gown——but there! —that's past." There was dead silence in the room for a few moments, then, "You could have saved me if you had wished," she said.

"*Saved you?*"

"Oh, not from this! This is nothing. Do you remember that night on the beach? I was screwing up my courage to go and speak to that man; but I looked at you, and saw you did not believe a word of it."

"Oh!" cried the little woman, with a sharp cry as of physical pain. "Surely I never said that?"

"No, you did not say it; but you looked as if you had found something better, don't you know? And your something better was too good for me."

"But, dear child, it is not too late. If I were you"—she threw back her head—"I would make a fresh start now—this very minute!"

The other nodded slowly. "I believe *you* would, even if you were dying," she said. "Oh, I know you have got hold of some thread in life, something that is worth having; but you don't seem able to put it into words much. Well, well, it doesn't matter! I don't suppose my soul was worth saving—and, I daresay, it was all bunkum after all. When you come to think of it, nobody ever has come back.—Is that you, Jack? Come in! Let me introduce you to my friend——"

She broke off with a laugh less musical than of old. "I declare I don't even know your name! Never mind; we are old friends all the same, I assure you. Well, what luck?"

The newcomer seated himself with a sigh of resignation, and looked at his watch. "There is a revival meeting," he said, "in the conventicle down the way, and a performance of 'Johnny's Mamma' in the Town Hall."

The beautiful lips pouted peevishly.

"'Johnny's Mamma'! I've seen it a hundred times. Never mind! It will help to pass the time. Good-bye, Miss—— Smith? I might have known it was Smith! Come along, Jack. We shall be awfully bored, but we'll show the folks a Parisian bonnet for once in their lives!"

THE KNIGHT AND THE LADY.

Mein Kind, wir waren Kinder,
Zwei Kinder, klein und froh.
. . . . . .
Vorbei sind die Kinderspiele,
Und Alles rollt vorbei.—HEINE.

I.

SHE was as winsome a little lady as heart could wish, and I don't suppose she ever looked sweeter than she did that autumn night in the gloaming, when all the brilliant colours of the sunset shone faintly back from her fresh white frock.

She had climbed half-way up the great wooden gate of the carriage-drive, so that her dimpled elbows could rest on the top. The smooth beech hedge swept round behind her, throwing its cool green tints into the folds of her baby skirt; and on the other side of the drive, the silver-grey pods of an old laburnum dangled caressingly above her dainty head. And well they might; for the battered sun-bonnet had fallen back, and the fluffy red-gold curls were blown about a face that reminded one of the budding moss-roses a few yards off.

"Happy laburnum!" I had said one day when I

found her thus—for the old gate was a favourite
watch-tower, and a small worn patch on the paint
of the centre bar bore witness to the frequent pressure of her baby feet—"happy laburnum! When
you grow a little taller, he'll be able to kiss you.
That's what all the other old trees are gossiping and
laughing about. Do you hear?"

Her face grew very solemn for a moment, and
then she broke into a scornful little laugh.

"Why, that's the wind!" she said contemptuously. "You talk like the fairy-books."

"And of course you don't believe *them?*"

She shook her head half regretfully.

"I haven't believed them since I was—oh,
such a *wee* little girl. I haven't believed them
since——"

"Since when?"

"Since I saw Auntie putting the things in my
stocking."

"You ought to have been asleep!" I said indignantly, for I had very definite ideas as to how a
well-organized child ought to behave in the great
affairs of life.

"I lay awake on purpose," she said placidly;
"but of course I b'etended to be asleep, or Auntie
would have gone away again." She sighed. "I
did so dreadfully want it all to be true—Santa
Claus, I mean—but it was no use if it wasn't
real."

"Child of the age!" I exclaimed with a smile and
a sigh. "No use at all, of course. Well, ta-ta!
Poor old laburnum! You'll hold up your head like

a man if you take my advice. There's an awful
snubbing in store for you if you don't."

The little lady nearly toppled off her perch in
the effort to see the presumptuous spray above her
head.

"Horrid old thing!" she said indignantly. "Do
you know it's *poisonous?* Nursie found me eating
green peas in the garden one day, and she said if I
ate one single laburnum seed by mistake—I'd
die?"

Her blue eyes grew round with horror as she
approached this climax; but that expression soon
gave way to an apologetic little smile.

"Of course Nursie's an old silly," she said with
the air of a mature philosopher who has reconciled
himself to the conviction that his fellow-countrymen
are "maistly fules." "I believe she thinks I'm a
baby still." This with a pregnant side-glance at me.
"As if pea-pods grew on trees, and were skinny and
knubbly like that!"

But here I am maundering on with my own
recollections of the little lady, when I only wanted
to tell the tale of the fairing she got from Duncairn.
Poor little lady! I heard her try to tell the story
herself the other day, in the gay, bright world that
has just claimed her as its own; and I loved her
none the less when the eager cultured voice broke
down in a childlike sob.

Yes, it was her watch-tower, that great wooden
gate,—the coign of vantage from which she looked
out with longing eyes on the forbidden world. Not
much of a world, I admit, if it had not been forbid-

den ! Only a dusty private road, separated from the turnip-field beyond by a great uneven bank, topped by scraggy ash-trees, and starred over with blue-eyed speedwells and yellow tormentilla.

Behind her lay the territory in which she was free to roam at will,—one of those rare old gardens, the very memory of which is a legacy of peace and rest to many a weary soul. A garden where the spacious strawberry-bed was bounded by old world roses; where an occasional hedge of sweet-peas broke the monotony of kail and brocoli; where, even in the show-beds under the sitting-room windows, dear old flowers that most of us have not seen since childhood straggled at random over the warm brown earth, and followed their own wild will.

But at this stage of her development my lady was pleased to consider that she had exhausted the possibilities of the garden. True, she had woven countless daisy-chains on the dear old lawn, where nobody presumed to think the daisies out of place; she had pinched her fingers with the passive Snap-dragon, and made him act the part of whale in the wondrous drama of Jonah; she and her dolls had made believe to dine on "rice and curry" from the marguerites, and on "mince" from the luxuriant tufts of red sorrel, which to be sure had no business at all in the cabbage-bed; she had captured a few unhappy caterpillars, in order to determine for her-self whether the story of their turning into butter-flies must not be relegated to the despised region of fairy tales, but had wisely decided on the third day that life was too short for an experiment so pro-

longed; she had even made attar of roses, with
liberal help from the tarred old water-butt beside
the tool-shed, and had succeeded in persuading herself for nearly two days that the gruesome compound
was going to prove a success; she had—— But no, I
cannot honestly maintain that she had exhausted the
true inwardness of the strawberry-bed. Such de-
lights, however, are apt to pall, even at the mature
age of six, and in my little lady's case their enjoyment was hedged in by divers restrictions which
prevented their being by any means always available.

So she stood on the gate, looking out on the forbidden world—as many a captive maid has done before her—a forlorn little beauty that only a knight
with a heart of stone could resist.

A long, long time passed—nearly five minutes
perhaps—and then an approaching figure came in
sight,—surely the quaintest little knight you ever
beheld!

He was shuffling along in hob-nailed shoes a size
too big for him, and he wore a shabby corduroy suit
several sizes too small. The elbows and baggy
knees were worn quite threadbare, and manifold
patches of varying date covered the regions of maximum wear and tear. And yet it had a beauty of its
own, that poor old suit. It had weathered sun and
rain, and outdoor play and toil, till bounteous Mother
Nature had almost come to look on it as one of her
children, and had warmed its shabby surface into
something not unlike the mellow tints with which
she clothes the walls and tree-trunks.

But, alas! "the trail of the serpent is over it all;" and, even if he had been a born painter, I fear the little knight was too much a man of the world to be consoled by his own artistic value. He knew well how great a gulf separated him socially from the little lady, for—although a sort of tàcit exception was made in his own particular case, on the ground that he was a "cannie laddie,"—he was aware that a well-defined rule forbade her speaking to the cottar-children unless some responsible person was at hand.

He saw her now, of course, the moment he came in sight of the gate; but, boylike, he pretended not to see her, while at the same time he clutched his old cap with an awkward gesture that might easily have been taken for an accident. From which you may guess that, although he was only a common Scotch laddie, this little knight of mine, he was rich in the possession of a good mother with old-fashioned ideas on the subject of "mainners."

The little lady grasped the top bar of the gate with her chubby, sunburnt hands, and, bending low over it to send her voice across the road, she called in a mysterious whisper—

"San-dy!"

The boy turned his head, smiled somewhat sheepishly, and continued his shuffling gait.

"*Sandy!*" she called imperiously.

No man on earth could have resisted that,—not even a man of nine; so he crossed the road rather doubtfully, and lifted an honest, brown Scotch face, framed with straight fair hair. It was not at all a

8

remarkable face; only serious, "cannie" (as the cottar-folk said), with sweet gentle curves about the firm little mouth.

  • "Cut me a switch!" said the little queen.

Oh, Rosie, Rosie, did you even then read the other sex by instinct? How could you possibly know Sandy's weak point, the straight road to his heart? How could you know that only the day before he had found a knife by the roadside? Old and rusty, it is true, and with the large blade broken across; but an honest knife still, and one that responded bravely to a long course at the grindstone.

Sandy's grave little face shone like a sunbeam, and, darting across the road, he hastily examined the undergrowth of the nearest ash, in search of a suitable switch. He chose a royal one at length, and the brave knife was already at work on it as he crossed the road again to her side.

"No, no, no!" she cried, with an impatient little stamp of her foot. "Don't peel the skin off; you'll make it sticky! And let the leaves alone, please," she continued more gently, mollified by his instant obedience. "I'll pull them off for myself."

He handed up the switch, and wiped the trusty . blade on his sleeve rather ostentatiously, hoping she would take notice of it; but my lady's cleverness, after all, had its limitations.

"They're gey teuch," he said deprecatingly, after a pause, pointing to the switch in her hand. "It's ill gethrin' them withoot a knife."

But the lady was examining the points of the

switch with a critical eye, and did not deign to notice his treasure at all.

So poor little Sandy was reduced to a direct attack. "It's an auld ane," he said humbly, holding it up to .her, "an' no by-ordinar bonny; but it's a braw ane to cut!"

She looked at it with fastidious eyes.

"It's very ugly," she said candidly. "You should see my Auntie's knife! It's a teeny-weeny thing the colour of bluey-white milk."

He did not answer immediately. He was too much of a philosopher not to have discovered before now that women cannot be expected to look at things from a man's point of view.

"Ay," he said slowly at last, "I've nae doobt it's bonny; but I wadna wunner if she'd no be muckle pleased gin she catched ye cuttin' switches wi't!"

This argument was irrefutable, and Sandy was emboldened to proceed.

"Noo mines," he said, "is no fit for the like o' her; but it's unco stoot; in fac'"—why not clinch the argument at once?—"it's like my faither's!"

But the little lady was once more absorbed in her switch. "There!" she said at last, holding it up in well-pruned elegance. "Next time Nursie takes me to see the pigs, I'll switch the flies off their backs! Sandy, mustn't it be dreadful to be a pig?"

Sandy gazed open-mouthed. His imagination was not equal to the strain she put upon it.

"They're so hidjus," she went on, "that's the first

thing; and then they're always in a mess,—that's
the second thing; and then—*I'm quite sure their tails
are no use at all!*"

Sandy listened in respectful silence to this lecture
on Natural History.

"It would have been so easy for God," she continued, "even if He wanted to make them ugly, to
give them proper tails. Look how the horses can
swish the flies off! And they don't need to half so
badly with their thick coats. I think its dreadful;
and then on hot days—Ugh!"

Sandy ventured humbly on a practical view of
the case, even although it was not strictly relevant.

"My Mither says whiles she disna ken what we'd
dae, wantin' oor pig. Mony's the time my Faither
himsel' hasna a bite o' butcher-meat frae Sawbath to
Sawbath!"

This was beneath contempt.

"Swing me, Sandy!" said her ladyship serenely,
moving like a crab to the end of the gate where she
would get the benefit of the maximum motion.

Sandy looked round doubtfully. "I doobt she'd
no be pleased gin she catched us at it."

"Who?" asked the child frowning. "Auntie has
gone away; she won't be back till to-morrow night.
Nursie is at supper."

"An' she's left ye here yer lane?"

"Oh no! Sarah is taking care of me; but she
met a gentleman she knew, and—I *think*—she's giving him some raspberries. You mustn't tell! Sarah
wouldn't be pleased if Auntie was to hear of it.
She's letting me stay up an extra half-hour, but she

made me promise not to go beyond the garden. I suppose," she added ruefully, "*you* can go to the farm as often as ever you like?"

He shook his head.

" It's fower ere I get hame frae the schule; an' then I hae my lessons to get, an' odd jobs to dae for my Mither."

"It can't be nice to go to school and get the tawse," she said meditatively; "but then there are such lots of things you can do! You can walk along the dykes, and wade in the burn, and climb the straw-sou, and ride in the corn-carts—oh, Sandy, it must be fine to be a boy!"

"Woa, Snowflake!" Sandy looked up shyly, breathless with the exertion of pushing the heavy gate. " I'm no carin' sae muckle aboot thae things," he said, with a little air of superiority, " but I'm gaun to the Fair the morn!"

It was well that the fiery steed had checked its pace, for the lady nearly lost her balance in the excitement of the moment.

"*Sandy! No!*" she exclaimed.

He nodded.

"Oh, Sandy, you lucky, *lucky* boy! I do want so dreadfully to go to the fair! I heard the servants speaking about it ever so long ago, and I begged and begged Auntie to take me. But she only laughed, and said it wasn't a place for little girls. Oh, why *didn't* God make me a boy!"

Sandy racked his brains, as many a wiser man has done before him, to find some suitable words of consolation, but in vain.

"Kirsty—that's my big sister"—he said at length—"her that's in the dairy the noo,—is seekin' a place; so she maun gang to the hirin', an' my Mither maun gang wi' her; an' Faither says there'll be room i' the cairt for me."

"What a *nice* father you must have, Sandy! Do you think—I don't s'pose—there'd be room in the cart for me too?"

Sandy shuffled uneasily from one foot to the other before he ventured to look up.

"There wad *that!*" he said emphatically, measuring the tiny figure with his kind, honest eyes. "But oor cairt's no the place for the like o' you. What'd yer Auntie say, missy?"

She tossed the curls out of her eyes. "Auntie's not here, so I can't ask her," she said loftily. "Never mind. I dessay your father wouldn't take me."

"I'm sure he'd be prood," cried poor Sandy; "but he'd no daur. He says there'll no be a horse in its stable the morn, nor a cairt in its shed. A'body 'll be on the road, an' a'body 'ud be speirin' at him hoo he cam' by the braw wee leddy. An' yer Auntie—— Na, na, Missy. It'll no dae. Ye maun e'en pit yer mind past it. Haud on to the yett, an' i'll gie ye anither swee."

But the joys of the "swee" had paled like a star in sunshine. Carefully climbing down from the gate, the lady put her knuckles in her eyes, and sobbed as if her heart would break.

Not noisily: Sandy could have borne it better if she had "howled like the wee lassies at the schule":

but this silent tearful misery was almost more than he could bear. Being only a man, he did not reflect that his heartbroken lady had not the smallest desire to summon Sarah and the "gentleman" from the raspberry bed.

So he held his cap in both his hands, and moved awkwardly from one foot to the other, repeating monotonously at intervals, "I wadna greet if I was you, Missy, I wadna greet." He thought it very brutal of Auntie to be so obdurate, and—in the bottom of his heart he longed to run away; but of course, for a true knight, such a course was impossible.

At last the lady dried her eyes with the air of one who makes a mighty resolution.

"I know what I'll do!" she said. "Nobody 'll take me to the Fair, so I'll go myself. *I'll walk!*"

"Hoot awa', Missy!" cried Sandy, glancing unconsciously at her dainty shoes. "It's juist no' po'sible. Ye cudna dae't. It's sax mile guid—sax mile an' a bittock!"

"I don't care," she said resolutely, though for a moment she was staggered. "I've got a big strong pair of boots at home, and I'm sure I've walked six miles often and often with Nursie. She keeps me out some days for hours and hours till I'm so——"

"Tired," she was going to say, but decided that a more advisable word might be found under the circumstances. Failing to think of one at the moment, she continued irrelevantly,

"I'm just as strong as—strong! Everybody knows I can walk far better than Auntie!"

"But, Missy," urged scandalized Sandy, "ye'll *no get*. It's no to be expeckit. Yer Auntie's awa, an' yer nurse that's left in chairge o' ye———"

"Nursie won't know anything about it," she said serenely. "Now that I'm a big girl, she sleeps in the little room off mine, and I'm awake hours and hours before she is. Oh, Sandy, how she does snore! I don't believe she'd hear me a bit if I got up early, and I'm sure I could dress myself for once. I can't get out at the front door," she continued reflectively, "for the big key is too heavy to turn; but the back-door is unlocked when the dairymaid gets up, and I'm sure I could slip out without anybody seeing me.

"Sandy, dear!" She drew him down towards her with a pretty caressing gesture. "Let you'n me go to the fair together! I'll meet you here quite, quite early, before anybody is up, and we'll have *such* a good time. Please! Please! You'n me, Sandy!"

"But they'll miss ye, my wee lassie," he said gently; "an', afore we was halfw'y there, a'body 'd be seekin' ye, an' there'd be an awfu' stramash!"

"Not if we started soon enough," she answered pouting. "Don't you see?—I just want a wee little peep of the music and dancing, and the merry-go-rounds, and the ladies in spangles. I don't care how soon they bring me away after that, and I'm sure I don't care if they keep me on bread and milk for a week!"

(Brava, little lady !—

"Sound, sound the clarion, fill the fife !
To all the sensual world proclaim,
One crowded hour of glorious life
Is worth an age without a name !")

"But of course," she went on cruelly, "you want to go in the cart."

"It's no that I'm mindin' sae muckle aboot the cairt," he said honestly, "but I nae ken what I'm to say to my faither. I'm loath to lee to him at ony time; an' he'd be sweer to persuade that I was wantin' the walk, for he kens fine I'm aye keen about the ridin'." There was a long pause before he continued in a very low voice,—"An' I was to get haudin' the reins mysel'."

Oh, selfish little lady ! Can't you retire gracefully even now ?

"You could always *come back* in the cart," she said. "But never mind; I'll go by myself. You won't tell?" she demanded with sudden eagerness.

Sandy hesitated.

"Na," he said at last, "I'll no tell; an'—gin ye gang—ye'll no gang yer lane nayther, Missy. I'll watch for ye here aboot sax the morn. It's no like ye'll be wauken; but if so be as ye're aye mindit to gang—we'll gang thegither. Guid nicht !"

II.

FOR the first time in his life, with the exception of one awful week when he had his first and only experience of "the toothache," Sandy lay awake that night for half an hour after he went to bed. True, as he had said, the chances were all in favour of the lady oversleeping herself; a healthy child, accustomed to breakfast at eight, was not likely to wake very early; still, there was an amount of uncertainty about the whole adventure which sent cold shivers down the little lad's spine. However he was big and strong for his years, and quite able to take care of the bonny bit thing till the people began to get drunk; and, of course, her friends would find her long before that. When they did find her—the very thought made him brace his muscles for a blow—of course there would be an "awfu' stramash," as he had told her, and then he must simply take the whipping and be done with it.

He would never be allowed to speak to the little lady again,—that was certain. Everybody would say he had presumed on the favour "Auntie" had shown him, and——here Sandy buried his face in the pillow, and, being a sensible boy, soon fell asleep.

It was no hard task for him to wake at sunrise. He was old, as well as big, for his years, and he often rose early to help his mother with her "chores,"—"sairwrocht" as she was with household cares and farm-labour combined.

So five o'clock found him out in the road, with

his flaxen head under the pump. He tried to be very quiet, but before he was fully equipped in his "Sawbath claes" his father turned uneasily in the old box-bed.

"What's ta'en ye, Sandy?" he asked sleepily. "Ye're sune up. It's no lang chappit five."

"Ay," said Sandy. "I'll pit on the fire for my Mither. She'll be thrang the day." (He blushed deeply at his own wickedness as he said this.) "It's a bonny day. I was thinkin' I'd juist step on, an' see if the berries are ripe in the den,—I daursay ye'll catch me up."

His heart nearly stood still with fright; but, fortunately for him, his father was too much of an epicure to rouse himself unnecessarily from that delicious state of physical relaxation which is half sleep and half waking. An hour or two later, however, the farm-labourer waxed eloquent on the subject to his wife.

"There's nae pleesurin' thae laddies ava," he said. "It's nobbut twa-three days sin naethin' wad please him but drivin' the cairt, an' here he is awa on his feet!"

"Weel, there's no muckle hairm i' that," said the mother, who always kept a particularly warm corner in her heart for her "cannie, mindfu' laddie." "Nae doobt he's awa wi' some o' the ither laddies. He's gey chief wi' Ritchie's An'ra the noo, an' *he* was to foot it. I'm houpin' he's ta'en a bit cake in's pooch. It's a gey lang road."

"Hoot, they'll juist be playin' theirsels, I'se war-

ran'. They'll no win faur—I wadna wunner but
An'ra's lippenin' to a lift frae hiz."

Meanwhile Sandy had mounted the hill towards
the "muckle hoose" in a state of no small perturba-
tion. No doubt she was sound asleep, the little
lady—unconscious alike of nurse's snoring and of
all the wild dreams of the night before. Sandy had
always been a quiet, steady laddie; but even he was
well aware of the blighting effect of the morning
light on plans that had seemed quite feasible at
bedtime.

Of course she wouldn't be there: the very idea
was ridiculous; and, as he came to this conclusion,
he felt an odd little throb of disappointment in the
midst of his mighty relief.

Could it be possible? Yes, there she was!—limping along with a face as white as a snowdrop, cloak
and bonnet all awry, and with one tiny boot and sock
clutched almost convulsively in her chubby hand.

"Oh, Sandy, dear Sandy!" she said, looking up
with two large tears just ready to escape from her
long eyelashes. "I have been so frightened!
Nursie stopped snoring, and I was so afraid she'd
wake up! I left my socks and boots to the last,
because I thought if there wasn't time I could go
bare-footed at first; but it does hurt so, Sandy! I
never thought a common road could be so prickly.
And I couldn't find the button-hook anywhere. Do
you think you'll be able to fasten them without?
I've got one boot on, you see; but it isn't but-
toned."

"That will I!" said Sandy bravely, concealing his doubts like a man. "But we'll no bide for that the noo, Missy. Juist pu't on onyw'y, till we get bye thae cottar-hooses."

So, hand in hand, they started on their moment-ous journey, the knight and the lady. They were very silent at first, and an occasional sobbing sigh bore witness to the terrors the lady had come through ; but, after all, Nature is a kind mother to the little ones. It was a flat, agricultural landscape through which they passed, and you or I might have longed for mountain and wood to break its dreary monotony ; but the children were more than con-tent. The unclouded sun overhead, the single row of scraggy trees by the roadside, the rippling burn, and the occasional late dog-roses, were enough to fill their tiny cups, without their knowing how or why.

So they gathered flowers, and cut switches, and chased the "flying bluebells," as Rosie called the azure-tinted butterflies, and enjoyed their common birthright to the full. Breakfast, of course, was quite a serious function. Sandy had secured a bit of oatcake, and Rosie had saved a biscuit from her supper the night before. These dainties were shared with the microscopic exactness of which only children are capable, and were followed by a raw turnip, together with a few unripe bramble-berries from the hedge, and some handfuls of water from the burn. Was not that something like a breakfast ! And all the time the sweet "caller" air caressed their heated brows, and swept away both memory

and forecast ;—so you see for at least one sunny
morning the knight and the lady knew what it was
to live.

To be sure no pleasure is wholly without alloy,
and the knight had a very bad ten minutes when he
tried to button the lady's boots. It really was the
very hardest bit of work he had ever attempted, and
the beads of perspiration stood on his puckered forehead before he had accomplished half of his task.
Fortunately the lady was graciously pleased to let
the matter rest there ; and, when the knight had
washed his bruised red finger-tips in the burn, they
continued their way.

They must have covered fully a third of the
ground when Sandy sighed deeply.

" I'll be back at the schule the morn," he said.

"I've begun lessons too," said she. "What do
they teach you at school, Sandy ? "

"Oh, juist a'thing," he replied with unconscious
satire—"readin', an' writin', an' coontin'——"

" I've got to subtraction," said my lady proudly.

" Have ye though ?   Weel I niver ! "

" How far have you got ? " she pursued

"Weel," said he unwillingly, " I'm a laddie, ye
ken, an' a muckle sicht aulder than ye, Missy. I'm
at compoon' long diveesion."

This was crushing !

" What's that ? " asked the lady faintly.

" Weel," said Sandy, scratching his head in great
perplexity, " diveesion is a wee thing like subtrawction, ye ken, juist as multiplication is maist the same
thing as addeetion—only different," he added con-

scientiously. "But there, what am I bletherin'
aboot? Ye've no gotten the length o' multiplication
yet."

"I know all about the multiplication table," said
my lady severely; "at least," she added as an afterthought, "I've got as far as two times nine."

"Weel to be sure! It's juist wunnerfu'! An'
what'll twa times nine be, Missy?"

He only wanted to help her to show off, but she
looked at him as though he had been convicted of
cheating at cards.

"That's not fair!" she said coldly.

"Is't no? Than we'll drap it. I hadna tellt ye
what 'compoon'' means."

"Tell me," she said, still without effusion.

"Weel, ye see, it's like this. In *simple* diveesion
—or subtrawction—ye juist pit doon the feegures on
yer sclate,—three, fower, sax, aucht, or whativer it
may be. But in *compoon'* subtrawction—or diveesion
—ye ken what it is ye're dealin' wi', an' ye pit doon
the like o' money. Tak' fowerpence frae saxpence,
or whativer it is that's in the buik." He was rather
proud of himself for finding so simple an example.

"Oh, I'd like that!" cried the lady, forgetting
her grievance in a moment. "I'll make Auntie
teach me compound—what was it?—compound long
division—to-morrow."

Sandy was sorely tempted to let this remark
pass unchallenged, but he was too conscientious for
that.

"I doobt that'll no dae, Missy," he said, with the
air of a man who will go to the stake for his convic-

tions. " Ye maun e'en gang through wi' the simples,
an' than commence wi' compoon' addeetion."

The lady thought it was time to change the subject, and she did so like a true conversationalist,
with no unseemly wrench.

" Do you know how much I've got to spend at
the fair, Sandy ? " she said. " A shilling and six-
pence penny ! " And she produced the three coins
in triumph.

" My word ! "

" How much have you got, Sandy ? "

" Weel," said he, looking rather unhappy, " I'm
no mindit to spen' ower muckle, for I'm savin' up to
buy a horse."

" A horse ! "

" Ay. My faither thinks I'll manage it by the
time I'm twinty. 'Mony a pickle mak's a mickle,"
he says. I've sax poun' the noo, an' maybe a wee
thing mair. It's maistly gey slaw wark coontin' the
bawbees, but I got a graun' lift when my graunfaith-
er deed. He left me five pun'."

" Oh, Sandy, how splendid ! " cried the lady,
moved to genuine enthusiasm. " A real big horse,
instead of the stupid old gate. Will he be like Snowflake ? "

" Ay," said the boy, with the air of a connoisseur,
such as his father might have assumed on tasting a
sample of wheat,—" no unlike Snowflake, but no sae
langnebbit, an' a wee thing braider i' the hench."

" And will you give me a ride, Sandy, as you did
on the gate last night ? You called the gate Snowflake, you know."

The boy's face fell. They had become such excellent friends in the last hour.

"Ye maunna forget, Missy," he said, "I'm no to
get it ere I'm twinty, an' I doobt ye'll no be carin'
muckle aboot a ride than !"

There was something irresistible in this argument,
and the lady's face fell too.

"But, Sandy," she said shyly, "perhaps by
the time you're twenty, you'll be—a gentleman!"

"Na, na," he said with honest Scotch pride, "I'm
no wantin' to be a gentleman. I'd suner be like my
Faither, an' mak' the finest furrow an' the straucht-
est stack i' the hail countra-side!"

Alas, for the cloud no bigger than a man's hand!
There could be no doubt at all that a shadow had
fallen upon the tiny "twosome," and now the shadow
began to darken.

"D'ye no hear wheels?" said Sandy suddenly,
stopping short, and putting down his ear to listen.
"Ay, it's a gig! Gang a wee thing forrit, Missy, in
front o' me, an' I daursay they'll no tak' muckle heed
o' ye. Carry this bit switch ower yer shouther, an'
pu' yer bannet weel forrit. Ye're in an awfu' mess
o' dust—that's ae guid thing—an' no vera like
yersel'."

In a few minutes the gig rattled past, and, fortunately, its occupants took no apparent notice of
the two little travellers.

"It's a man an' a wife," said Sandy presently,
"but I dinna ken wha. I dauredna lift my een till
they were bye. Nae doobt the gig's been loaned

9

them, an' it's ill kennin' folk frae the luik o' their backs on Fair day!''

" Wha's yon?" remarked the driver of the gig to his wife, when they were past.

" I'm no that sure. The laddie's like Tamson's Sandy, but I nae ken wha the wee lassie can be. She disna favour the Tamsons ava."

The children drew a breath of relief, but before long a spring-cart came up, and this time a woman leaned over to speak.

" Wha's yon ye've gotten wi' ye, Sandy?" quoth she.

" A lassie," said cautious Sandy.

" I see fine it's a lassie, but what'n a lassie?"

Then poor Sandy, driven to desperation, was guilty of the one piece of unjustifiable rudeness of which I ever heard him accused—such trite rudeness, too, unrelieved by a single spark of originality.

" Ask yer granny!" he said, with as bold an air as he could muster.

A shout of laughter from the cart greeted this retort. Humour of the crudest type is allowed to pass muster on Fair day.

But the baffled questioner did not join in the laugh.

" My word!" she exclaimed angrily. " He's no blate! An' they say the Tamsons' Sandy is that canny an' fair-spoken. I niver!"

" Hoot, wumman, it's the Fair!" said her husband soothingly, and so the matter dropped.

Thus danger Number Two passed by, but although the little lady had held up gallantly hitherto, there could be no doubt that her strength was beginning to flag. She denied vehemently that she was tired, and she still talked gaily of merry-go-rounds and " ladies with gold spanglies "; but, as Sandy looked at her drooping dusty little figure, he began to feel quite sure of what he had feared all along—that she would never reach the Fair at all.

He was still looking at her, with a very pitiful feeling in his honest heart, when a great cloud of dust came up behind them, and, when it settled—behold the figures of Mr. and Mrs. Thomson and the lady's nurse !—not to speak of poor old Snow-flake, patiently wondering why he had been lashed into such an unconscionable lather.

At first it was impossible to distinguish anything in the violent altercation that ensued; but at last the nurse succeeded in dismounting from the cart, and—as is the way with nurses while an explanation is pending—shook her little charge violently by the shoulder.

" I wunner *at* ye ! " cried poor Sandy with trembling lips. " It wasna her blame—a wee bit thing like yon ! "

" An' ye're no feared to staun' there an' say it was *your* blame ! " shouted Sandy's father, white with rage, yet amazed, in the midst of his indignation, that a lad who had never needed a thrashing in his life should have earned one so richly now. " There'll no be ony Fair for you, ma man. Ye'll gang straucht hame, an' change yer claes, an' when I come hame the nicht—*I'll pay ye !* "

This was indeed an appalling threat; for although Bill Thomson was a decent, well-doing, kindly man in the main, it was not to be expected of human nature that the night after the Fair should find him in a peculiarly conciliatory or reasonable frame of mind.

Sandy turned as white as a sheet of paper; but, selfish as my little lady was, this was more than she could bear.

She shook off her nurse's hold in a moment, and, darting up with crimson face and clenched fists to the huge, passionate man, she stamped her tiny foot on the dusty road.

"It's not his blame!" she shouted, quivering with anger, and unconsciously making use of their own expression. "It's not his blame, and you know it! It's *my* blame. He wanted to drive Snowflake. He didn't want to bring me a bit; and I made him, I made him, I made him! I said I'd come alone, so he had to take care of me. And—and—and I made him promise not to tell— *so there!* If you whip him, or send him home, or say a single word to him, I'll "—she gasped literally for breath—" I'll KILL YOU!"

And, having thus delivered herself of all the points in the evidence, having even got safely through a most impressive peroration, counsel for the defence broke down in a torrent of tears.

"Is that true, Sandy?" said his mother, putting her arm round the trembling boy.

Now Sandy had never lied to his mother in his life; and being, as I told you, only a common Scotch laddie, and no gallant French gentleman—being, moreover, much too young and inexperienced for a heavy *rôle* like that of knight in so trying a drama, —he hid his face in his mother's shawl, and sobbed out a most unchivalrous " Ay ! "

" Just to think," cried Nurse, still white with fright, " o' that hussy, Sarah, never lettin' on till we missed her that the bairns was together last night. I'll gie her a hearin' once I get hame ! "

" Weel," said Sandy's mother cautiously, " I've nae doot ava that Sarah's gotten a fricht—*as weel's yersel' !* "

But the hint was lost upon Nurse.

" I'm that pleased," she said, " that I didna telegraph to the missis. There's no need now for her to ken onything aboot it."

" Hoot, wumman ! " said Mrs. Thomson. " Honesty's aye the best policy. Tak' my advice, an' mak' a clean breist o't the meenit she pits her fit ower the door. She'll be wantin' a word wi' wersels as weel, I'm thinking ! "

Nurse had come on with the Thomsons to save time, but had left word that the governess cart was to follow as soon as possible, so there was no difficulty about getting home. And so it was settled, with more immediate justice than we are accustomed to meet with in human affairs, that Sandy should go on to the Fair, as originally arranged, and that the lady should be conducted ignominiously home by her nurse.

I think I need scarcely inform the reader who has followed her fortunes thus far, that, under these trying circumstances, she conducted herself with due dignity, as a heroine should, flatly declining to excuse or incriminate herself in any way till Auntie should arrive.

III.

THE poor little lady had sobbed herself to sleep that night, and Auntie and I were still sitting over the drawing-room fire, congratulating ourselves and thanking Heaven that the adventure had ended no worse. The fire had burned low, and we were talking of going to bed, when the door burst open, and our motherly old cook came in with a white, scared face.

"If you please'm," she said, "they say wee Sandy at the cottar-hooses is deein', an' he's awfu' keen to see Miss Rosie."

"*Dying!*" exclaimed Auntie. "What do you mean? He was well enough this morning."

"Ay, but he'd an awfu' accident at the Fair. He was on ane o' thae muckle swees, leanin' atower to speak to the laddies below,—an' he fell. He was kin' o' stunned like at the first, but he's himsel' the noo; only—they say—the doctor's feared his neck's broke."

"And does the doctor think there is any immediate danger?"

"Ay. He niver thocht the laddie'd live to get here, but the Mither, puir body, couldna rest till she got him hame; so they brocht him on a shutter. The doctor says it's no a case in which he'd like to

be unco sure; but he's no expeckin' him—to bide
wi's—till the morn."

"Then of course Rosie must go at once," said
Auntie hastily. "Tell Nurse to put on her warm
dressing-gown, and wrap her up in a blanket.—No,
stay. I'll go myself. You'll come with us?" she
said, turning to me.

Poor Rosie was sadly scared and disconcerted
at being wakened out of her first sleep.. I doubt
whether such a thing had ever happened to her in all
her baby life before.

It was the grieve who had brought the news,
and now, as he lighted us down the dark road,
Auntie tried to prepare her little niece for what she
was to see. This was no easy task, for, beyond a
general idea, picked up mainly from the servants,
that God was responsible for most things, and might,
or might not, be inclined to listen to human prayers,
—the child had received no religious training at all;
and the eclectic knowledge of Scripture, witnessed
by her familiarity with the story of Jonah, had by
no means been calculated to fan the flame of devo-
tion. For Auntie was one of those people who believe that only a mature intelligence should grapple
with what she called "the problems of religion."

The cottage consisted of a but and a ben, and we
"went ben" at once, while the grieve prepared the
family for our visit. We drew back in a moment
when we found the doctor in the sitting-room; but
the house was so small that it was impossible not to
hear every word he said,—for he had brought with
him his nephew, fresh from college.

"I don't see why you should suspect a cervical
fracture, uncle," the young man was saying. "There
is no paralysis, and his breathing is practically all
right."

"That's true, lad," said our dear old Æsculapius,
whom a happy chance had brought to the spot a few
minutes after the accident. "But I got a creak
once that I didn't like, and I'm sure neither you nor
me is wanting to get it again. Besides it's not for
nothing that he's holding his head so stiff. I've got
it now between sandbags, and I've told him to keep
it steady (though that wouldn't have been much use
if Nature hadn't been beforehand with me, as she
mostly is). But we must make some better arrange-
ment for the night, in case he falls asleep, puir laddie! I've told his mother it may come any minute,
and—if it comes—it's like to be over before she
knows."

At this moment Mrs. Thomson entered the tiny
passage in which we stood, and, after a vain convulsive effort to speak, beckoned to us to follow her.
It is little to say that none of us will ever forget the
sight that met our eyes as we entered the kitchen.

By the smouldering embers of the fire sat the
father, ill at ease in the unaccustomed "braws"
donned for the fair, his whole attitude one of the
uttermost dejection. The light of a single tallow
candle fell on the bed where the little patient was
lying, strangely straight and stiff, but otherwise not
half so changed as we had expected to find him. On
one side his Mother stood by the head of the bed,
looking at him—Ah, how she did look! Surely her

very soul was flowing into his!—and on the other
side sat the young minister who had lately come to
the parish, with one hand stretched out towards the
boy, the other grasping a well-worn Bible.

A curious fit of shyness seemed to come over the
little lad as we entered the room. Unable to turn
away his head, he laid one hand across his eyes,
while with the other he groped stiffly about the
counterpane.

"I brocht ye a fairin', Missy," he said timidly.
"Whaur is't, Mither?"

Half-blind with weeping, the poor woman put
something into his hand, and he held it out to the
little lady whom Auntie had placed on the foot of
the bed. Surely half the pathos of death lies in the
weird touches of comedy that cross his path to the
very last. Solemnly Rosie held out her hand, and
solemnly she took possession of a gingerbread man,
and a bit of the crude red confection which is a
staple commodity at the Fair.

"It's naethin' by-ordinar," he said humbly, recovering from his shyness, now that the longed-for
ordeal was over. "No what I wad ha' likit; but
they wadna let me bide——"

"Na," said his mother. "It was efter they had
him on the shutter, and he'd begooed to come to
hissel'; but the doctor had tellt me—— Naethin'
wad please him but he maun get a fairin' for Missy.
I'm sure I juist gruppit onythin' that cam' to my
han'. I canna even richtly ca' to mind that I p'yed
for't. It *is* a puir bit thing! Ye maun e'en excuse it."

"You *dear* little boy," said Auntie, kneeling down
by the bed, and stroking the rough brown hand.
"You shouldn't have spent your money on Rosie.
She has lots of toys. When you get well——"

Here she broke down; but now Rosie, who had
been sitting half dazed, suddenly found voice,—

"And he didn't mean to spend his pennies,
Auntie. He's saving up to buy a horse!"

"Na, na," said the boy hastily. "Hae they no
tellt ye? I'm no gaun to get better, Missy. The
meenister says," he added, with a shy smile, "that he
wadna wunner an they gied me a horse when I get
there. He's been readin' me an awfu' bonny scripter
aboot the white horses. I'm no sae feared o'
Heaven, an it's like yon."

For just one moment the minister looked rather
shamefacedly at Auntie. She was a beautiful woman,
and he was very young, and they had had some
wondrous discussions of late; but criticism was
very far from Auntie's eyes just then.

"I am sure you deserve a horse if you want one,"
she said, "you little hero!"

He pointed to the lady at the foot of the bed.

"She was pluckier than me the day," he said
simply. "I've been beat by a lassie."

"*That* you haven't, darling! Rosie has told me
all about it, and I'm sure she is as sorry as I am for
the trouble she got you into. If Rosie grows up to
be half as brave and good as you are——"

Here Auntie broke down completely, and a
troubled look came over the little face.

"I was aye mindit to be guid to my Mither when

I was big. She's been sair owerwrocht, puir Mither!
But I'm thinkin' God maun ken fine that He hasna
gied me the chaunce."

The doctor had entered the room, but I don't
think there was one of us who could have found
speech to answer this, when Rosie's worldly little
voice broke in upon the silence.

"But you must get well, Sandy; indeed you
must! I like you better than all the other boys—
Ronald and Harold and Hugh. They're so rough
and selfish, and they won't have girls in their games.
If you'll only get well, Sandy—when you're big—
I'll—I'll marry you, even if you're not a gentleman!"

Did we laugh or cry? Both I think; but the
little knight on the borderland took the situation
very seriously.

"Ye're unco guid, I'm sure, Missy," he said
simply; "but ye're no for the like o' me. It's no
that I couldna wark for ye. I could that! But
ye'd aye need a wumman body to dae for ye, and
I'd no like to see ye wantin' the bonny bit things
ye've been used to. Maybe," he went on, changing
the subject with delicate tact, "the meenister wad
read us yon bonny chapter again."

And without opening his Bible the minister began in a deep sympathetic voice,—

"'And I saw heaven opened, and behold a white
horse, and he that sat upon him was called Faithful
and True, and in righteousness he doth judge and
make war. His eyes were as a flame of fire, and on
his head were many crowns; and he had a name

written, that no man knew but he himself. And he was clothed with a vesture dipped in blood ; and his name is called the Word of God. And the armies which were in heaven followed him upon white horses, clothed in fine linen, white and clean.' "

Did he think the next words were too stern for so young a disciple ? I do not know, but after a moment's silence, he fell back upon the same allegory, as it issued from the lips of the prophet, in whose mighty heart and brain it first took form.

" ' And he said, Surely they are my people, *children that will not lie*——' "

He paused again for a moment, and the poor mother broke in eagerly, " That's him, sir, that's Sandy ! It's as if it was wrote for him !" And then the minister went on,

" ' ——so he was their Saviour. In all their affliction he was afflicted, and the angel of his presence saved them : in his love and in his pity he redeemed them : and he bare them, and carried them—all the days.' "

The little lady listened with rapt attention, straining her ears to catch every word ; and who knows what vague, grand image formed in her baby mind ? As for the little knight, he forgot his injury, and with a hasty, unconscious effort, turned to speak to the minister. In a moment he remembered, but it was too late. Even as he fell back, before he had time to guess that the summons had come, a change came over his brave little face. . . .

I think his young visitor scarcely noticed the

change, for the doctor hastily signed to us to leave the room, and we went.

Shivering with excitement we made our way up the dark avenue to the house.

" Auntie," whispered the heathen little lady, forc- ing her head out of the blanket and gazing all around, like a chicken from under its mother's wing, " has the man on the white horse come to fetch him ? "

Poor Auntie ! It would have taken a wondrously pure Agnosticism to stand the blast of a furnace like that.

" I believe he has, darling," she said, clasping her treasure more tightly. " ' He shall gather the lambs with his arm, and carry them in his bosom ' ! "

An hour later, when the little lady was sound asleep once more, Auntie stopped on the stair, candle in hand ; and I saw she had been seized by one of those odd relapses into cynicism, with which her friends were so familiar.

" I always knew Rosie was a witch," she said lightly, " but the amount of discrimination she has shown in the last thirty hours——"

Here the cynicism broke down, and the cynic made good her retreat.

IV.

It was New Year's Day, and a party of bright young girls were gathered in Rosie's pretty boudoir waiting for afternoon tea.

" Leap Year," said one of them, taking down a

calendar from the mantelpiece. "Now's your chance, all of you!" And they jested as young girls will, to whom life (in the orthodox social sense) is a "joke that's just begun."

"I wonder," said a dreamy voice, "whether any woman ever did avail herself of her privilege?"

"Of course!" said Rosie calmly.

A shout of indignation and surprise greeted this speech, for Rosie was far from being in the habit of giving away her own sex.

"And, to hear her talk, you would think she knew something about it!" laughed one.

"I know this much about it,—that I have done it myself!"

"You!"

"Proposed to a man!"

"Your first season, and the ball at your feet!"

"Nonsense!"

"Nevertheless it is true," said Rosie quietly. "I was six years old, and he was nine. He was dying, and I said, if he would get well, I'd marry him. I would have done it too," she went on, looking round her royally, "if he would have had me,—though he *was* a farm-labourer's son! His mother is one of my best friends to this day. I was a spoilt ill-mannered little minx; and he—— I wish some of our fine gentlemen could learn *manners* from him! No well-worn tricks; none of the 'little way' which we women are supposed to be quite unable to resist; no surface veneer;—only real chivalry and inborn fine breeding as deep as his brave little heart!"

So then of course they made her tell the story, as

I have tried to tell it to you. There was dead silence when she finished. She had risen towards the end, and had walked over to the window; but she was Auntie's own child, and now she turned, and brought us back with a jar to

"The C Major of this life."

"Oddly enough," she said, "we were at Duncairn last summer. The Fair came round while we were there; and oh, the noise and the squalor and the tawdriness! There was no escaping it. It seemed to blast the country for miles around. *Sic transit gloria mundi!*"

"Ay—*mundi!*" I answered thoughtfully. "But it seems to me that Sandy's memory is wondrous green."

THE STORY OF A FRIENDSHIP.

But thou and I are one in kind,
  As moulded like in nature's mint ;
  And hill and wood and field did print
The same sweet forms in either mind. . . .

And so my wealth resembles thine ;
  But he was rich where I was poor,
  And he supplied my wants the more
As his unlikeness fitted mine.—TENNYSON.

I.

THE docks have a poetry of their own when impartial night throws her uniform dark domino over fair and foul alike when the red and green lights fall in spangles on the water, and the flare of torch, or perhaps the gleam of moonlight, makes an impressionist picture out of every commonplace group. The docks at night would be a not unfitting scene for the opening chapter of a love-tale.

But this is no love-tale that I am about to tell ; it is the simple story of a brief Bohemian friendship ; and it begins—fittingly enough, perhaps—not in moonlight and glamour, but in the prosaic, shadowless glare of an unclouded September noon.

The good ship *Puffin* was getting up steam, and

its belching funnel radiated a sickening intolerable
heat: the well-scoured planks glowed in the sun, the
paint and the metal fittings scorched the unwary
hand like redhot iron, and the creak and rattle of the
crane added a final note of unrest to the general
glare and discord.

"Do come under my sunshade, Ned!" said a tall
young girl. "This heat is perfectly killing."

Her companion—a man of perhaps five and thirty
—raised a delicate, sunburnt hand to put the proffered shelter aside. He was standing on deck with
one long leg thrown lazily over the arm of a wooden
seat.

"Heat suits me," he said, with a touch of irritation in his voice; "and, if it didn't, it would be almost
worth while being grilled to gather first impressions
of one's fellow-passengers. It's for all the world
like putting into a lottery."

She let the dainty, lace-frilled parasol fall on her
shoulder, and looked round with a low laugh.

"Mainly blanks this time, I fear!"

"Perhaps. You are young and hard to please;
and your *rôle* in life does not happen to be merely
that of spectator. But there's a certain interest in
the thing itself apart from the chance of a prize. Do
you notice the difference of opinion that seems to
exist as to our destination? These business men
come on board with as little ado as if they were
stepping into a city omnibus; and to see those
weeping schoolgirls, one would think we were bound
for——" He paused.

"The Antipodes?"

10

"Ay. Or that our jovial captain was old Charon himself." He paused again, and smiled rather grimly. "Who knows? Perhaps he is—for some of us!"

"*Ned!*" The girl frowned impatiently, and hastened to change the subject.

"Your 'schoolgirls' are pretty mature," she said. "You ought to have a chaperon. It is astonishing how every small shopkeeper nowadays must needs send his daughter to Germany to study music."

"Why not? Where is Edith?"

"I don't know. Tipping the steward to see that you don't fall overboard, I should think."

"She is quite capable of it. Tell her it is high time you were going on shore. Think what it would be for me to be saddled with both of you, just as I am looking forward to a little peace!"

She smiled with the quiet assurance of a girl who knows her own value. "Don't be uneasy. We have no desire to miss the tournament. And here comes Edith at last to set your mind at rest. Do I look as sweet and cool and willowy as that? I often think, Ned, how grateful you must feel for your sisters—when you look at other people's!"

"Oh, I do," he said quietly. "The thought of their back hair brightens my darkest hours.—Good Lord!"

A cab had just driven up, and from it was alighting a young girl. She seemed to be about eighteen, though the short, scrimp gown of heavy plum-coloured stuff scarcely bespoke so mature an age. Her brow was moist, her cheeks crimson with heat;

and an old-fashioned jacket was thrown open, reveal-
ing an uncompromising row of bright metal buttons.

"Oh, the pathos of her!" murmured Edith from
out a cool cloud of lace and cambric.

But the new arrival, fortunately for herself, was
as yet wholly unaware of her own pathos. All she
knew was that she meant to catch that steamer, and
she was too inexperienced a traveller to feel sure
even now that she was safe. So, with dogged determination, unconscious of the undisguised amusement
in the eyes of the lookers-on, she took a basket, a
tin hat-box, and a bundle of wraps in one hand;
and carefully grasping a violin-case in the other, she
proceeded to thread her perilous way across the
narrow gangway.

"Go it, Sturdy!" said Ned under his breath, and
he went forward, with such haste as his languid
nature allowed, to offer his help.

But the well-meant act only awakened her to a
tardy, painful self-consciousness.

"Thank you; I can manage," she said stiffly,
though with a catch of fatigue in her voice; and, by
dint of a mighty effort, she deposited her traps at
the top of the companion-way.

The young man returned to his sisters with a
comical light in his blue eyes.

"That is what you call the snub direct," he said.

"Minx!" said Sybil softly.

"Nonsense!" corrected Edith. "She is accustomed to help herself, that's all. Poor little soul!
I wish she wasn't quite so hot."

"So do I." Ned took off his straw hat, and

passed his hand through his straight brown hair. "She has raised the temperature on board by several degrees."

"Well, miss, *you've* run it pretty close!" said the porter, dropping a large tin box with a bang on deck.

The girl glanced uneasily at her ill-used box, and then turned to the porter with a sense that an apology was due somewhere.

"I know," she stammered awkwardly. "I couldn't help it. My train stopped in the tunnel for forty-seven minutes. They said——"

But the porter, having secured his meagre tip, naturally did not stop to hear what they said.

"Well, good-bye, Ned dear!" said Edith, offering him her soft pink cheek in an incidental, perfunctory way. "Do get proper food, and don't stay in the North after the cold weather begins!"

"Steep your soul in Wagner," said Sybil, "and avoid *Heringsalat*—if you can."

Ned just touched the fair cheeks with his lips, then lifted his hat, and looked after the graceful retreating figures with very genuine admiration. The little girl in the plum-coloured gown was sitting close to the gangway, so for a moment she necessarily formed a part of an otherwise charming picture.

Yes, he did feel grateful for his sisters—when he looked at other people's!

II.

LUNCH on board was a dreary affair that day. The saloon was stifling, and everyone seemed more or less depressed. Even the man whose *rôle* in life was merely that of spectator could wring from this first social gathering only the mild form of amusement to be gained by revising his conception of his fellow-passengers, now that he saw them for the first time without their headgear.

"Odd," he reflected, "how in some cases the upper part of the face makes no difference, while in others it gives the lie to the mouth and chin. I hope I don't go about the world dumbly exclaiming, 'Oh, wretched man that I am!' What a head little Sturdy has! Is it genius or a tendency to hydrocephalus? I wonder why people with that particular shade of sandy red hair always choose that particular shade of inflammatory red gown. And what demon can have prompted the brass buttons?"

The captain, to be sure, was in excellent spirits, as captains are wont to be,—answering impossible questions with imperturbable good humour, and striving in the intervals to enliven the little party of "schoolgirls," collapsed and unselfconscious as these were under the first fierce throes of homesickness. The only woman on board who struck Ned as being in any way eligible from the point of view of companionship, a young married lady travelling with her little boy, left the table before the soup was removed. She seemed to be suffering from a strong preconceived notion that she ought to be sea-sick.

Altogether he was thankful when the meal was over and he was free to escape, free to bask in the sunshine on a luxurious deck-chair with a handkerchief over his face, and a copy of Keats within easy reach of his hand.

He must have fallen asleep, for it seemed only a moment before his meditations were disturbed by a peal of rippling laughter. The schoolgirls must surely be coming to life again. Yes, there they were, comfortably ensconced under an awning on the captain's bridge, laughing and chatting as gaily as if there had been no tragic parting only an hour or two before.

"Chameleons!" ejaculated Ned. "No more sleep for me this afternoon." And his conclusion proved perfectly right. The ripple of laughter went on with scarcely a break till it seemed to him that a tiny stream of it was drawing nearer to where he sat. It was a very tiny stream—mentally he stigmatized it as a giggle—and he was not a little surprised when it broke over him with a plash.

"May I ask if you are courting a sunstroke?"

He removed the handkerchief from his face, and looked up calmly with wide blue eyes. Chivalry was not one of the virtues on which he prided himself, so he was in no hurry to respond. Moreover, although he had travelled a.good deal, he had rarely travelled alone, and he had never realized that young girls did this sort of thing.

Yet there was something quite attractive about

the speaker's face,—a fresh, sweet *beauté de diable*
which made no pretension to anything more remarkable. He had no objection at all to entering into
conversation, but, before he had found the reply he
sleepily sought, another voice broke in,—

> "'In the days of my youth,' Father William replied,
> 'I thought it might injure the brain ;
> But now I am perfectly sure I have none
> I do it again and again.'"

Ned turned his eyes languidly to the second
speaker. There was no difficulty in classifying her
—a typical *soubrette*, with red cheeks, large round
eyes, diminutive nose, and a mass of touzled hair.
Few men feel themselves at a loss in dealing with
this particular type, and, as it chanced, her quota-
tion supplied him with the answer for which he
sought.

"'Curiouser and curiouser,'" he said, looking at
her gravely.

But the girl who had spoken first was not prepared to be taken on her companion's level.

"I hope you will forgive the liberty we have
taken," she said with a pretty blush. "The fact is
we are all so homesick and the sea is so unexpect-
edly calm, that we thought of having a little.con-
cert to-night to cheer us up. Some of us play and
sing a little, and—and we are all quite sure you are
musical, so we thought you would not mind our asking your help."

He smiled pleasantly. "You flatter me," he said.
"I shall be delighted to turn over your leaves."

"Is that all you can do?" asked the *soubrette*.

In her social circle at home audacity was considered to be her forte, and she had cultivated it accordingly.

"That is all."

"Then of course you can't do that decently. But we don't believe a word of it, you know. Look here, will you sing for us?"

"Sorry I can't."

"Then what is your instrument?"

"I don't know. When I was very young, and felt the absolute necessity of converting my energy into sound waves——"

"Well?"

"I found the toilet comb a fairly satisfactory medium."

She laughed, then tapped her high-heeled shoe impatiently on the deck.

"Look here," she said again, "we don't know you, you know."

"Oh! Thanks. I confess I was forgetting the fact."

"So you might just give us some idea how much urging you usually take. If it's a case of fetching camp-stools, it would be kinder to say so at once."

He had half risen from his comfortable chair, but was by no means prepared to relinquish it.

"No," he said candidly. "I think camp-stools would be a mistake." Then he turned to the girl who had spoken first. "I am sorry I can't be of use," he said; "but you will find me an excellent listener."

" Humph !" ejaculated the *soubrette*. "Never mind, Miss Lawrence. We still have the professional to fall back upon."

"The professional?" said Ned, with languid interest.

"Yes; don't you know? The girl who arrived late, with big box, little box, carpet-bag, and bundle —*and* violin-case—on her shoulders. Looks musical, doesn't she? I say,"—she lowered her voice to a whisper,—"do you know how she is employing her time this lovely afternoon? Studying German ! Her particular genius seems to be for doing things at the eleventh hour."

" Enviable woman !" said Ned. " My particular genius is for *planning* to do things at the eleventh hour, till my resolutions are disturbed by hearing the clock strike twelve."

"Well, I think you have the best of it. All the German she'll learn on the voyage won't do her much good."

" Nonsense, Miss Brown !" interposed her companion good-naturedly. " How do you know she is studying German ? "

" I can see from here. Her pages are all broken up into exercises an inch deep. '*Der Vater ist gross. Die Mutter ist gut.*' You know the sort of thing."

" A whole philosophy of life, in fact," said Ned with a twinkle in his eye—

" ' He for God only ; she for God in him.' "

The girls looked puzzled, and he regretted his
far-fetched observation.   What intelligent women
Edith and Sybil were, with all their limitations!

But Miss Brown saw she had missed a point, and
hastened to change the subject.

"Do come and help us to tackle her," she said.
"I believe she is strong-minded."

"Then my sex is clearly out of it;" and, just
lifting his straw hat, he resumed his lounge and his
book with a sensation of considerable relief.

And then he found himself wondering how solemn
Sturdy would enjoy the baiting that awaited her.
But there! She was a girl, of course, and *bourgeoise*
at that.   No doubt she would be highly flattered by
the request, and only too pleased to trot out her
répertoire of pretty pieces.

But here he was mistaken. "Solemn Sturdy"
only looked up from her book to give a brief refusal.
"I never play in public," she said.

"Public!" exclaimed Miss Brown.   "Call this
public?"

The girl coloured, but stood to her guns. "It is
to me," she said simply.

"But I don't see what is the use of studying
music at all," said Miss Lawrence persuasively, "if
you don't mean to give pleasure to other people."

The girl opened her lips to speak; then closed
them again.   "There are other uses," she said
shortly.

"Oh, I know! I am used to hearing talk about
Art for Art's sake, and all that sort of thing. I am
afraid I must be a very commonplace person, and

quite unworthy of true Art; but it always seems to me a pity when superior people throw cold water on the simple pleasures that crop up by the way——"

"It's a thing any fool can do!" put in Miss Brown tersely.

"We don't ask them really to enjoy things that are beneath them," went on the other, taking a leaf from her companion's book; "but sometimes I think it would be worth while to make believe a little bit. It is very weak and frivolous, of course; but we do want to be happy in our own way, not in theirs."

She paused for a moment, awaiting a reply; but the girl did not look up, so the two companions walked away.

"One to you, Sturdy!" thought Ned. "I wonder how you like that?"

She did not leave him long in doubt. In another minute she had walked up to the two girls, blushing furiously.

"I didn't mean not to answer," she said, her voice quivering with the effort the action cost her. "I was thinking. You said some very true things just now. I *was* thinking only of myself; and—and—I will play to-night if you like; but I know I shall do it very badly."

"Well played, Sturdy, by Jove!" was Ned's emphatic mental comment. And it pleased him to fancy that from that moment the conversation of the trio was on quite a different level. They ceased for the moment to be merely "schoolgirls," and almost became human beings.

"But, oh, my child," he said regretfully, "you are

sadly out of proportion. Why that beetroot red?
And what a hat for the North Sea!"

Then he stretched himself with a yawn. "So we
must sit out this blessed concert after all!"

It did not prove so great an ordeal as he had
anticipated. Several of the girls played well—as
girls do nowadays—and one or two of the men threw
themselves into the entertainment with commend-
able zeal. But the feature of the evening was un-
doubtedly "Sturdy's" performance. Her violin was
cheap and harsh in tone, and her nervousness was
ridiculously out of proportion to the importance of
the occasion. Indeed the moral effort it cost her to
play at all might, under other circumstances, have
enabled her to lead a forlorn hope, or to face the
tortures of the Inquisition. But, apart from all this,
it was easy to see that her ear was indifferent, and
her whole method hopelessly bad. Her kindly lis-
teners scarcely knew where to look as she played;
the ignorant simply suffered; the initiated saw no
glimmer of hope or promise; but Sturdy scraped
doggedly on to the end.

It was over at last. She evidently realized that
it had been a failure, for she turned a deaf ear to
the well-meant conventional remarks that followed
it, and her lips were set firm and hard as she deliberately returned the showy new violin to its showy
new case.

"Is that a 'Straddledarius'?" said Ned playfully,
for the mere sake of breaking the awkward silence.

"Oh, of course!" she replied with unnecessary

bitterness; and, unconsciously holding her head very straight, she made her way up the companion-way to the darkness and solitude of the deck.

Poor little Sturdy!

"Well, if that's what you call Art for Art's sake," said Miss Brown, "I prefer to give my friends a little Philistine pleasure;" and, seating herself un-asked at the piano, she dashed into a swaying irre-sistible waltz, which covered poor Sturdy's fiasco more effectually perhaps than the kindest intentions could have done.

III.

IT was shortly after midnight when the steamer began to roll, and, an hour or two later, Sturdy awoke in her berth with that unearthly sense of strangeness and loneliness which almost makes the inexperienced traveller feel as if he had awakened in another world.

The lamps were burning low in the cabin, and from every peg a gown or cloak was swinging mys-teriously to and fro like the pendulum of a clock. The dash of the waves past the port-holes seemed suggestively near; and it was a relief even to listen to the noisy monotonous rattle of the screw, which seemed unwearyingly to reiterate that all was going well on deck in spite of the wind and the darkness.

For a time Sturdy lay steeped in a sense of lone-liness and home-sickness; but at last this was broken up, as a breeze breaks up enshrouding mists, by a vague haunting recollection. Surely there was something else, something more definite, about which she ought to be fretting, than her mere loneliness? Ah, yes, to be sure, there it was! No need to go in search of it. Why had she been such a fool as to attempt that *Bolero?* It was too trying! She had played it so well the day before she left home, and now—she never wished to hear it again as long as she lived! Of course she would never see these people any more, so after to-morrow it would not matter; and even now—if there was a real storm, they would be sick and frightened, and would forget all about that miserable concert.

And, having thus, in a figure, set Rome on fire to cook her poor little chop, Sturdy composed herself to sleep once more.

It was broad daylight when she awoke to see a tangled head peeping through her curtains.

"I say!" said Miss Brown's cheerful voice.

"Yes?"

"I have been lying awake for the last hour try- ing to think what the 'other uses' of violin-playing are. Do you think I could understand if you ex- plained them to me?"

Sturdy did not stop this time to reflect what was the right and honest thing to say. She took the first weapon that came to hand.

"When people are fortunate enough to give as much pleasure by their music as you do," she said coldly, "they don't need to think of other uses."

Miss Brown's round eyes grew rounder with sur- prise. "You *are* queer," she said candidly. "Do you know, yesterday afternoon I thought you were going to turn out pious?"

The other blushed painfully, but would not admit that the words struck home.

"I know," she said. "You thought you had only to put your penny in the slot, and take out your nice little cake of butter-scotch."

Miss Brown made her way to the looking-glass in search of a hairpin, but presently came back again

"Look here," she said. "Was that original—what you said just now? It was clever, you know."

"Nonsense!"

"And you don't look clever a bit."

"So I have often been told."

"I don't see any fun in being clever myself. Men like you far better if you are jolly."

"I don't see that that has anything to do with it. Is it nearly breakfast-time?"

"Quite, I fancy; but my watch has gone wrong." She gave the dainty enamelled toy a vigorous shake, and looked up with eyes full of serious perplexity. "Do you think the engine-man will be able to put it right for me?"

Sturdy smothered a laugh in the bedclothes. "If not, I would try the stoker," she said. "Do you mind letting me get up?"

Breakfast had already begun when the two girls entered the saloon, and their appearance was a matter of some interest, as the sea was by this time sufficiently rough to keep all the other ladies in their cabins. Moreover, each of the two had acquired a definite individuality the evening before in the eyes of the other passengers—Miss Brown by her frank audacity, Sturdy by her ludicrous and pathetic failure.

As soon as the meal was over, Miss Brown ensconced herself in the deck smoking cabin, with a little circle of admirers round her; while Sturdy sat uncomfortably perched on a high wooden seat in the open, her country-shod feet dangling some inches from the ground, and her eyes fixed on the book which had afforded Miss Brown so much entertainment the day before.

Ned was amused by the contrast between the two girls, and mentally sketched an impressionist description of them for Sybil's benefit. It was his custom to do this when separated from his sisters; but—lest he should appear too incredible in his character of brother—it is only just to add that very few of these descriptions were ever committed to paper.

And then he began to wish that the lady with the little boy had been able to come on deck. He was depressed, and inclined to be sea-sick, and, manlike, he wanted someone to interest and amuse him. Anybody would do. He spent a few minutes on the captain's bridge, but the deafening wind drove him down on deck again.

He was not in the least degree tempted to join Miss Brown's coterie; and the plum-coloured gown was certainly not attractive either, even though the

vulgar hat had been replaced to considerable advantage by the hood of a dark grey cloak. Moreover, the owner of the gown had twice already
repelled his commonplace, conventional civilities;
and, although he justly attributed this to mere
girlish *gaucherie*, he had no desire to lay himself
open to snub number three. The bait was not
sufficiently tempting. True, the girl had given
some sign of possessing rather a fine moral vein
the evening before, but one might talk to her for
hours without striking that particular vein again;
and if, by ill luck, one struck music instead——!

So he paced up and down till it became almost
impossible to retain a footing on the wave-washed
deck; till Miss Brown, with the roses all fled from
her cheeks, had been assisted down the companion-
way; till he and the plum-coloured gown retained
sole possession of the field.

A sudden lurch of the vessel made him stagger,
and he wondered whether his companion felt as
acutely miserable as he did.

Apparently not. She had just raised her eyes
from her book, and the expression of her face as
she gazed absently over the heaving grey water,
recalled to his mind — incongruously enough it
seemed—a rapt young nun whom he had seen one
day at Lyon through the grating of a queer old
chapel.

That transient expression gave her face a note
of distinction that almost startled him—it was so
curiously at variance with his previous conception
of her; and he began to wonder what her book

II

could be. Not German exercises surely. What a pity she was not decently dressed, and a little less self-conscious!

But in spite of these obvious drawbacks her placid self-sufficiency and complete disregard of the buffeting elements were prevoking, and at last he stopped in front of her, balancing himself with difficulty, and wrapping his Inverness cape round his lean figure.

"You are plucky," he said.

No one could have resisted the charm of those clear boyish eyes, but unfortunately their very frankness had the effect of making her self-conscious, and she made an obvious effort to pull the scrimp skirt over her clumsy boots. She was angry too. She felt quite sure that this languid, superior-looking man would not trouble to speak to her when women of his own set were present; so why should he go out of his way to be agreeable just because they chanced to be alone?

"I don't see any occasion for pluck," she said.

"I think I could find you a more sheltered seat if you would let me."

"Thank you; I am quite comfortable here."

This was so obviously impossible that his face broke into a broad brotherly smile.

"I can only congratulate you on your book then," he said; "it must be enthralling."

"It is."

Her expression changed, and her eye fell lovingly on the page.

He took this as a sign that the interview was

over, and staggered away in no very amiable humour.
He asked so little of women as he went through life,
and it happened very rarely that they failed to give
him as much as he asked!

" Little stick ! " he said to himself. " She is not
so attractive that she need hold herself so dear ! "

He smoked a cigarette, and then, looking at his
watch with a yawn, he decided to go downstairs.

But just at this moment the wind caught his
companion's paper-covered book, and threw it in
half-a-dozen pieces across the deck.   Before he had
realized the situation, she had sped on an awkward
chase after the farthest fragment ; and, by dint of a
desperate scramble, they gathered up the remainder
between them.   The shabby grey cover fell to his
gun, as he afterwards expressed it ; and, before returning it to her, he glanced frankly at the title,—
*Die Erziehung des Menschengeschlechts, von Gotthold
Ephraim Lessing.**

" Jove ! " he exclaimed, forgiving and forgetting
in a moment the undignified exertion to which he
had been put.   " Is that the sort of literature
with which you while away the time on a stormy
voyage ? "

He was smiling again, but this time his face bore
witness to such genuine surprise and interest that
she answered eagerly,—

" Thank you so very very much. .I was afraid it
was gone for ever, and another copy would never
have been the same.   Have—you read it ? "

---

* *The Education of the Human Race*, by G. E. Lessing.

"Not in the original. You have the advantage
of me there. I have read Robertson's translation."

"I don't read German well," she said colouring,
"but this is worth digging at."

"Rather. I am afraid my knowledge of the
language is too limited to be utilized even as a pick-
axe." He turned over the leaves as lovingly as she
might have done herself. "The fellow was a poet
as well as a seer. He put his heart as well as his
head into this." He paused, wondering whether it
was worth while to give utterance to the thought
in his mind. "A book written with the intellect
only, affects me like a picture on which the artist
has 'lavished all the wealth of his paint-box,' as
the novelists put it, without producing a bit of real
colour."

Was it really the same girl who stood looking
up into his face, hanging on his random words with
such breathless interest? The vulgar unbecoming
dress had somehow vanished out of the picture altogether; even the homely features were merged in an
expression of living interest, compared to which
beauty itself might well have appeared tame.

At last she drew a long breath. "It seems to
me just wonderful," she said in a low voice, "though
I have only spelt it out line by line. Perhaps, as
you have read it, you would be so very kind as
to explain one or two things I didn't quite understand?"

"Oh, come!" he said, his blue eyes dilating with
a comical expression of alarm and amusement. "I
shall begin to regret that I owned up to having

read it. It seems much more likely that you can help me."

"Don't laugh at me, please!" she said. Why, there were actually tears in her eyes! What a queer little customer she was! Robinson Crusoe could scarcely have looked more excited when he came upon the footprint in the sand. "I never could have said what you said just now. I didn't even understand it all, and yet it seemed so true."

He laughed softly. He may be forgiven if Gretchen's words passed through his mind—"Why, that is what our pastor says,—only in rather different words."

"You must have read so much, and seen so much," she went on; "and I—mine is such a *little* world! I thought I never should meet the people who like the books I like!"

He looked down at her from his great height with a pleasant smile, amused at the turn affairs had taken. As his admiration for her grew, he realized more fully what a child she was.

"Come and sit in that sheltered corner I told you of," he said kindly, "and tell me about the books you like."

And that was how it began.

IV.

A man unspoil'd,
Sweet, generous, and humane;
With all the fortunate have not—
MATTHEW ARNOLD.

SURELY there are few things on earth so altogether desirable as a rare old friendship—issuing,
not from glamour and ignorance, but from well-tried
confidence and knowledge; animating us, not with
the heats and chills of fever, but with the quiet constant glow of vivid life, providing us, now with
fresh springs of energy, now with rest and healing
waters after labour and defeat; throwing back to us
an image of ourselves which we recognize, and yet
would fain live up to; taking us thankfully for what
we are, and yet ever unconsciously reminding us of
what we would be. Restful in its very essence is a
friendship like this, though constantly stirred through
its depths by a silent spring of effort to attain more
nearly its own ideal.

And yet, when all is said, there is a charm about
new friendship too, with its shallow transparency, its
pretty leaps and bounds, its constant sparkle of sur-
prises. In youth we find it full of infinite possibilities. In manhood hope and interest are not so
easily roused: experience has proved most things to
be mediocre, and the true exception occurs so seldom
that we have almost ceased to believe in its existence.
Yet, surely, although it is only the tyro who is always
ready to believe he sees the phenomenon which his

handbook marks "very rare," the wise man will be disposed to walk warily, in science as in life, keeping his eyes and mind open even for that which he scarcely expects to find.

But at this time, of course, neither Ned nor Sturdy had any thought of friendship. As iron sharpeneth iron, so their minds worked upon one another; and yet the simile fits them ill, for his mind was as tempered steel compared to her rich crude ore. It was natural that she should hear in all his criticisms the ring of true genius, for, broadly speaking, she had read only books, not books about books. Here at last was life,—here was such conversation as she had pictured when she had read of the *Noctes Ambrosianæ*, of the old dramatists at the Mermaid, and of the Lake poets at the Swan.

And, somewhat to his surprise, he found undoubted charm in her. talk too. It was so impossible to predict what her views would be about anything, and yet she was so honest in all her inconsistencies. He thought he had never met such a curious mixture of humility, insight, conventionality, and downright priggishness.

"And what is taking you to Germany?" he said, when they had talked of books galore; and his eyes brimmed over with that quiet smile which always seemed to have a trace of raillery in it. "Simply the search for culture and for kindred souls?"

She frowned, but only with the effort to answer honestly.

"I want to make my life *tell*," she said slowly.

"It seems a dreadful thing to have only one life, and to let that slip away. Do you know what I mean?"

There was no smile on his face now as he looked rather grimly over the grey water.

"Unfortunately," he said, with just a touch of bitterness in his usually mellow tone,—"or fortunately perhaps for long-suffering mankind—the Fates have not given it to all of us to 'make our lives tell.' Some of us are fane to be content if—

> 'From day to day our little boat
> Rocks in its harbour, lodging peaceably.'"

She glanced up quickly at his delicate, intellectual face. She would not have dared to follow up the opening he had given her, but he had not realized how often tact takes up her abode behind the least likely exterior, and he hastened to retreat to safer ground.

"And why Germany in particular?" he asked genially.

She tossed back a little streamer of hair from her forehead, and answered almost defiantly, as though she were well used to opposition on this score.

"There is so much *good thought* in Germany. I want to get into the heart of it. And there is the music, and—living is cheap."

"I am glad to hear it."

"Oh, not for you! But I think I can do it very cheaply,—and earn something by teaching English. You see, my people have already kept me for a year at a London boarding-school."

He raised his eyebrows. Was this the product of a London boarding-school? "And didn't you get a feast of culture there?" he asked, amused.

She shook her head seriously. "I think I got more *culture* from the public library at home, with its Carlyle and Smiles and George Eliot, and Blackie's *Self-Culture*. Boarding-school was all chocolate cream and lemonade, don't you know? French and dancing and water-colour painting and——"

"Violin-playing," he suggested mischievously.

She blushed so painfully that he was ashamed of the uncalled-for thrust, especially as she obviously had not the *savoir-faire* to parry it.

"I shan't play the violin any more," she said at last humbly, surprised to find how much less sore she felt on the subject than she had done an hour or two before. "It ought not to have needed last night to teach me that. But my Mother was so proud of it, and I—I thought if I could learn even a little, it would give me a better position as a teacher."

There was a moment's pause while he reflected what a brute he was.

"So that is how you mean to make your life tell?"

She nodded. "It seems absurd now, I know; but—I have such a wonderful picture in my mind of what a teacher might be, and some people are teachers who haven't even got that."

"A few," he answered drily.

"And if one tries and tries to make the very most of oneself——" She broke off abruptly.

"But don't you mean to specialize a bit? It is all very well to make the most of yourself; but you can't teach everything."

Her eyes shone with the perception of a deeper meaning in his words than he had meant them to bear. "I know. Of course one only ought to teach the things that set one's own mind on fire; but it is difficult to get your foot on the ladder when you have no influence at all. It is not a question of what you have got, but of what other people want. You can get a good price for the shadow; the substance has no market value at all."

He laughed good-humouredly. "It is a pity you weren't more fortunate in your boarding-school. They do that sort of thing rather well nowadays. Where was it?"

"At Cromwell Park."

"*Ah!*" Then perhaps there was some excuse for the remark about the substance and the shadow.

But the emphatic monosyllable was not lost on her.

"You see, down in the black country one doesn't know; and indeed it was my own fault if I didn't learn a good deal, for they took us about to see things, and we sometimes heard a good lecture or a good concert or a good preacher. But I was thirsty, don't you know? They always seemed to be just letting me wet my lips when I wanted to get a good drink."

He laughed. "Like that remarkable child," he

said, "you were constrained to amuse yourself with
pebbles, while the great ocean of truth lay all undis-
covered before you."

"Yes," she answered ruefully, half entering into
the spirit of his chaff, "and they wouldn't even let
me fill my basket with pebbles!"

"Ah! It is a mistake, you see, to have a larger
basket than other people."

But this time he had gone just too far. "Oh,"
she said, suddenly waking up into full self-consciousness, "I was so longing to hear you talk, and now—
how I must have bored you!"

"On the contrary. You have whiled away the
time delightfully. I am afraid the story of my aimless driftings would fall very flat after yours."

But he wanted good-naturedly to set her at her
ease again, and he talked on for half an hour, so
simply, so picturesquely, that it did not occur to her
till long afterwards how rarely in the story of his
wanderings he referred directly to himself.

He talked to her of Cambridge, till she heard the
plash of oars on the river, and the solemn pealing of
the organ through the lofty arches of King's; till
she saw the smooth-shaven lawns, and smelt the
heavy scent of the syringa in the college backs. He
talked, too, of his first winter in Italy, of how he had
looked out from his third-floor window on the stretch
of blue water with its strip of yellow sandstone; and,
beyond these, on the sage-green olive slopes and the
grey limestone precipices of the Carraras, gradually
shading off into the dazzling white of the snowy
peaks.

His enthusiasm for colour and beauty was a revelation to her. Cambridge she understood, as she understood Germany. The very names were full of the suggestion of eager life and intellectual progress. But Italy!—Italy seemed asleep or dead. Surely one little human life was too short for mere Italy!

It was with no deliberate intent that Ned avoided all unnecessary mention of himself, nor was his silence on this subject merely a question of his riper years. Such personal talk was at all times as foreign to his nature as, when she was roused, it was easy and natural to her. He was one of those rare souls, who, even in an introspective age, instinctively live not in their own moods and feelings, but in the world outside, and in the thoughts of those "who gave us larger hopes and larger cares." So natural was this habit of mind that he scarcely recognized it himself, and perhaps for this reason he was moved to greater admiration than most men and women would have been by the strong individuality of his little companion, and by her dogged determination to "make her life tell."

And so he talked, and so she listened, as Desdemona might have listened to the Moor, till the luncheon bell brought them back to the present again—to the deserted deck and to the grey North Sea.

V.

THE sea became much calmer during the afternoon, and one by one the passengers struggled up
on deck, looking not a little washed-out, and rather
indifferent as to the details of their personal appearance.

A few young men, in a rebound of high spirits,
started a game of quoits, and Ned threw himself
into it heart and soul, though, under the conditions,
it was rather a question of chance than of skill. He
belonged to the well-marked class of men who have
a knack of looking superior to their surroundings,
without in any way suggesting the idea that they
are aware of the fact. When the game was over,
his eye fell on his little acquaintance, as she leant
against the bulwarks, watching the whirling white
trail in the wake of the vessel. She turned with a
bright smile as he came up.

" That's right ! " he said, sitting down and crossing his legs as comfortably as might be. " I didn't
feel sure that I wasn't going to be suppressed again,
like the dormouse."

" Suppressed ? " she said wistfully. " *You !* "

He laughed. The game had proved exhilarat-
ing. " One would think, to hear her talk, that she
had not done it systematically for twenty-four
hours."

" Was I horrid ? I am so sorry "

" You were quite right. In a general way, when
a girl is travelling alone, the best thing she can do
is to keep herself to herself."

"It wasn't that," she said eagerly. "Not with you."

She ought to have stopped there, of course, but her naturally quick perceptions had been only very partially developed. "Do you think I don't know," she went on quietly, with suppressed feeling, "that I am only a plain ill-dressed girl whom no man is likely to speak to for his own sake? I knew you only did it out of kindness."

I suppose few men would have enjoyed the situation she forced upon him; but the blue eyes had never looked more limpid, more absolutely impersonal than when he turned to reply. The very undercurrent of quiet amusement seemed gone from them for the moment.

"And 'what ails you' at kindness?" he asked gravely. "Do you make a point of never doing a kind act yourself? Suppose I did do it out of kindness?"

She laughed rather bitterly. "Why, then, of course—it was very kind of you!"

There was a pause, during which she groped her way to his point of view, and saw the matter impersonally.

"Of course," she went on apologetically, with a sudden sense of her own smallness, "if it had occurred to me that you knew infinitely more about the things I like than I do myself, I should not have cared whether it was kindness or not. I mean—I should have accepted the kindness gladly and gratefully—as I do now."

She paused again.

"I only want men to understand that I quite realize—that I can't compete—with Miss Brown."

He laughed. "You are severe. No, I am afraid you can't."

"Miss Brown's name slipped out. I didn't mean to be spiteful. I meant I can't compete with—with other girls. And I have made up my mind to that, and am content that it should be so, if only men wouldn't sacrifice themselves, and make believe."

"I don't know that I am qualified to speak for my sex," he said drily; "but it seems to me that what I have always cared most about in young girls is that they should be pleasant and unselfconscious, and take life simply. When you come to think of it, there are more ways than one even of suppressing people."

He looked up with his comical smile, and saw that he had said enough. Indeed she winced so perceptibly that he thought she was offended. Well, what then? She had laid herself open to it, and he was not going to retract. If she declined to compete with other girls, she must not expect pretty speeches.

She looked out over the sea for a minute or two, deliberately measuring the meaning of his words, deliberately trampling underfoot the pride and resentment and shyness, which stretched like a prickly undergrowth across her path. Then she turned to him with a smile, a smile that almost startled him with its half unconscious revelation of her mood.

It was not distinctively a woman's smile; still less was it that of a child. It was the smile of a comrade who frankly accepts a helping hand, and, by its aid, climbs to a higher level.

Now Ned had not intended to proffer any helping hand; it was not in his nature under any circumstances to pose as a moral guide or preceptor; he had simply given natural expression to a mood that was half amusement, half irritation. It was something quite new to have his random utterances taken *au grand sérieux* in this fashion, and he did not altogether like it. It savoured too much of what he was wont scornfully to characterize as "soul-outpourings."

However, to do the child justice, she had not spoken; she had merely smiled; and perhaps it was not her fault if her smile spoke more plainly than words. So he adjusted his estimate of her once more, and — remarked that the weather was improving.

"Those two seem to be getting on, don't they?" said one of the passengers. "Scarcely a case of 'birds of a feather' either."

"I don't know," said Miss Brown placidly. "She's not such a fool as she looks. She said something about butter-scotch this morning that was really rather clever. I have made a note of it for my own use in future."

"Butter-scotch?"

"Yes; and that reminds me I have left my caramels in the saloon. Do you mind fetching them?"

She fastened an unnecessary eyeglass on her tip-tilted nose, and looked across at Ned and his friend.

"So that's the girl who doesn't care what men think of her! I wonder what they are talking about?"

She pricked up her ears to listen, but the conversation was dead. Sturdy had killed it, as earnest young women will at times, by becoming too painfully personal. She longed to return to their former easy and pleasant footing, and was too young to realize that for the moment she had made that impossible. Her best move now was simply to go away, but of course she did not know that.

Fortunately just at this moment a spoilt little boy on board came to the conclusion that life was not worth living unless he was allowed to catch fish over the bulwarks; and, having received the requisite permission, he proceeded, as was natural, to catch a passenger instead.

"It's well for you that that infernal machine of yours didn't chance to take hold of my gills, young man," Ned said good-humouredly, but, before he had extracted the hook from his coat-sleeve, the boy's mother came up to apologize.

She was not beautiful, and she was still looking pale and weak after a violent attack of sea-sickness; but, from the moment she appeared on deck, she seemed in some unconscious indescribable way to raise the whole social standard of the little company. Sturdy's crudities became more manifest; Miss Brown's ill-breeding more intolerable. Even the men who were out of earshot became more careful of their words, as they watched her sitting there, and one and another strolled past on the

12

chance of being able to render her some trifling service.

The lady chaffed her little boy for his clumsiness, and addressed a few remarks to Ned with the easy assurance of an attractive woman whose position in life is indisputable, and to whom the homage of men is as much a matter of course as the air she breathes. She might have struck a still higher note, perhaps, if she had included Ned's little companion—who so obviously belonged to a different social class—in her casual remarks; but her omission to do so seemed to the girl herself perfectly natural and fitting.

"I think—I have a letter to write," said the latter awkwardly to Ned. "Good—good-night!"

She wrote her letter dutifully and then dropped her head on her arms.

"Oh," she moaned, "*what* a teacher I should make if I looked and spoke like that! How quiet she is—how graceful—how" (poor Sturdy!)—"how ladylike! And I—oh, dear God, what a clodhopper I am!"

And Ned, conversing placidly with his new companion, did not ask her whether she had ever heard of Lessing. He took her for what she was and found her very restful and soothing. When she had gone away and left his thoughts free to revert to his friend of the morning, he shrugged his shoulders philosophically.

"It would ill become an old bellows-mender like me," he said, "to find fault with girls for doing men's work; but if the woman of the future really means to live at that pressure, who on earth is to keep us all sane?"

He seated himself at the saloon-table, and opening the heavy leathern writing-book, he saw to his surprise the modest grey cover of the *Erziehung*.

" Hallo!" he said, " she must have fallen asleep!" and, turning over the leaves of the book, he tried to recognize his favourite passages. Presently he came upon some pencil jottings on the fly-leaf at the end, and turned to them in the hope of getting a little fresh light,—

" Surely, surely, if God ever began to educate the human race, he is educating it still; and great and noble men and women, such as Huxley and Darwin and Harriet Martineau, are not thwarting his purposes, but working them out. We have been gradually taught—Lessing tells us—to believe in the oneness of God, in the immortality of the soul; and if we are learning now that *the earth is the Lord's* it is due more to science than to anything else. . . . Science, Art, Religion—are not these just the colours that the prism casts on the wall? and, as all these colours must be blended to produce the kindly light —so, surely, science, art, religion—all the bits of thought and work and insight man has heaped together—are but broken lights of God."

It would be impossible to describe the panorama of varying expression that passed over Ned's face as he read. But, as he finished, the habitual look of quiet philosophic amusement had settled down again.

" Huxley and Darwin, and Harriet Martineau!" he ejaculated. " These be thy Gods, O Israel?"

Then he read the pencilled lines again.

"Art!" he said. "And what do you know of art, my child, when it ceases to illustrate *The Pilgrim's Progress?* I will lay my first groschen that your favourite picture is *The Man with the Muckrake!*"

Half an hour later, when he carefully stowed his long limbs into the confines of his berth, some lines of poetry glimmered tantalizingly just out of reach of his memory. In the midst of the effort either to remember or forget them he fell asleep; but he woke a few hours later to find the stanza floating free on the surface of his mind :—

> "' Give strenuous souls for belief and prayer !'
>   Said the South to the North,
> ' Who stand in the dark on the lowest stair,
> While affirming of God, He is certainly there,'
>   Said the South to the North."

VI.

I would have you be . . . like a fire well-kindled, which catches at everything you throw in and turns it into flame and brightness.—MARCUS AURELIUS.

IT was a grey November morning, and Ned was standing in front of the Conservatorium, chatting to one of the professors.

A knot of men students in queer little round felt hats lounged on the door-step, discussing the merits of a new contralto who had made her first appearance in the Opera House the night before; and from

time to time a young woman passed in or out, looking
anxious or indifferent, depressed or elated, as the
case might be.

Presently a girl came out with a quick, firm, unselfconscious step. She looked neither depressed
nor elated, but her whole expression was a study of
eager vitality. Ned declared afterwards that he
would have recognized her in the wilds of Arabia
simply by the way in which she grasped her cum-
brous old-fashioned portfolio.

Her face rippled into a radiant smile when she
met his eye; and the two men lifted their hats with
a common impulse.

"Do you know the English Meess?" asked the
professor.

"I crossed with her on the steamer. I forget her
name."

"Meess Dunbar. She is my best pupil."

"What!" exclaimed Ned, startled out of his mood
of lazy indifference.

"*Doch!*" said the professor doggedly. "She is
no Englishwoman. Your English ladies breakfast at
noon, and cannot have a lesson till two; but she—
she comes before eight every morning, and she is of
a perseverance—no!"

"Oh, no doubt. That I can well believe. But all
that does not make her musical."

"*Musical!*" repeated the professor contemptuously. "Your musical English ladies think they
know more than we do. Miss Dunbar has not got
to *music* yet. She could do nothing for it that she
was trained in England. Of course she came to me

and played some absurd piece—Weber's *Perpetuum
Mobile!*" He chuckled at the recollection. "I let
her play two lines, and then I throw it aside. 'That,'
I exclaim, 'is mere illusion. It were better you had
never learnt the piano!'"

"To which she?"

"She regards me with a smile. 'I know,' she
says quite simply, 'I have come to you to learn it
now.' 'Good!' said I. 'You put yourself in my
hands. It will be three months before you play another piece.' But I was wrong. At the end of six
weeks Miss Dunbar had a *touch!* Ah, but she is per-
severing, industrious!"

He turned away as he spoke, and Ned looked
after him with mingled envy and contempt,—envy
of a man who had mastered technique, contempt for
one who could attach to it so disproportionate a
value.

From time to time in the months that had elapsed
Ned's thoughts had drifted back to his sturdy little
friend, and he had wondered, without any definite
desire to renew the acquaintance, whether their paths
would cross again. But now he found himself swinging along at a very creditable pace, with a keen look-
out ahead in the direction she had taken. There
seemed little chance of his overtaking her in
these busy thoroughfares, and it was with some
surprise and a good deal of amusement that he
saw her at last looking into the window of a
large *Conditorei*, with a lean purse in her uncertain
hands.

"Well," he said, holding out his hand, and assum-

ing his most fatherly air, "how goes the human race?
—'still in the go-cart'?"

She started as if she had been caught red-handed
in a crime. "I don't know," she stammered con-
fusedly: then, recovering her wits,—"I hope the
whole is progressing better than this poor little
unit."

"Oh, come! I have just been hearing great
things of you."

"From Herr Waldstein?" Her face beamed and
crimsoned with pleasure. She longed to know just
what her teacher had said; but was too shy and proud
to ask; and indeed Ned would not have thought it
right to tell her. "She would never see the remark
in its true proportion," he thought. "Art for her is
nothing but technique just now."

She turned to leave the window; but he held
back.

"Don't let me interrupt you," he said, with the
old, wide-eyed smile. "I would not interfere with
the commissariat for the world."

She winced again, and then, with a sudden luminous recollection, bethought herself of what he had
said about taking life simply.

"I am awfully hungry," she said bravely. "You
see, I have to breakfast at seven on my music days,
and they only send me up one *Brödchen.*"

"Poor little starved thing! Let us go in."

But she shut the shabby purse resolutely with a
snap.

"No," she said firmly, "I can't afford it, and it is
a bad habit to get into. It is yielding to the flesh.

In fact "—she blushed—" I *vowed* I wouldn't spend
my money like that."

"Don't you find it rather exhausting to bring
such mighty principles to bear on such trifling
affairs ? "

"They are not trifling to me," she said apologetically; "or rather, they are all the more important
because they are trifling. I don't see how I can
expect the human race to grow any better if I give
way to a little temptation like that. Besides "—she
paused—"two of those cakes would pay for a Bilse
concert."

"But I am awfully hungry too," he said men-
daciously. "I was just wishing I could find someone to drink a cup of chocolate with me; and you
and I have two whole months of experiences to
discuss. Come! Your vow does not cover deeds of
necessity and mercy. Look at those *Windbeutel*
and *Apfelkuchen*. They are just yearning for appreciation."

Vanity was not one of Ned's faults, and, least of
all, vanity where women were concerned; but she
had made no secret of her pleasure in his society,
and he could have guessed which way her inclina-
tions pointed, even if her face had not borne pathetic witness to the effort it cost her to be true
to the traditions of a narrow upbringing and an
unlovely girlhood.

"No, no," she said ungraciously, as she turned to
walk on. "I mean—don't let me keep you; but I
am not really hungry, you know; and I ought to be
at my practising place by now."

"Don't you practise at your diggings?"

"No. There are far too many of us. I go to the wareroom of a small manufacturer."

"Straight from the Conservatorium?"

"Oh yes!" she laughed shyly. "Sometimes I run most of the way, in case I should forget some of the things Herr Waldstein has told me."

"By Jove! I don't wonder he is delighted with his pupil."

"I am delighted with my teacher," she answered eagerly. "It is an inspiration to have lessons from him."

"Whew!" He raised his eyebrows. "Inspiration is a big word. Waldstein's technique is first-rate. It seems to me that the German school is crushed to earth by the weight of its technique just now."

"Do you think so?" she asked surprised, as if the idea were quite a new one. "I am not in a position to say. I think one must master technique before one can judge of its value."

The blue eyes dilated with a humourous smile. "That is severe. On the other hand, it must be a tremendous sell to spend years in drudgery, and then wake up to find you have simply been walling in 'the nothing you set out from.'"

"Yes," she answered absently;—"I wish you had been at my lesson this morning. I 'had practised one of Mendelssohn's *Lieder ;* but, although I knew the notes, I hadn't grasped the idea a bit. Herr Waldstein let me plunge right through to the end, and disgrace myself hopelessly before the two other students; and then, without a word, he played the treble alone on his own piano. It was a revelation to hear how he brought out air and accompaniment both in the right-hand part,—sustained singing notes above, and crisp chords below. It was wonderful."

"No doubt," said Ned, smiling; "but I suppose there have been one or two fellows since Mendelssohn, who could have done as much for you."

She had been "standing up to him" so well that he expected a frank retort; but she collapsed into one of the odd fits of humility, which always made him feel himself a brute.

"Of course," she said awkwardly. "I forgot how widely your standpoint differs from mine."

"As widely as the standpoint of the onlooker differs from that of the genuine worker."

"Yes," she responded sadly. "You are on a vantage-ground, surveying the building as a whole; while I am studying—the grain of the stones in the porch."

He turned to look at her with frank admiration for an appreciative metaphor, and, for the first time, it struck him that the plum-coloured gown had given place to one of shaggy homespun which was quaintly becoming to her independent figure. Her face, too, was different. Its curves were less childlike than they had been two months ago, and there was almost a touch of *chic* in the poise of the resolute chin.

"What splendid use you are making of your

time!" he said with a pang of envy. "You look as if you lived on live birds."

She laughed and shook her head.

"Nothing so recognizable," she said; "and, oh, I haven't done one-third of what I planned to do in the time."

"One-third! I call that brilliant. When I used to make plans, I never accomplished more than $.oox$ of the original design."

"And x equalled?"

He shrugged his shoulders. "Oh, x was so far from the decimal point that the equation wasn't worth working out."

"Poor Algebra!" she said, "that knows no equality, only quantity;" and then she was ashamed of being too clever. "Are you studying music now?" she asked shyly.

"Not at the Conservatorium. I am scraping away at the cello a bit, and dipping into harmony, and—frequenting the opera. Fine house, isn't it?"

"I haven't been inside it yet. Oh, I mean to go. I want to hear both *Lohengrin* and *Tannhäuser ;* but I should like to learn a great deal more first. This is my—destination."

Her eyes expressed a doubtful invitation, and he followed her with rising curiosity through a squalid doorway into what appeared to be the living-room of a large family. The atmosphere was close and offensive; food, cooking utensils, and unwashed dishes lay about in hopeless confusion; and three or four dirty children were clamouring for the bread which a slatternly mother cut from a long brown

loaf held against her breast.   The whole scene
struck Ned as being a hideous travesty of the well-
known picture of Werther's first meeting with
Lotte.

"*Guten Tag!*" said Miss Dunbar pleasautly.
"*Ein englischer Herr ist heute mitgekommen.*"

"*Ach so!*" replied the woman, bowing; and she
hastened to add with an eye to business, "*Vielleicht
möchte der Herr die Claviere probiren.*"

"*Oh ja, gewiss.*"   Ned's answer came rather
stiltedly, and he felt an uncomfortable sense of his
companion's superior fluency in speaking the language.

The girl hastily led the way through a door at
the farther end of the room into a dreary best parlour; and thence into the wareroom, where some
eight or ten cheap and showy pianos stood awaiting
a purchaser.

Ned laid his hand against the ice-cold tiles of the
stove, and thought of his own pleasant sitting-room
overlooking the Thiergarten.

"Your surroundings are picturesque in a broad
sense, certainly," he said; "and the local colour of
your home letters must be excellent.   How many
hours a-day do you spend in your—barracks?"

"Five as a rule.   Sometimes more."

"And is the stove never lighted?"

"No.   The room is very dry."

He sat down and struck a few chords.   "Jove!
The tone isn't half bad.   And now you are going
to initiate me into the true inwardness of Mendelssohn."

She looked at him. "I wonder," she said slowly, "whether I shall ever learn not to make a fool of myself."

He did not seem to hear. His long fingers were producing some fine arpeggios from the cheap instrument. Then he rose languidly from his chair, his fair face devoid of all expression.

"I have never had much sympathy," he said, "with the morbid desire to appear wiser than one is. It is too much fag, for one thing. Let the world call me a fool and be done with it! When you come to think of it, the desire is just a bit of intellectual or moral vulgarity, isn't it?"

Her face was very grave. "I don't think I quite know what you mean by vulgarity."

He laughed. "Rather a fundamental hitch that. Vulgarity, to my mind, is veneer,—want of simplicity."

She nodded slowly. "Did you ever think how much easier it is to be simple, as you call it, when all the conditions of your life are beautiful in themselves? If my life was furnished with oak, I should have no use for veneer."

"And if my life was furnished in deal, I should be content to keep it well scoured. I should not pretend it was oak."

Her face flashed into sunshine. "That is self-evident," she cried, "when you put it so; and yet I believe I have been groping blindly after it for years."

"Then I am sure you have been very near it sometimes," he answered half abashed,—"nearer than most of us perhaps. And now no doubt you are longing to turn me out. Good-bye."

Later in the day he made his way to a house in a very different part of the town, and was duly ushered into a comfortable English drawing-room. A graceful woman lounged idly in an arm-chair by the fire.

"That's right," she said languidly, holding out a pretty white hand. "I haven't seen you for a fortnight, and to-day I am bored to extinction. Sit down, and tell me what you are doing with yourself."

He looked round the room with an amused smile. "I have just been making a call," he said, "in a very different drawing-room from this. Do you remember the bright little girl with the tawny hair who crossed with us to Germany?" And he drew a highly-coloured picture of dogged little Sturdy in her odd surroundings.

The lady laughed and stifled a yawn.

"Upon my word," she said, "you *are* good to that child. Don't you realize that you are turning her head?"

He looked down thoughtfully at his unfashionable hat. "It wouldn't be a very easy thing to do," he said. "I don't think you quite understand her. She is not an English rose, I admit; but I am greatly mistaken if she is not a regular young oak-tree.—I'll have one more quarrel with fortune if she doesn't get space to grow."

He walked over to the English fireplace, and turned his back to the cheerful blaze. "Do you

know," he said,—"if I were a woman—I should
think it a thing worth doing to give a little girl like
that a chance. She is the most receptive creature I
ever met."

The lady's laugh had a ring of annoyance in it.
"Really, Mr. Beresford," she cried, "you are *impay-
able!* By the way, what did you think of the new
contralto? She sang flat once or twice; but, apart
from that, her voice seemed to me perfectly gor-
geous."

VII.

"THERE'S a lot of liver left over from dinner to-
day," said Pauline, the maid of all work.

"Well, God knows I am glad to hear it!" was
Fräulein's reply. "We'll use it for supper to-night.
The girls have been eating the very hair off my head
lately."

Sturdy slipped past the kitchen door unobserved,
and, frowning, ran down the long stair.

How petty it all was! Must one really die and
be buried before one could escape from the sordid
groundwork of life? Germany had seemed so ideal,
so romantic, before she came,—all music and art,
and literature, and development ;—and, now that she
was here, the shoe pinched just the same.

She was genuinely sorry for Fräulein's worries,
and she understood only too well the look of pathetic anxiety that followed the course of the dish
round the circle of growing girls; she never asked
for a second helping without feeling herself a brute;

but healthy, hungry youth would assert itself in spite of the most heroic resolutions.

Ah! Life seemed brighter now that she had reached the keen frosty air. The last brown leaves had fallen from the trees in the square, and the winter evening was darkening fast. Thank God for her music, her work, her dreams! Poor, poor Fräulein!

The girl drew her shabby cloak more closely round her, and sped like a hare through the unfashionable streets. *Vita brevis, ars longa;* and, quite apart from that, it was desirable to lay up a store of animal heat before facing the chilly "barracks."

The wareroom looked bare and desolate, and the pianos cast great shadows on the whitewashed walls, as she trimmed her ill-smelling lamp by the light of a succession of matches. These little discomforts were nothing to complain of, but unfortunately one of the pianos had been moved into the best parlour for the benefit of another student, and Sturdy now had to practice her simple studies as best she might, counting aloud to drown the crashing chords that resounded through the wall.

"One, two, three, four. One, two, and three, four!" till her fingers grew stiff and her voice grew weary.

Suddenly the volley on the other side of the wall ceased, and the door between the two rooms opened.

"*Gott!*" ejaculated a fair-haired German girl. "Didn't you know your lamp was smoking?"

Sturdy slipped from her chair and turned down the flame. "No," she said simply, "I hadn't noticed."

"*Gott!*" exclaimed the girl again, with a look of genuine commiseration for the *kleine Engländerin*, whose perseverance was so sadly out of proportion to her talent. "You may have my room now if you like. I must hurry home to supper. We are going to the opera to-night."

Sturdy looked up with more of reverence than of envy for a mortal so highly favoured.

"Thank you very much," she said humbly.

She felt the unspoken pity keenly, and recognized the justice of it. Would it end in nothing after all, this visit to Germany, of which she had hoped so much?

Well, she was in for it now, and must make the best of it. Work was the cure for this mood. To work, to work!

"One, two, three, four. One, two, and three, four!"

It was thus that Ned found her when, attired in a great fur-lined coat, he dropped into the barracks an hour or two later.

"Miss Dunbar," he said abruptly, "I want you to go with me to *Lohengrin* to-morrow night. I have two seats, and the other fellow can't go."

If he had broached the subject gradually, she would probably have refused. As it was, she sprang to her feet with a spontaneity that would have given valuable hints to a stage *ingénue*.

13

"Really?" she cried. "Really? Oh how good of you to think of me!"

The sunshine in her face seemed to brighten the whole dreary room. Ned felt like a schoolboy on the eve of a spree.

"These things begin absurdly early here," he said apologetically. "I am afraid you will miss your supper; but we'll pick up a bite somewhere." He thought it judicious to pass lightly over this part of the programme. "Shall I call for you here—or at your lodgings?" He added the alternative doubt-fully, with a man's natural reluctance to face a *posse* of women when he only wants to see one.

"Oh, don't trouble to call. I'll meet you at the place."

"No, no!"

"Then come here. I'll be ready, never fear!"

"All right! Say half-past five. I suppose you'll have to take your hat off,"—he smiled at the novel experience of giving a woman instructions in such a matter,—"but you don't need to dress."

She went with him to the door, and then, throwing on her old cloak, ran home like the wind.

"Girls," she cried, bursting into the room where the boarders sat over their books, impatiently await-ing the call to supper, "I am going to the opera to-morrow!"

"*Nein!*"

"*Mein Gott!*"

"*Du lieber Himmel!*"

"Quite right, too!" said a sprightly large-eyed French girl. "You have worked like a hero, Mis-

schen, and you have scarcely so much as been to a
Bilse concert. Who are you going with?"
Sturdy set her lips.
"A friend," she said, "an English gentleman."
"That is charming. Where are the seats?"
"Well, naturally I didn't ask."
"But you will wear your velvet dress, in any
case?"
"No. I shouldn't think so. I hadn't thought
of it."
But this folly was overruled in a moment.
"Nonsense, Misschen!"
"And it is so becoming!"
"You are stupid! What do you suppose you
have got a pretty dress for?"
"And you will let me do your hair?" said the
French girl coaxingly. "You mustn't drag it back
like that. I'll make it a little fluffy in front, and
twist it into a simple Greek knot behind. You will
look perfectly charming."

And so it came about that Ned's companion at
the opera the following evening was one of whom
no man need have been ashamed. The quaintly-cut
gown of deep Gobelin blue had been chosen by her
schoolmistress in London, and was the one garment
poor Sturdy had ever possessed which made any
pretensions to beauty. Happy accident, or the re-
straining influence of her French friend, had prevented her from adding any jarring note in the
shape of ribbon or cheap jewellery; and her whole
expression and bearing were so transfigured with

happiness and excitement as to form a fruitful subject for conversation among the boarders during the
evening.   They had often found her *neidlich*, they
agreed; but to-night she was really charming.

And, indeed, no ordinary girl, whose life contains
its due sequence of pleasures, can form the least conception of the intense capacity, the fierce thirst for
enjoyment, which Sturdy carried with her, when, with
beating heart, she ran down the long dimly-lighted
stair.   No wonder her face was a poem; no wonder
it suggested to Ned the rush of life one feels all
around on a glowing day in spring after rain.   Her
winter had been so long, poor Sturdy!   In her wild-
est dreams she had prayed only for starry nights
and Alpine peaks; and now behold—for a few short
hours—sunshine and morning and a smiling green
valley at her feet!

I must not attempt to describe the events of the
evening as they appeared through her temperament.
If I did, I might seem to be borrowing a page from
the Arabian Nights, whereas everyone knows the
comfortable café where they supped, and everyone
knows the bright effective Opera House as it looks
on gala nights, when its crowded tiers are aglow with
gay costumes and expectant faces.

The emperor and empress were in the royal box
—"*der greise Kaiser ;*" no one guessed then in what
quick succession he was to be followed by "*der weise
Kaiser*" and "*der Reise-Kaiser*"—and Sturdy found
herself for the first time in her life under the same
roof with royalty.

Not for one minute through the long evening did

her delight and interest flag. Of course the opera, as an opera, was far above her comprehension; and yet, in an emotional unconscious way, she drank it in as Wagner meant she should, yielding up ear, eye and soul in one to the great complex whole of his ·creation.

Singers and orchestra surpassed themselves that night; Brandt was superb; Mallinger and Niemann renewed their best days. But, for Sturdy, the orchestra had no existence; the music came from everywhere, was in everything; Elsa and the others were not opera-singers, they were real,—the only real people in the world; and the whole thing meant, not recreation nor amusement, but life,—the distilled essence of human life.

At last the dove flew off, drawing after it all that had made the little world of Brabant a very kingdom of heaven; the curtain fell; and Sturdy found herself back in the emptying, darkening Opera House, —back in the work-a-day world, where life was so complex and so slow that one could not see its plan.

She turned to Ned, her eyes brimming over with tears. "Though I should live to be an old, old woman," she said, "I shall never have another night like this."

Ned had enjoyed the evening too, though in a very different way. It would be idle to deny that there had been moments, both at the café and in the Opera House, when his friendly interest in his little companion had threatened to develop an emotional side which might have been all the more dangerous because he considered himself so entirely proof against its advances. It is difficult to be absolutely self-contained in the presence of such a redundancy of throbbing young life. ᐧIndeed, if the girl had possessed even the simplest and most laudable instincts of coquetry,—my story might have had a very different name.

VIII.

WHEN Sturdy awoke at half-past six next morning, she felt an even greater disinclination than usual to get up; but five minutes later she sprang out of bed with a bound.

"It would be too terrible," she said, as she groped for her match-box with shaking hands, "if a great moral and mental and physical treat like that was to make one less fit for the duties of daily life."

From which it appears that even a superficial study of "Huxley and Darwin and Harriet Martineau" does not necessarily suffice to disturb the original bias of a Puritanic mind with the logic of natural laws—such as that of the Conservation of Energy—in the spiritual world.

She drew aside the window-blind and looked out. Nothing was visible save a blurred street-lamp, and two great snow-flakes melting on the pane.

"Slush underfoot," she said with a shiver. "That means thick boots and a short skirt."

She took the old plum-coloured gown from behind the chintz curtain which did duty as a wardrobe, and threw it on the bed; then, with her teeth set hard, she poured the ice-cold water from the ewer.

Washing is a prolonged operation when one's basin is what in England would be designated a small pie-dish ; and there is no denying that life looked very dark while the operation lasted. So dark that a whole new crop of severe moral resolutions had to be twisted into a great knot of sandy hair,—with the result that the knot was tight and rather uncomfortable, and very unbecoming.

There had been little time to discuss the opera on the way home the night before, and it would probably have occurred to most women that Ned might look in to the barracks in the course of the day, but such an idea never crossed Sturdy's mind; so when he actually arrived about noon, the consciousness of her own plainness and general commonplaceness marred even the glad spontaneity of the greeting to which he had been looking forward. The sun was shining brightly now, and the streets were drying fast, so the short skirt and heavy boots had lost even such beauty of fitness as they had possessed in the early morning. Without any doubt the glamour of the night before was gone.

Ned was disappointed of course, and yet his disappointment was mingled with relief. After all, this was her true self ; and he respected her the more for going on her simple dogged way quite independently of him. They had seemed very near for a little while the night before, and now they seemed very far apart. Well, so much the better ! How indeed could it possibly be otherwise ?

They exchanged a few conventional sentences awkwardly, at arm's length, so to speak. He had come with the full intention of discussing *Lohengrin*, but now he felt a curious reluctance to broach the subject. And yet he did not want to go away. He wanted to throw fresh fuel on this eager mind, and watch it burn. He wanted to see what she would make of her life.

"Very tired?" he asked kindly.

"Not a bit," she replied, and she thought she spoke the truth.

"It was a real charity to go with me last night. It does one good to hear the mother tongue after this eternal guttural jabber."

"Doesn't it?" she responded quickly; "and yet it is surprising how little barrier the difference of nationality makes after all."

"No doubt that is your experience—picking up the language with the extraordinary facility you do."

She smiled. She was used to compliments on this score.

"Do you know, even now I don't follow every word of a sermon unless I sit quite near the preacher."

This gave the flagging conversation a suggestive fillip.

"What church do you go to?"

She blushed, unable now as always to answer a question superficially.

"In the morning I go to please my people at home. Our minister gave me an introduction. It is

not exactly a church. They meet in a sort or school-
room——"

She hesitated, and was relieved that he did not
press the subjèct. "In the evening I go to please
myself. I have heard Herr Prediger Stöcker of
course," — she smiled — "and Paulus Cassel, and
Hossbach——"

"You are catholic!"

"One learns to be," she said with the profound
philosophy of eighteen. "In the afternoon——"

"In the afternoon, I suppose, you complete the
epigram and go to please your Maker?"

"*Im Gegentheil!*" she flashed back, and then
blushed with shame at her own flippancy. "In
the afternoon I go to the National Gallery."

"Well done! I wish you would take me with
you next Sunday."

"Oh!" she cried, "would you? would you? It
would be an education for me. I know so little
of art. When the other pupils at the studio talk of
values and balancing and impressionism and temperament, I feel as if the rest of the world was
breathing air while I was buried alive."   ·

"What studio?" he asked abruptly.

"Herr Lulvès'. I have been working there twice
a-week lately."

A look of profound depression came over his
sanguine face. "By Jove!" he said drearily, "you
are a wonderful woman." Then, metaphorically
speaking, he gave his own personality the con-
temptuous kick to which it was so well accustomed,
and returned to the matter in hand.

"Sunday afternoon, then," he said cheerfully.
"What time do you go?"

"Any time," she said; but her face had lost
the bright assurance of a moment before. "There
can't——" She hesitated.

"There can't what?"

She blushed painfully. "There can't be any harm
in it."

He turned his great blue eyes full upon her.

"What harm should there be?" he asked coldly
and innocently. "Does your landlady object?"

"Oh, no. She says I am so '*ernst*,' so unlike
other girls. She never enquires into my comings
and goings."

"Sensible woman! So even a German *Hausfrau*
is capable of flashes of insight. Then where is the
difficulty?"

She looked miserable.

"I don't see any," she said; then added desperately, "it—it isn't—customary."

He took a turn up and down the room, perhaps
to conceal a smile, and then seated himself on a
broken-backed chair, languidly crossing his legs.

"Look here, Miss Dunbar," he said; "I am old
enough to be your father, so suppose we abjure the
customary for a few minutes, and indulge in a little
plain speaking—just to clear the air. You told me
some months ago that you didn't profess to compete
with other girls, and any fellow who wasn't an ass
could see that you spoke the truth. Well, when
an ever-watchful Providence saw fit to wreck my
constitution some years ago, it decreed that I should

cease to compete with other men, and—the position
suits me admirably. I haven't a grain of—sentiment in my composition. So you see we have one
thing in common. Each of us is at loose ends, so
to speak, as regards the other sex. The winds and
waves of life have thrown our ˈboats alongside for
a bit, and in due time we shall drift apart again.
Can you tell me why, in the name of the height
above or the depth beneath, we should scruple to
extract what amusement or interest or benefit we
can from our brief companionship ? "

In the name of these mighty things, of course, the
"customary" sank into nothingness, and she would
not have been herself if at the moment she had even
thought that, in addition to the height above and the
depth beneath, there were divers little craft round
about.

He rose from his chair again, and strode up and
down thé room. Even the events of last night
formed a welcome relief from this.

" But I wanted to hear your opinion of *Lohengrin*,"
he said. " Did it come up to your expectations ? "

" Oh, you know ! It far surpassed them. And
yet—in one way I was disappointed. I could not
have *liked* it better, but I felt that I wasn't *appreci-
ating* it. It was too big to get into my mind."

He smiled, well pleased.

" Well, if we can't have opinions, let us at least
have impressions. One can't avoid them."

" No," she answered thoughtfully. Then suddenly she turned on him,—" Wagner must have had
a very low opinion of women ? "

He laughed—a hearty laugh of amusement and surprise.

" Why ? "

" I don't know which is worse—Elsa or Ortrud."

"You don't mean that."

" I do—at least I almost mean it. I don't believe one woman in a hundred would have been such a fool as Elsa was."

He raised his eyebrows.

" Do you mean by that that not one woman in a hundred would have had Elsa's spiritual insight?"

She did not answer. Her honest face revealed in a moment that he had taken her out of her depth.

He looked at her calmly. She was too clever and too independent to require any quarter, so he went on drily and relentlessly,

" I don't fancy Wagner intended *Lohengrin* as a brochure on the woman question."

She coloured. " I didn't suppose he did," she responded warmly, dropping back at once into the schoolgirl.

Her words and tone jarred on him indescribably, and he became more acutely aware of her unprepossessing appearance. Was this really the glowing sentient thing who had sat by his side last night? For the first time in their intercourse he was moved to trample on her, to make her feel her own limitations.

" The reply is unworthy of your honesty, Miss Dunbar," he said coldly. " It seems to me that is exactly what you did suppose. What I meant to say was that Elsa in Wagner's conception is not

only a woman, any more than Lohengrin is only a
man.   She is a human soul."

He paused, half ashamed of his own priggishness.

"And Lohengrin?" she said eagerly.

"Is the spiritual element in life, I suppose. Elsa
has faith to see the invisible, but she has not faith
to lean her whole weight on it. The time comes
when she must have it translated into the tangible.
The problem came to her in that particular form,
but it comes to all of us in one way or another; and
you tell me that ninety-nine women out of a hundred have not only eyes to see the invisible, but
faith to turn their backs upon the substantial obvious pomps and vanities, and trust themselves, body
and soul, to what in most moods seems only a rain-
bow bridge."

She was altogether at his mercy now so far as
the argument was concerned, but she had forgotten
everything else in the new vista he opened up.

"Go on!" she said, almost under her breath.
"Oh, do you think *Lohengrin* will soon be given
again?"

He shook off his rare ill-humour in a laugh.

"It seems to me," he said reflectively, "that a
great artist uses the whole question of sex as a
means, not as an end.   He doesn't revel in it for its
own sake." Then he broke off abruptly. The days
had not yet come when men discussed such questions with young girls.

"It is refreshing to see a woman stand up for
her sex," he said in a lighter tone; "but a woman
who looks at life, who looks at every work of art,

through the medium of her sex, only shows how
subject she is to its limitations."

Sturdy drew down her brows. "I should like to
think about that," she said. "It sounds very true,
but it doesn't walk straight home like what you
said about *Lohengrin*. I think an artist is bound on
the whole to keep even the petty balance between
the sexes pretty level."

"On the whole perhaps, but not in each individual work; his canvas may not be big enough to
get it all in. Don't condemn Wagner till you have
at least heard *Tannhäuser* as well."

"Oh, Wagner!" she said simply. "I wasn't
thinking of *him*. That was only my ignorance."

"Well, good-bye," he said. "You won't thank
me for wasting so much of your time."

"Good-bye," she said shyly, taking his proffered
hand. "Would—would three o'clock suit you on
Sunday? I should *love* to come."

Half an hour later she made her way home to
dinner. One of the German girls opened the door.

"*Ach!*" she cried in some dismay, surveying the
shabby old frock. "Then you haven't seen the
English gentleman to-day?"

"Yes, I have," said Sturdy, hastily pulling off her
weather-beaten hat.

"*So!*" with a glance at the unbecoming *coiffure.*
"I suppose he isn't young?"

"No, he isn't young."

"Hm. Married perhaps. What a pity! We were
hoping last night that something might come of it."

IX.

"WHY, Misschen, you have made tremendous progress!"

It was a bright frosty morning, and Sturdy sat by her bedroom window making hasty impressionist sketches of chance figures in the square,—a couple of mongrel dogs harnessed to a vegetable cart, a group of children at play, a sleigh gliding over the snow.

At that particular hour—in accordance with a formidable time-table on the wall—she ought to have been at the barracks, practising; but she had sprained her left wrist the week before in the endeavour to acquire a bit of technique to which her master attached great importance.

She had ignored the pain on the morning of her lesson, and had played the study in question with great spirit; but when she got to the end, a sudden intolerable twinge had warned her to say regretfully before a fresh programme was prescribed,

"I think I have hurt my wrist."

"And very sensibly done!" he had responded calmly. "Sprain your wrist every week, if you do it to such purpose as that."

Then he noticed the whiteness of her face and the trembling of the ill-used hand.

"Bandage it tightly with a cold-water cloth," he said, "and don't practice any more for three days."

So she sat curled up at the window, sketching the figures in the square.

She laid down her pencil and drew a long breath of content. "Why, Misschen, you have made tremendous progress!" she repeated to herself softly; and then, "Sprain your wrist every week, if you do it to such purpose as that!"

Yes, she was getting on, and her German was progressing better than either music or drawing. She ought next autumn to be able to get quite a good situation,—perhaps fifty pounds a year!

The money was a very important item to poor Sturdy. It was the outward and visible sign of the extent to which she had attained her ideal; and it meant, not only food and clothing, but all the dimly apprehended culture for which her whole soul longed. It was the medium by which she was to be developed all round, that she might lay something worth having on the altar of her lifework.

Yes, she was very happy. She was getting on; and this day in particular was all gilt and red letters, for was she not going with her friend in the evening to see *Faust?*

She had read the drama for the third time the night before, scarcely seeing in it the trite story of seduction, of which it has become the type; and her whole being quivered still in sympathy with Faust's perplexities and Gretchen's sorrows.

"Letter, Misschen!" said one of the boarders, opening the door. "But don't raise your hopes. It is not from home."

It was the first local letter Sturdy had received, and she scanned it eagerly. The handwriting was strange to her,—clear, cultured, flowing, a thing of

beauty in itself,—and might have been that of either
man or woman.

But alas for the contents!

"DEAR MISS DUNBAR: I enclose two tickets for
the performance this evening. I am sorry I have
caught a chill, and shall not be able to go. If this
queer Teutonic Æsculapius succeeds in patching
me up again for a little space—as he seems to
think he can—I hope you will tell me some day
how you liked it. They say Klein is a splendid
Mephisto.

"Yours sincerely,
"EDWARD BERESFORD."

The hand that held the letter shook, and Sturdy's
face turned very white. "*If* this queer Teutonic
Æsculapius succeeds in patching me up again—for a
little space—as he seems to think he can"——Was
it a joke? or did he really mean it? Often when
he was speaking it was impossible to tell, and now
she had not even his eyes and voice to guide her.
The measured steady handwriting gave no clue.
She thought with a pang of his thinness, of his occasional cough, of the hands and face that looked
so transparent now that their summer coat of sunburn was gone. Could he be really ill?—seriously
ill?—in danger?

He had given her his address, and to her it
seemed a very imposing one. Would it be possible
for her to brave that fine façade and ring the bell,
and enquire how he was? Perhaps his sisters were

14

with him,—those lovely elegant girls she had seen
on the steamer; and, if so, they would resent the
interest of a shabby little bourgeoise. On the other
hand, her friend might be alone,—and he might—be
going to die.

An hour later she was making her way up a
staircase which seemed to her simply palatial. The
steps were carpeted with heavy matting, the balus-
trades cushioned with crimson velvet, and at every
turn a bronze figure held aloft a large lamp. Her
voice shook for very shyness when she enquired for
the sick man.

"Are you a friend of his?" asked the landlady
eagerly.

"Yes." What else indeed could she say—being
there?

"*Gott sei Dank!* Then you will come in and see
him? Oh, it is not a time for standing on ceremony,
I assure you. The doctor says it is most unfortu-
nate that none of his friends are here.—A charming
English lady with a little boy did call one day; but
it seems they have gone to Vienna.—There is a great
deal of old-standing mischief in the lungs, the doctor
says; but there is no reason why he shouldn't get
over this particular attack, and be practically as
well as he was before, if only he could pick up heart
and take nourishment. He won't eat: I believe he
can't: it is positively touching to see him try. And
I have made him such excellent soup! Come in, do,
and cheer him up a bit."

Sturdy shrank selfishly from the spectacle of pain
and weakness; but the good *Hausfrau* left her no

option in the matter, and another minute found her
face to face with her friend.   .

Solemn and large-eyed, Ned lay in his comfortable bedroom, deliberately looking death in the face,
and trying to persuade himself that he did not care.
His was not the Christian temperament which glories
in infirmity; by nature he was a pure Greek; and all
his life he had hated with unspeakable loathing even
the mention of the unwholesome or pathological in
mind or body. It seemed the very irony of fate
when his fine physique was undermined by the inroads of an insidious disease; but the disease entirely
failed to crush his indomitable spirit. He refused to
accept any conventional view of the situation. As
long as it was possible, he ignored the fact that he
was ill at all, while congratulating himself on the
leisure his delicacy gave him to indulge his particular
tastes in Art and Literature. Even those who knew
him best found themselves unable to form any just
estimate of the plans and hopes and aspirations that
lay buried beneath his gay, light-hearted exterior.
He himself would have said there were none. He
elected, and to a great extent his constitution made
it easy for him, to walk on the heights of his nervous organisation; but, when one of Nature's knock-
down blows made this impossible, he had far to fall,
and the depths were dark indeed.
    And so he lay in bed, deliberately looking death
in the face, and trying to persuade himself that he
did. not care.
    He had been a fool, of course, to remain in the

North so long, but there was no use in going back
on that now.   The die was cast.   Should he write to
his people at home, as his landlady wished?   No, no.
The doctor *said* he might get over this attack in a
few days; and although, no doubt, the doctor lied,
it would be too ridiculous to make a fuss about nothing.   Let things drift!   Let things drift!

An English lady—Miss Dunbar—was anxious to
see him.   Might she come in?

His first impulse was to refuse.   It was too humiliating to be seen like this.   On the other hand,
the thought of Sturdy's bracing personality came to
him like a whiff of air from the happier world behind
him,—and he said yes.   It was so characteristic of
her to take him by storm in this fashion, he thought,
little guessing her anguish of mind at the prospect.

But her anguish was short-lived.   At the sight of
suffering so real, all the mother in her rose, and put
to flight the awkward, self-conscious girl.

"I am so sorry you have been ill," she said in an
interested but thoroughly matter-of-fact way, sitting
down by the bedside as she spoke.

"You must be," he replied with the ghost of a
smile, "if you have left your beloved barracks to
come and tell me so."

"Don't give me any credit for that;" and with an
instinctive feeling that she must not talk of him, and
a natural tendency to talk about herself when no
other subject was pressing, she told him the story
of her sprained wrist, and of what the professor had
said.

This naturally suggested other sayings and doings of the professor in question, some of which had become part of the tradition of the Conservatorium. Sturdy took care that they should lose nothing in the telling, and she was relieved to see, as she chatted on, that Ned's smile became more frequent and less death-like.

He admired her tact in taking his condition for granted and asking no questions.

"And what are you doing with your time?" he asked at length.

"I was sketching some dogs in the square this morning. It was great fun." And, with a real moral effort, she produced the shabby little sketch-book from the pocket of her cloak.

Very feebly he held out a delicate, blue-veined hand.

"Take off your hat," he said, "and tell me about your pictures."

She needed no second bidding, but she was startled to see how weak he was.

"Wait one moment," she said, "while I fetch your soup. Your landlady said it was time."

"No, no," he began querulously, but he suddenly realized that he was hungry. In some indescribable way the nerve tension had relaxed, and he felt that he could eat.

"*Gott sei Dank!*" exclaimed the good woman when she heard the request. "Wait one moment, Fräulein, a glass of good red wine will do him no harm."

It was astonishing how his heart revived as he

sipped the savoury soup; and all the time, with delicious unselfconsciousness, Sturdy sat curled up in
a big easy-chair at the foot of the bed, chatting and
laughing in a low pleasant voice, and almost forcing
him to laugh too.

If he had really occupied the centre place in her
life—if, in fact, she had been in love with him—his
profound depression must have dominated the mood
of a woman so much younger than himself; but, fortunately for him at the moment, her affection and
gratitude and admiration left abundant room in her
mind for a deep interest in her own life and plans.

"Why don't you go to Girton?" he asked suddenly. She shook her empty hands.

> "How pleasant it is to have money, heigh-ho !
> How pleasant it is to have money ! "

"But there are entrance scholarships."

She blushed as if he had read her thoughts. Was
not the paper of regulations among her most cher-
ished possessions?—laid up in cedar, yet falling to
pieces from frequent perusal ?

"I know," she said, "but they leave one a great
deal to make up. It seems impossible at present,
and yet—I can't shut the idea altogether out of my
dream world. I may earn enough in time."

"Have you any pupils here? I remember you
wanted some."

"Two," she said,—"a governess and a clerk."

"A clerk? A *man?*"

"Yes."

"Humph!" he ejaculated indignantly. "What

does the fellow pay you?" He wondered whether she would resent the question.

She *felt* it evidently, but did not resent it.

"Ten marks for twelve lessons."

"Nonsense! What an infernal niggard he must be!"

She rose.

"It was I who fixed the price," she said simply; "and—I am afraid I am making you talk too much. Good-bye."

"In other words, 'What the devil are my affairs to you?'"

She laughed assentingly, but had not the *nous* to retain an advantage, even when it was given to her by the adversary.

"No, no," she said. "If you are good enough to care——"

"Will you come back?"

"If I may."

"When?"

"This evening if you like."

He was feeling a great deal better, but he knew by bitter experience how his whole tone of mind would gravitate to lower levels as night came on.

"And what about *Faust?*" he said.

"Oh, bother *Faust!* I mean—I had forgotten. It was more than kind of you to send me the tickets; but you must have lots of other friends who would be glad to have them, and I—would rather come to you if you care to have me."

"You are awfully good to me," he said humbly. "I wish the old bellows-mender was worth it!"

She flashed over him a glance that was a tonic in itself. " *Worth it !* " she said.

From that morning Ned began to mend ; his appetite improved, and his temperature gradually ceased to rise in the afternoon. He was thankful he had not written to his friends at home ; and his gratitude to Sturdy was quite out of proportion to her deserts, for she counted it all pleasure and profit to spend an hour or two in his society each day. He had told no one else that he was ill, and for a week her daily visit was the pivot on which his whole life turned. The landlady, too, received her with open arms, and gradually fell into the practice of sending in fruit or chocolate and cakes for the delectation of the bright little English miss, who obviously was not over-burdened with this world's goods, and who showed so frank an appreciation of the delicacies in question.

As was natural under the conditions, all that was best in Sturdy's character came out, and she proved to be one of those people for whom it is an excellent lesson to learn their own value. Each day Ned thought her simpler, sweeter, more womanly. It was curious how completely their positions were reversed for the time : she was the light-bringer now, and he sat in the narrow confines of his lot, and watched for her coming.

And so convalescence came, and drifted them apart again.

" Excellent ! " said the doctor one evening, as he examined his clinical thermometer by the light of the reading-lamp. " But you must not run the risk of another attack like this. The grey North is no place for you from November to May. If you keep as well as you are now, there is no reason why you shouldn't start for San Remo in the beginning of the week."

"All right!" said Ned, "I have a friend there who is expecting me;" and, with a pang of regret, he realized how impossible it would be for any other friend to fill poor little Sturdy s place in his life. Of course that feeling would pass in a week or two; but, for the moment, it was pleasant to give himself up to it, to exaggerate her merits and the extent of his indebtedness to her. What a plucky, loyal little soul she was! One would lose faith in human nature if she proved unworthy of a trust. And what a headpiece—for a woman! He would have liked to kick the confounded little cad who was taking twelve lessons from her for the price of one. It was infamous!

She had promised to come in this evening, but of course the rain would detain her. How it did dash against the windows! Ah, well! they must make the most of the three days that remained—Friday, Saturday, Sunday.

A quick rap at the door, and an eager face looked in.

"Why, Sturdy," he said with shining eyes, "you have never ventured out on such a night!"

She smiled, surprised.

"Is that my name?"

He nodded, conscious for the first time that he had used it.

"Of my very own earning?"

"Assuredly."

"I like it," she said decidedly. "Please don't ever call me Miss Dunbar again. You didn't think a little rain would keep me away, did you?"

An affectionate word was on his lips, but at that moment she removed her cloak, and, with a quick revulsion of feeling, he exclaimed irritably,

"Whose livery do you wear?"

"Livery?" she repeated, startled.

"Yes. If you are not in livery, what induces you to wear those atrocious brass buttons?"

She coloured. "It is an old frock," she said apologetically. "The night is so wet."

But Ned was suffering from the irritability of the convalescent, and moreover he had to pay the penalty of his recent rare indulgence in emotional idealization.

"What has its age got to do with it?" he said. "One would think gowns developed brass buttons as humanity develops silver hairs!"

She laughed in spite of herself. "The dressmaker put them on," she said, "and I suppose I just took them for granted."

"Just look across at your reflection in the pier-glass—a detestable piece of furniture, by the way—and analyze it as you would analyze a picture in the National Gallery. One——"

"Oh, don't!" she cried, wincing.

He stopped abruptly.

"Go on," she said desperately. "It is awfully good of you to take the trouble."

"On the contrary. The subject has preyed on my mind for months. I shall sleep to-night. One can't judge of colour in this semi-darkness, but look at the lights. The gown is in obscurity; the face in semi-obscurity; the high lights of the picture are constituted by——"

"I see," she said, with profound conviction. "It is appalling."

"And if you will study the subject by daylight, you will see that, on the one hand, that inflammatory dye has no beauty of its own; while, on the other, it robs your face of all the colour it habitually possesses,—of course you have been walking in the rain just now;—moreover, it makes your hair look absolutely commonplace; whereas the other evening, when you wore that blue thing, it looked almost—striking."

"I am going to get a new frock," she said shyly, "the first I ever chose for myself. My uncle has sent me the money to buy one as· a Christmas present."

"What fun! I wish I could help you to choose it. Mind you get a colour complementary to your own, not hard like navy-blue, nor cold and chalky like some of the greens they are beginning to wear. It must be something soft and sympathetic,—something you don't mind seeing repeated in the shadows of your face. Do you understand?"

"Theoretically. I will try to work it out."

"Thank you. You can't think what a relief it is to have got that said."

"I am sure you might have said it long ago!"

"I wonder. You have an astonishing gift for retiring into your shell just when one begins to think one has got hold of you."

"I never thought of applying rules of art to a thing like that," she added reflectively. "The fact is, art is a bit of you; with me it is a graft at the best—like most other things. I must have jarred on you a dozen times for once that I saw I had done it—and that was often enough!"

He raised his eyebrows, and shook his head with mock resignation.

"Ah, yes," he said, "it has been a sore trial, a winnowing dispensation!"

Then he turned on her almost brutally.

"Are we going to be intense?" he said. "If so, I'll take a back seat. It's not my specialty."

She reversed engines with a suddenness that surprised him. "By the way," she said lightly, "I meant to tell you when I first came in that this was pay day, and my pupil insisted on making it fifteen marks. He said my teaching was cheap at the price."

"So I should think! Even so it is outrageous. Do you know, Sturdy, I have been thinking a great deal about that Girton business. I am sure, if you go the right way to work, you can't miss it. Tell me what you have done in Latin and Mathematics?"

X.

NED was gone.

"Work is the cure for this mood!" said Sturdy, and she worked harder than ever.

Work was the cure for most moods, according to her simple philosophy; and, if one must have a panacea, it would be difficult perhaps to suggest a better.

When Christmas came round, all the boarders went home, and she was left alone with Fräulein and Pauline, the maid of all work. Poor Fräulein did her best to give the English girl some idea of what a German Christmas means; and a pathetic little *Weihnachtsbaum* duly shed forth its feeble rays from the third-floor window; but I fear the festival would have been rather a dreary one, had it not been for the arrival the day after Christmas of a mysterious packet bearing an Italian postmark. The packet contained a few fine photographs of great Italian paintings; and, although Sturdy would have been the first to say that she did not "appreciate" them, she studied them with a rapturous affection which can scarcely have been entirely without reward. Along with the photographs was a slip of paper on which were inscribed the words— *Del vostro affettuoso amico.*

Sturdy had learnt no Italian, but she understood that.

"I wish I were worthy to be his friend!" she said regretfully. "I must make a fresh start, and work very hard in the new year."

And so the days passed into weeks, and the weeks into months.

In February her funds began to run low, so she left the boarding-house, and went to live in a furnished room. It was cheaper to make her own coffee twice a day, and dine at an unpretentious restaurant; and, moreover, by that time she had mastered the simple vocabulary of the boarders, most of whom were younger than herself.

"When spring comes I shall be able to work much harder," she said; but when spring came, kindling the trees into a soft green glow of life, it found her reproaching herself unceasingly with her laziness. In truth the child was growing very tired.

One day early in May she had trudged home from the barracks, weary and out of heart, when she found a letter awaiting her. Ah, me! It is only in youth that we get just that kind of joy out of letters,—the joy that makes us linger over the handwriting on the envelope, guessing the mood in which the letter was written,—the joy that makes us read it slowly, so slowly, because (although each subsequent reading will discover something new) there is a subtle flavour about the first which we shall never find again.

And this is what she read,

"MY DEAR STURDY: Do you recognize the handwriting, or have you forgotten the old bellowsmender altogether? If not, you may be kindly interested to hear that he is still wheezing along the flinty pathways of this lower world—very very far

in the rear, of course; but still sauntering along in
his own fashion, with ample time to observe all you
poor wretches who will insist upon running.

"Are you running, I wonder?—only running?
Or have you long since gone off in a fiery chariot of
spontaneous moral combustion? The very recollection of your *force* is exhausting,—infectious too. It
doesn't give a fellow a fair chance when a disagreeable duty is on the *tapis*.

"Tell me where I can see you on Sunday afternoon.

"Your worthless but grateful patient,

"NED."

A curious flush came over Sturdy's eyes as she
read, but she did not encourage the tears. It was
much more characteristic of her to make a hasty
critical survey of the room, instinctively looking at
every detail with his eyes. How proud and glad
she was to have a place of her own to receive him
in!—she who, in the exercise of her hospitality
hitherto, had always been dependent on the will or
caprices of others.

It was a very plain, shabby little room, to be
sure, but she had ceased to be ashamed of her poverty,—at least where he was concerned. A neat
chintz cover converted the tiny wooden bed into a
sofa by day, and the worm-eaten washhand-stand
folded up into a side-table.

On her way home from church on Sunday she
bought a crisp little *Napfkuchen*, a few pennyworths
of whipped cream, and a great bunch of daffodils;

and then she gave all her energies to the making of the coffee.

She hung over the battered old pot as though the welfare of an empire were at stake, and she had just convinced herself that the result was an unqualified success, when the door opened and Ned walked in.

His face had regained its becoming coat of sunburn, but Sturdy still saw in the great blue eyes something of the look that had appalled her that bright December day. Even to an inexperienced child like her, he could never again be quite as other men are.

She feasted her eyes frankly on his great lanky brotherly figure.

" I never expected to see you again," she said.

" Thought I'd be under the mools ?" he responded with the old mischievous smile. " It is astonishing how much it takes to kill me."

" Oh, how can you ?" she cried, disgusted at her own stupidity. "I meant—I thought your beloved Italy would not let you go."

" Her embrace *was* becoming a trifle fervid. That was what drove me away."

" But you have had a good time?"

" Oh, first-rate. I found my abortive grunts on the cello were immensely appreciated by an amateur orchestra, and even my stray chips of German seemed impressive when viewed through an Italian atmosphere. I have come back to rub up both; but they recommend Dresden this time. They say the place is not so bad as its china."

She did not answer. What more could she possibly ask than this one priceless afternoon ?

" Well, I do call this jolly!" he cried, dropping
into an old-fashioned arm-chair. " Have we really
got the field to ourselves ? And does the aroma that
greeted me on the stairs really issue from this very
room ? Why, Sturdy, what an afternoon we'll make
of it ! "

She smiled. In her infinite content it did not
occur to her to speak.

" You must have no end of news to tell me. No
sugar, thanks. What a don you must be by now!
How is Herr Waldstein ? "

" Disgusted with me. I seem less and less able
to please him as I get on."

" Ah ! " This was precisely what Ned had anticipated, and it was characteristic of him to let her see
it. "Swears, does he?"

"Oh, no! I wish he did! That is the trying
part of it. He sees that I do my best, and he must
feel that he wasted his time on me at first. He
often gave me more than my share of the lesson. It
is an awful experience to fall short of anyone's expectations."

" I can imagine you find it so. And what about
the teaching? How is—my friend, the clerk ? "

A deep blush spread slowly over her face.

" I don't teach him now," she said rather jerkily,
but with the air of one who dismisses a subject.

Ned looked down on her with the calm smile
which might have seemed cynical to anyone who
did not know him.

15

"Ah! Asked a little too much, did he?"

She looked as if he had performed a feat in thought-reading. "However did you guess?"

"I can't think. And yet on second thoughts it seems to me that I have heard of that sort of thing happening before."

"It never happened to me before," she said frankly; "and it was a horrible shock."

"But I can't think why a commonplace little episode like that should have put a stop to the lessons. I hope you were not so much taken aback that you omitted to tell him he must look on you as a sister?"

She laughed, but did not answer. "I have had another pupil, however. The baroness, in whose family my little governess teaches, is taking lessons from me herself. She has had a dozen."

"Oh! she was not deterred by your exorbitant terms?"

The ready blush returned to the girl's face.

"We didn't say anything about money," she confessed uneasily. "She gave me sixty marks yesterday. I did refuse at first, but she made me take it. I hope I did right."

He laughed softly. "And how about your drawing?"

"Oh, I don't know. I am at a standstill there too. The truth is—I seem to have just wakened up to the fact that my life is a failure; and it is not a cheering discovery to make." There was no affectation in her tone; she was evidently making as light as possible of a mood that was weighing her down.

He raised his brows. " Really ! " he said with a curious light in his eyes. " Now I suppose you are the first man who ever made that discovery about himself. It is worth making a note of. Most of us are crushed by a sense of our own stupendous achievements and success."

She smiled, amused at his tone, but abashed once more at her own tactlessness.

" I'll tell you what it is, though," he exclaimed with a sudden change of manner, " you are looking pale, and—yes, I declare you are stooping. Why, Sturdy, you are unworthy of your name. And you know you will cease to be a moral inspiration if you turn your life into a treadmill. Why are you living alone like this ? "

" It is cheaper; and I was tired of the other place."

" And are you being properly fed ? "

" Oh, yes ! Really and truly I am. And I am not alone. My landlady is always ready to talk when I care to, and she speaks beautiful German. She has seen better days."

" I know. They all have."

" I can't think why I should be done up just now. There is every reason why I shouldn't be."

" My dear child, you must want a change apart from everything else. You can't go on for ever like the brook. Can't you go to the country for a week ? The Whitsuntide holidays are coming on."

She shook her head. " I don't know anyone in the country. One of the boarders kindly asked me

to go home with her at Easter, but I wanted to get
on with my work."

"That people should still be so young!"

"And besides, I couldn't very well afford it. The
journey was long, and I should have had to get a
number of little things that I can do without here.
You see, I didn't know that I should have a windfall of fifty marks."   :

He folded his arms on the table, and looked
across at her, frowning.

"I am going for a leisurely tramp through Saxon
Switzerland before settling down in Dresden," he
said. "I wish I could take you with me. They say
it is lovely at this time of year."

The light leapt up in her face at the very idea
of such a thing. "I wish you could," she said
simply.

"You don't know any nice, neutral sort of person
who would do the chaperon business, I suppose?"
he suggested doubtfully.

"No; and besides, I should have to travel third-
class by slow train, and I couldn't afford hotels; and
even then my fifty marks wouldn't go very far."

"I think we might compromise that if we could
manage the chaperon." He began now to look at the
matter from his own point of view as well as from
hers,—to think what an ideal travelling companion
she would make, with her fresh naïveté, her thirst
for enjoyment, her pretty deference to his greater
experience. It was slow work travelling alone; and,
although other companions could no doubt be found,
he dreaded the pity and patronage of his own sex.

It would be too humiliating to have to cry for quarter at every hill, to be always the first to propose an hour's rest, or to cavil at the hardships which, *corpore sano*, he would have welcomed with a rapture of which strong men had no conception. Now Sturdy —Sturdy had been down with him in the Valley of the Shadow, and no word of explanation on that score would ever be needed between her and him again.

The pain and abnegation in his face wrung her heart.

"In any case a girl would only be a drag on you," she said craftily.

"Humph! The difficulty would be much more likely to lie the other way."

"Do you mean to say that you would really be willing to take me?"

"Do you mean to say that you would really be willing to go?"

"Why not?"

The blue eyes dilated with amusement.

"'It isn t—customary.'"

She blushed. "I know I said that once, but I have been thinking a great deal on the subject since. If I lived in a big gracious cultured world, I should be willing to be bound by its capricious rules and regulations; but in my particular cramped little corner the smug smile of approval is a deal too dear at the price."

She had risen to her feet unconsciously, and now stretched her arms with a long sigh of relaxation. "I must get breath where I can. I must live my own life; and if, in consequence, people will have none of me, I must just make shift to do without their society. It is not as if I were the sort of girl men think about. No one who looks at life 'with larger other eyes' would say I was wrong; and I can't afford to consider the rest."

He felt centuries old as he looked at her eager face. How odd it must seem to be so young—to have life all before one like that!

"I wonder," he said kindly, "whether I ought to let you judge for yourself. You are very young, and at this moment you are quite out of touch with the world. An hour at home might make your view of things very different."

The light died out of her face, and he realized with a touch of wonder that she was only a plain woman after all.

"Listen," she said, seating herself again. "I know you hate heroics, but I should like you just to have some idea of what my life has been. I have lived most of the time in a manufacturing town in the heart of the black country, among people—oh, I wonder what *you* would say if you knew the things they talked about!—hour after hour, always and always! Occasionally I paid a visit to my uncle and aunt in another manufacturing town, and there it was just the same—only more so, as you would say. Two years ago I went to boarding-school by the midland route. There were some fine views on the way, if one could only have stopped the train now and then to look at them!—At the end of a year I went home again, and a few months later I came to

Germany. That is all I have seen of the world. All my life I have dreamt of forests and mountains and glens, but I have never really *seen* them. And now you give me a chance to see them for the first time with your eyes——"

" No, no!" he said. " They would be a poor exchange for your own, Sturdy."

" But there are two things I will not have. I will not have you stinted in the luxuries you are used to, and I will not have you spend a groschen on extras for me. It may be silly to draw the line just there; but you must give me the satisfaction of drawing it emphatically somewhere. Would sixty marks do, do you think?—or—or seventy?"

" Easily," he said somewhat recklessly, "so far as that goes. We must spend the first night in Dresden; but after that we shall sleep at little country-places, where you can get a room in a cottage if you like; and all our meals will be *al fresco* and *à la carte*. You can spend exactly what you choose."

" Then you really mean to take me?"

He looked perplexed. " God bless my soul, child, I shall be only too glad, if you are sure you want to come.

Sturdy was very far from being a plain woman just then. " Don't you see," she said persuasively, leaning forward in her chair and clasping her knee, " don't you see what an education it would be for me? It would widen my horizon for all the rest of my life."

His face brightened; and, springing to her feet,

she clapped her hands with the most girlish movement he had ever seen in her.

"Who says life's not worth living?" she cried.
"Oh, it will be lovely, perfectly lovely! I shall
dream of it day and night till it comes."

Half an hour later she went with him to the
door. They had made all necessary arrangements,
but she still seemed to have something on her
mind.

"And—my frock?" she stammered desperately at
last. "Is it—what you meant?"

"It is an inspiration!" he said heartily. "So
that is why your room was full of the suggestion of
willows and birches and alders and all sorts of shim-
mery things. And I see you have learnt how to
treat that tawny mane of yours. You are a woman
of genius, Sturdy."

XI.

DID ever the sun shine before as it shone that
fresh May morning? There was no doubt about it,
no uncertainty, no coquetry on the part of fair young
Nature. Without waiting for tears and entreaties,
she threw abroad with unsparing hand a glorious
expanse of blue, and smiled down on her children
with all the warmth and brightness of her great
mother heart.

The night-watchman duly earned his *Trinkgeld*,
and Sturdy gave it with all good will; but it was
money thrown away so far as she was concerned.

Five o'clock indeed! The first glimpse of daylight had found her on her knees at the window, her heart full of thanksgiving for so great a boon. She slept with one eye open after that—What if the night-watchman should forget?—And, before the door-bell rang, she had warmed her coffee, and was packing the tiny satchel which constituted her luggage. She was almost startled when she caught sight of her face in the glass. "Yes, yes!" she cried, nodding back to the radiant image, " if this is the end of all things—it is worth it. You and I can never complain!"

It was good to see other tourists astir ; Sturdy was still too young to be exclusive in her enjoyments; and oh, how good it was to see the carts coming in to town laden with the birch and poplar that were to decorate the houses for the festival! She kept quoting to herself, " The mountains and the hills shall break forth before you into singing, and all the trees of the field shall clap their hands," which of course had nothing to do with the case— except in her own mind.

Even she was rather appalled, however, when— having met Ned at the appointed corner — she caught sight of the crowded excursion train.

"Oh, how could I let you in for this!" she groaned in self-reproach.

He nodded reassuringly. "All right !" he said, " we'll manage."

And it was all right, unless something was morally wrong, of which she had no suspicion. All she could say was that the guard seemed unusually interested in their select party, and hastened to unlock a special carriage when they came up.

"What luck!" she cried in delighted surprise; and Ned was well content·to agree with her.

Then her face grew grave. "Don't you think," she said shyly, "it would be simpler to settle up as we go along? Do you mind telling me what you paid for my ticket?"

His exclamation was not intended for her ears.

"I do, very much," he growled. "Look here, Sturdy, you will drive me mad if you go on like this. Let us pay for things alternately. I have taken the tickets. Now it is your turn. We want—— Hang it, what do we want? Don't you think we should have a time-table?"

"I do," she responded drily, "and I see one sticking out of your pocket. No, no," she continued coaxingly, "I am frightfully sorry to worry you; but it can't be helped. Please don't think I don't see how much greater the kindness is on your part when you let me—have my own way!"

This was somewhat involved, but it served its purpose, and he remonstrated no more. For the rest of the tour money matters were settled between them with strict accuracy as a matter of course.

Ned's rooms in Dresden were already taken, and he had found no difficulty in obtaining possession of them a few days earlier than the date originally agreed upon; so he conducted Sturdy there at

once, and then betook himself to the nearest
hotel.

" I will call for you in half an hour," he had
said, "and we will lunch on the Terrasse. You
will like that, won't you ? "

Sturdy, of course, would have liked anything
just then, but the sight that greeted them when
they ascended the broad stone steps was one to
gladden the heart of even the *blasé* tourist.

The Whitsuntide sun overhead seemed to charm
forth every latent touch of colour in town and
tree and river ; gay little pleasure craft plied up
and down ; and on the fine spacious terrace a
crowd of people in fresh spring attire lounged
and strolled and ate and drank and smoked—and
basked in the sunshine, like lizards on a mellow
south wall.

The whole scene was somewhat of a contrast to
Sturdy's garret in a back street of Berlin !

She had gone through many searchings of heart
on the question of dress. The temptation to don
the pretty new gown which Ned had admired
seemed at first to come straight from the evil
one ; to wear it on a walking-tour was to abjure
all the most sacred principles of her upbringing ;
but, on the other hand, gratitude was a moral
duty too, and the only way in which she could
show her gratitude to her friend was to do him
as little discredit as possible. So the green gown
was duly laid out on Friday night. A simple
sailor hat, rejuvenated with a fresh ribbon, was
too obviously suitable to require much meditation ;

and Sturdy had completed her preparations by the poor woman's invariable extravagance—the purchase of a new pair of gloves.

Of course in the end she did not enter into any sort of comparison with well-dressed women; but—in that cosmopolitan gathering—she looked at least like a wholesome purposeful English girl.

Ned had mixed but little with his kind of late years, or he might well have been recognised by some chance lounger. As it was, the strange couple passed almost unnoticed. To any but the casual observer the combination might have seemed a curious one, but there was safety in the fact that Sturdy, as she expressed it, was "not the sort of girl men think about."

Indeed she became a little too painfully aware of this fact for her own peace of mind, as her eye dwelt on the elegant women of all nationalities who flitted about the terrace like birds of rare plumage. Not one of them, she reflected, would look out of place in Ned's society. Though unconventional in the details of his attire, he could rank with the best; whereas she——! At the Conservatorium, the studio, she had a niche of her own, but what was she doing here?

His cheerful voice broke in on her doleful musing.

"Well, madam, shall we fall to?—you to your dinner of herbs, and I to my stalled ox? Does this table meet your views? *Kellner!*"

But that first meal was certainly not a success. A good holiday is very apt to make a false start.

Sturdy was now fairly in the grip of an uncontrollable fit of shyness, and Ned—well, Ned was only a man after all, and he found himself wondering what in the world had induced him to play this extraordinary prank.

All through the afternoon the stiffness lasted. Her over-acute perceptions exaggerated the vague dissatisfaction of his mood, and at the picture-galleries she scarcely dared to open her lips lest an ill-advised remark should add to the irritation against which she imagined him to be struggling.

And then, almost with relief, she saw the well-known lines of physical weariness on his face.

"I am tired," she said quickly. "I should like to go to my own rooms and rest a bit."

His face brightened, and he looked at her with the old fatherly smile.

"Tired!" he said kindly. "You, Sturdy! Well, I hope you will make a note of the fact in your diary. First time in your life, isn't it?"

"Not quite; but I am afraid you won't find me a very energetic companion. I feel so lazy somehow."

"Poor little soul! The child has simply been working herself to death. Never fear, Sturdy. My demands on you won't be heavy. Go and lie down for an hour or two, and we'll meet about six in our own corner of the Terrasse."

But, when she reached her apartments, it was only to pace untiringly with furrowed brow up and down the long length of her luxurious sitting-room.

" It is no use," she said desperately at last. " I must go back to Berlin to-night."

Why, Sturdy, why? Do you regret that you have compromised that poor little reputation of yours, which nevertheless is of more value than you can even imagine just now?

Not so. For better or worse that view of the question never so much as entered her mind. She was only afraid that there was not enough good stuff in her to stand the strain of three or four days' companionship,—afraid that she would irritate her friend, rasp him, worry him, with her gaucherie and stupidity and ugliness.

She was overstrained, of course, with all the excitement of expectation in which she had lived through the last few days; but she had not learned to allow for that; and she only attained something like peace of mind by resolving to tell Ned as soon as they met that she must return to Berlin that night.

Poor little Sturdy! It was a heroic resolution in its way, and, having made it, she laid her head on her arm for a quiet cry; but before the tears had time to come, the heroine was fast asleep.

It was not characteristic of her to be late for an appointment, and the look of relief on Ned's face when she appeared induced her to postpone for a few minutes the weighty communication with which she was charged.

" I am so sorry," she said simply. " I fell asleep," and then she sat quite still, and so unwittingly gave herself up to the soothing magic influences of the evening.

Such an evening! The sun was setting radiantly, but the air was still warm and soft, and the distant strains of the orchestra seemed to her to give voice to a scene that was wanting in nothing else.

Night came on slowly that cloudless Whitsuneve; but at last, as the shadows darkened, gay lamps flashed out among the trees on the terrace, and the river was all alive with vivid touches of red and green.

"Oh," she cried at last, "what a *good* thing frivolity is!"

Ned heaved a sigh of relief.

"Come, that's right! I was afraid you were going to be intense."

"I am afraid I was—a little," she confessed penitently. "I was going to say that all these pretty things—the lights and the music, and the rustle of the wind among the trees—only make me *more* determined to do something,—not just to drift."

He helped himself to *compôte*.

"The physical excitement of adolescence, my child," he said calmly. "We all have to go through it. It just happens to take you in that particular way. But there is nothing to be alarmed about. It will pass. Have some beer; it is an excellent sedative."

"Sedative!" she repeated scornfully. "I have been taking sedatives all my life. I mean to *live* now. We are always complaining that we ask for bread and receive a stone; but it happens occasionally too that someone says, ' It is not bread you want;

it is air. Breathe!' That is what you have done
for me. You have given me air."

He slapped his poor chest with a laugh that
seemed to her sadder than tears. "Come!" he
said; "I appreciate the metaphor keenly. I have
so little accommodation for air myself!"

Wildly she searched for a suitable reply, but the
obvious thought that many men have sound lungs
for one whose moral presence is to his fellows like a
mountain breeze came limping into her mind too late
to be of use.

His eyes overflowed with quiet fun.

"Well, my child," he said, "if you have quite
given up the search for that pleasing platitude, we'll
go indoors to the concert. There is something coming on that I want you to hear.

"You must not imagine," he continued cheerfully,
"that my acquaintances are neglectful of my best
interests. Whenever it gets wind that I am laid up
with a chill, the tracts and booklets begin to pour
in. I am stacking them in the cellar now at home.
I have a pretty good idea how a man feels who is
dying by inches in the desert, with the birds of
prey—— Come, make haste! They are beginning
that *Pizzicato*."

And it was not till Sturdy awoke next morning
in the sunshine that she bethought herself of her
heroic resolution.

XII.

BUT I lay down my pen in despair when I think of the days that followed. It is easy to write a record of journey and resting-place, of the trifling incidents of travel; but what idea can such things give of the way in which these two walked hand in hand into the temple of nature? From one point of view, of course, Ned had everything to give. His was the eye that saw the great white clouds surge seething up as if from a giant's cauldron, that read the subtle secrets of light and shade, and all the wondrous mystery contained in the brooding mellow glow of the atmosphere. He was the one to see the brilliant touch of colour in a cranny of the wall, or the mass of soft green tracery escaping from beneath a dripping stone. Sturdy saw nothing at first, —the tide of life and beauty swept over her head and surged in her ears, making her stupid and speechless; but it is something to initiate into the mysteries of one's religion a novice of such receptiveness.

And all this in Saxon Switzerland?

Even so, fastidious reader; all this in Saxon Switzerland; and I don't suppose it was needful to go so far. A bit of breezy moorland where the cotton-grass flutters in the wind, or a clover-field and hedgerow in June, have done as much for some men. There are those who can enter the kingdom even through a needle's eye.

It began that Sunday afternoon, as they sailed up the river in the soft radiant sunshine. Those

16

wooded heights, broken here and there by field and
vineyard, or ruddy sandstone cliff, wear many festal
garbs as the year rolls round; but I think one comes
at last to love them best as the travellers saw them
that day,—with the evening light playing through
tracery not yet quite concealed by tender green, calling into view, and then throwing into deeper shadow,
the mystical recesses behind.

The sun had almost set when the fortress of
Königstein loomed into view. "Not a minute too
soon," said Ned, "for my retina is in a state of extreme collapse;" and then Sturdy ventured to confess that for the moment she had almost drunk her
fill of beauty too.

"So we'll make straight tracks for the inn, my
child, and get them to recommend a decent cottage
for you."

But they were reckoning literally without their
host. The glorious weather had tempted forth an
even greater number of tourists than usual, and not
only were the inns full to overflowing, but there was
not a bed to be had in the place. For half an hour
they tramped about, verifying the landlord's statement to this effect, and then with delight they espied
an amateur-looking notice of a room to let.

But the notice proved somewhat deceptive. The
woman who answered their knock assured them with
beaming face that she had let her room hours before.

"*Herr Gott!*" she went on to her husband in a
loud aside, "was it not like English people to expect
every convenience at the eleventh hour when they
had not taken the least trouble to secure it!"

"Can't you at least take my sister in ?" said Ned. "She will put up with the couch in the kitchen here, or anything,—won't you ?"

But the woman shook her head. "A gentleman has bespoken that already," she said. "I daresay he wouldn't object to my making up another bed for *you ;* but the lady——"

"There is only one thing the lady can do," interrupted the *Hausherr,* looking up from his supper. "A friend of mine has a barn where tourists—oh, *ganz vornehme Leute,* I assure you—have been glad to sleep before now. Your *Fräulein* sister "—this with a curious glance at Sturdy, of which she was quite unconscious—"would find the straw very comfortable and beautifully clean."

"No, no," began Ned emphatically; but Sturdy laid her hand on his arm.

"Please, please!" she protested with sparkling eyes. "I should like it of all things. Don't say no!"

So he consented at least to inspect the barn. It was approached by a sort of hen's ladder, and proved to be a queer old place,—large and draughty and fairly clean, "but not quite up to modern notions of a boudoir."

"Rats?" he enquired in expressive Volapuk.

"No," was the doubtful response, "or very few. Two other ladies are going to sleep there."

This altered the aspect of affairs ; and indeed it was a case of Hobson's choice, so they were fain to accept the owner's somewhat exorbitant terms.

Ned looked rather unhappy, but his great blue

eyes brimmed over with laughter as they turned away.

"Well, this is the rummiest go, Sturdy," he said. "Invaluable to you who are so bent upon 'living.' Of course it will add enormously to your market value as a human being to have gone through the traditional heroic experience of sleeping in a barn. Consuelo did something of the kind, if I remember rightly; but I am afraid you will have to paraphrase the episode a bit in your home letters."

She laughed lightheartedly. Even home letters seemed a long, long way off just now.

They walked on in silence, following the course of a babbling brook along the foot of the valley. Steep hills wooded to the very top crowded in on every side of them, and, although the sun had set, the sky seemed as light as day above the gloom of the fir-trees.

The air, too, was still steeped in noontide warmth, so they supped and rested in the garden of a wayside restaurant; and then strolled back in the vivid moonlight, watching the tiny waterfalls flash out white and dazzling from the deep, shadowed pools above them.

"Let us go down to the Elbe again," said Ned. "The night will be long enough at the best in those princely quarters of ours. The river ought to be lovely just now."

And so it proved.

The moon had risen high above the fortress, and the surrounding hills and trees were reflected in the water with a distinctness that was almost unearthly.

A ferry-boat was moored to the shore, and they took possession of it at once, Ned stretching out his long limbs in the bottom, while Sturdy curled herself up in the stern. And the boat rocked to and fro in the silence of the night.

It was a long time before either of them spoke.

" I wish——" said Sturdy at last.

" Yes ? "

" I am very sorry, but I do wish you would tell me who is your favourite poet."

" Spare me, my child ! And yet I suppose one must pay the penalty of bringing a young woman out in the moonlight. I know yours, if that is what you mean."

" Who ? "

" Browning."

" However did you guess ? "

" Curious, isn't it ? Such an unusual taste in the youth of the present day ! "

" I can guess yours too," she boasted recklessly.

" Fire away."

" Oh—Blake—or Rossetti—or one of those people that life is too short to read."

" They would be flattered, I am sure, by the description. No, madam, my tastes happen to be primitive. If it will do you any good to know it, my favourite poet is Wordsworth."

" *Wordsworth ?* "

" Even so. Never heard his name, I suppose ? "

" Oh, yes. We used to read his poems at school. *Lucy Gray* and *We are Seven* and 'the lamb behind the hedge.'" She paused, and continued with emphasis, " No, I can't think what you see in them."

"Doubtless. So most of the trippers think, I suppose, who this very Whitsunday are trampling down the creamy tufty umbels in Grassmere church-yard, and chucking their orange-peel into the 'murmuring Rothay.'"

"Of course I know he has written fine things," she answered with some natural resentment.

> " ' They flash upon that inward eye
> That is the bliss of solitude.'

"That is by him, isn't it?"

"Is it?" he responded tantalizingly with the nervous susceptibility of the fervent disciple. "One of his less known poems, I think. How does it go on?—

> And then my heart with pleasure ups
> And dances with the buttercups,

or something to that effect."

She did not answer.

"He is a beast, isn't he, Sturdy? Never mind. You and I will have a dip into Wordsworth one of these days, and see what we can make of him. I didn't say I believed in his plenary inspiration."

The sound of passing footsteps startled them, and they turned their heads to see a man and woman with arms thrown round each other affectionately.

Ned settled himself into a comfortable attitude again. "Curious," he said philosophically, "the tendency people show at holiday times to walk about in couples."

"Very curious."

"Isn't it a comfort, Sturdy, that you and I haven't the smallest tendency to be—sentimental?"

"Great comfort," she assented conventionally.

"Now these poor souls imagine they are enjoying the moonlight and the hills and the trees and the river, but all the time they are only enjoying *themselves*. What they are pleased to call their love blots out all the subtle shades that are a joy to you and me. I think we have the best of it, don't you?"

"I am sure *I* have the best of it," she answered humbly, and then went on with dogged conscientiousness. "And yet you know I don't quite agree with you. I think it is a temptation of the devil to shut out sentiment altogether. When all is said, sentiment is one side of life, and we are bound to foster it—while we keep it in subjection—even though there seems little prospect that it will ever—get a chance—to bear fruit."

He did not dare to follow this up. It might mean anything or nothing; but of one thing he was certain,—Sturdy formed a very attractive picture curled up there in the stern, with the moonlight frosting the willow-green gown, and he was almost beginning to feel the inroads of sentiment himself.

The silence was so long that he was constrained to drop a plummet into its depths.

"In tune with your surroundings, little one?" he asked.

Her answer came dreamily, after a pause.

"Absolutely."

"Can you give them a voice?"

She laughed shyly. "I can tell you the words that were in my mind, though they were not Browning's—nor Wordsworth's. Look!" The moon stepped out grandly above the fir-trees without so much as a wisp of white cloud in her train. "'That we may walk with perfect hearts before Thee now and evermore!'"

Ned felt an inconsistent, unreasoning sense of disappointment.

"What a confirmed moralist the child is!" he said almost irritably.

"That is not morality," she answered quickly. "I suppose it is what you call—sentiment. I should think the very stones in the river must feel to-night that the Lord has lifted up the light of His countenance upon them."

The year was at the Spring; the world was white with a wealth of blossom; and Sturdy rejoiced in the blossom without so much as hearing the whisper of fruit at its heart.

It was not a night to be soon forgotten by either of them.

"You at least have the advantage of being picturesque," Ned remarked half enviously. "I am simply, prosaically squalid."

And there can be no doubt that she had the best of it. The flood of moonlight outside streamed through every hole and cranny in the old-world barn; the place was very quiet, yet "full o' noises";

and from time to time the sleepers were startled by the hooting of an owl away up among the cobwebby rafters overhead.

Sturdy slept like a child,—waking up now and then to count her happiness, but soon falling asleep again to dream of it once more.

XIII.

How the sun did stream through the chinks of the barn next morning!—and what a world met Sturdy's eyes when she threw open the rickety door! She hastened to make such a toilet as was possible under the circumstances, and then went to meet Ned at the inn.

Life did indeed seem very good. The air was so fresh, the coffee so fragrant, the sunshine so full of glee and expectancy, and the tall lanky figure—bending over its Baedeker, unconscious of her approach—surely the one of all those men that any woman might choose to be going to meet.

Certainly few of them had such a greeting to bestow on their womankind.

"Well, little lass!" he cried, springing to his feet with unusual energy, and placing a chair for her. "Is it all right?"

Her beaming face certainly did not betoken much amiss.

"I am longing to hear your adventures. Were there any rats?"

"Oh, I forgot about the rats. No, I don't think so. Only an owl. Such a dear owl!"

"And was the straw very hot and prickly about your ears? I blamed myself so for not lending you my big silk handkerchief."

"What a very kind thought! But I didn't want it at all, thank you."

"And did you contrive to get any sleep?"

"More than I needed. I was happy enough to lie awake all night."

"You are a woman to go through a siege with, Sturdy."

He had been standing over her, looking down at her bright face with eager interest, but now he dropped into his chair again, and called for coffee.

"Lovely morning, isn't it?" he said.

"Oh," she cried, "the air is like music. It is all that I can do to keep my feet from dancing."

"I have been discussing our itinerary with the landlord, and he strongly advises us to drive the first part of the day. Your time is so short, we should make the most of it. So I have ordered a trap—will you come with me, or does your Independence elect to follow on behind?"

"My independence may 'gang its ain gait,'" she answered, smiling. "I shall do as I am asked."

Her eyes sparkled with naïve delight when the "trap" appeared.

"Is that for us? Why, I never drove in a carriage and pair in my life before!"

"Then I hope you won't judge of the experience by this old shanderadan." But he looked at her

almost envyingly as he thought how often he had
loathed the monotony of his daily drive in the luxurious barouche at home.

"After all,". he said with a sigh, "half the world
has things, and the other half enjoys them."

They drove up the hill to the fortress, catching
a glimpse every now and then of the sunny Elbe
valley between the trees, and the smiling country
beyond. Then they passed under the ominous-
looking portcullis, and found themselves in what
seemed to Sturdy a very focus of history.

Ned was not a little amused by the conscientious
method with which she attacked the fortress. She
borrowed his watch, as hers had no second-hand, to
time the jugful of water on its way down the well,
and she duly drank her share of the tubful they saw
drawn up. Not all her amazement at the beauty of
the view from the ramparts could prevent her from
studiously identifying the place where the chimney-
sweep climbed up, and also the spot where the
Englishman threw himself down. ("An Englishman, of course," said Ned with a shrug.) She carefully examined the tree under which the captives
concealed the knotted string of towels that was to
prove the means of their escape; and she strove to
secrete a tear—so he declared—at the sight of the
white cross in the little cemetery away down beyond
the fortress walls. She was hard at work over the
remains of Gambrinus and the beer-cask when Ned
insisted on driving on.

His friendly chaff and her shy good-humoured
acceptance of it drew them nearer together than the

prettiest speeches could have done, and there was little need for words between them as they drove through the balmy golden air. How different the wooded slopes looked to-day in the friendly sunshine! No longer gathering close round the valley, full of gloom and mystery, but standing back and laughing up to the blue sky overhead. An unbroken line of firs fringed the ridge, but lower down the dainty birch and beech tossed out their fresh spring tracery against the darker green behind.

Then the rocks began to rise like gigantic pillars, too steep for vegetation; but from every cleft or cranny some willowy green thing raised its daring head; and, away up in mid-air, the sun flashed through the spray of a waterfall as it leapt from rock to rock, transforming it into a shower of diamonds.

It was well perhaps that, after they had stopped to bait at Schweizermühle, their route led them through flat, uninteresting country, and so gave their receptive powers a chance to recuperate; but their joy was great when they found themselves among the pine-woods again.

"Now we are in Bohemia," said the driver, pointing with his whip to a green and white post, followed almost immediately by a black and yellow one.

"Only now?" thought Ned, with an odd little smile.

But Sturdy sprang to her feet, and looked round as though she expected the trees to be of a different colour. "Are we really?" she cried—"*really?* How

wonderful!" and then her enthusiasm ran almost too
deep for words again, as they passed a rude shrine
by the roadside.   Two peasant women stood before
it, crossing themselves devoutly.

"It is as if we had gone back hundreds of years,"
she said with bated breath, "into the days of romance and chivalry and beauty.   It is like *Quentin
Durward* and *Anne of Geierstein* and—and *Faust*.   It's
like—why, it is just like *Tannhäuser!*"

"It is something to hear an appreciation of medi-
ævalism from you, my child, who are so emphatically
the product of your age."

Her face fell.   "Am I that?   I suppose so.   Some
people are the product of their age because they
don't get the chance to be anything else."

At that moment the driver alighted to adjust a
bit of harness.

"Odd," he said with a shrug of his crooked
shoulders, and a movement of his head in the
direction of the shrine,—"they still keep that up;
and our own people are not much better.   They
still believe Moses knew how the world was made."

Ned's eyes grew round.   "And don't you?" he
asked with quiet amusement.

"*Herr Je!*   We have a reading-club even in Königstein, *mein Herr*.   Most of them only read nov-
els and stories, but I take out the books that tell
how these rocks were here millions and millions of
years ago, how we men have developed bit by bit
without any *Herr Gott* at all,—and the Bible is children's tales."

Involuntarily Ned looked to Sturdy for sympathy,

and their eyes met in a quick flash of mutual comprehension that was worth hours of theological dis-
cussion.

Naturally it was lost upon the driver. He
mounted the box, but turned to them again loqua-
ciously.

" I try to open their eyes a bit, but you can't put
a quart into a pint pot. We have great arguments
in the inn-parlour sometimes. The beer is good and
the company is good; and they make me talk and
forget the time till I have to bustle home in a hurry.".
He shrugged his shoulders and winked to Sturdy. " I
haven't much to say for myself then. My wife does
the talking for me."

He laughed and whipped up the horses.

Ned turned to his little companion with a half
apologetic smile. " Poor Sturdy," he said, " so much
for your mediæval world ! "

"Another product of the age!" she responded
cuttingly; "but I don't seem to have much in common with him somehow. And he doesn't affect my
mediæval world; he only makes me listen all the
harder for the *Pilgrim's Chorus*. It is not poor
Sturdy; it is poor Darwin ! "

" Ah, I forgot that Huxley and Darwin and Harriet Martineau were 'broken lights' of yours! But
why 'poor'? Is it not the very acme of success to
have our views ground out on a barrel organ or
piped on a penny whistle? Doesn't it stir your
blood to think that fifty years hence it may be your
pet theories that are echoing on the heights of
Königstein ? "

"Or yours."

"*Ah!* No, my child. The gods have given me
many good things; but a stake in the chances of the
future is not one of them."

"Oh, why don't you write *now?*" she broke forth
impetuously,—"you who see so much and think so
much? It is such taste to keep it all to yourself
when the world is so thirsty!"

He laughed—a long low laugh of real enjoyment.

"Poor little Miranda! 'How features are abroad
she is skill-less of.' The dwarf only looms through
the mists of your inexperience, my child. You
haven't the smallest notion how clever people are
now-a-days."

Her face fell again. She was thinking of her
own prospects as a teacher. Then—

"There are better things than cleverness," she
said defiantly.

"True. Kingsley's moral is becoming something
musty. Oh, I don't mean to say that your strong
suit may not turn out to be trumps when you come
to play your cards; but I think we were talking of
my hand at the moment, not of yours,—a vastly
different thing. When you are my age—I can feel
now the force of the smile with which you will look
back in the light of a mature and cultivated intellect.
'Poor old fellow!' you will say. 'All he did in the
end was to appreciate some scraps of the work of
other men.'"

She could not rise to this.

"And all of Nature's, surely," she responded
lamely.

He shook himself. "Think so?" he said lightly. "That was handsome on his part, considering how scurvily Nature treated him. So this is Schneeberg. I fear you must bid farewell to your fellow-product of enlightenment."

He looked the poor little figure up and down as he paid the fare.

"*Degeneration : a chapter in Darwinism,*" he said quietly.

They had determined to dine at the top of the High Schneeberg, and Ned accomplished the pull manfully. Sturdy quickly learned not to keep too near him as they climbed, nor to make many remarks that involved an answer; so there was no needless expenditure of the labouring breath, and she was relieved to see, when they reached the summit, that, though tired, he was not exhausted.

Indeed, he attacked the soup and *Kalbbraten* with unusual gusto, and his spirits soon bubbled over into wild superficial criticism of their fellow tourists, his face all the time as grave as if he were discussing the differential calculus. It was a mood that she did not appreciate, though she tried hard to fall in with it. She was growing fast, but humour with her was a bud that blossomed late. Just now life seemed too intense, too short, too beautiful for nonsense. She did not realize the educational value to herself of these playful moods of his; though all the time she was learning with characteristic receptiveness to look at things from his social and intellectual plane, —such a different plane in every way from that to which she was accustomed!

"It's an odd thing," he said at last, frowning, "I can't raise my eyes without being gorgonized by a pair of tea-saucers a few yards off, and I seem to have seen them before. I don't suppose you can throw any light on the question?"

Sturdy waited a moment before looking up, and then, as she found the "tea-saucers" fixed full on her face, there came to her the smell of ropes and of brine, the vision of the grey North Sea.

She dropped her eyes, and spoke very quietly.

"It is Miss Brown."

He drew down his brows. "I seem to have heard the name before," he said, "or to have met with it in fiction. Any particular Miss Brown?"

"Don't you remember? She crossed with us to Germany."

And then he drew down his brows in good earnest.

"Confound her!" he said under his breath. "Well, we have no time to lose if we mean to do justice to the view and catch our train at Bodenbach. Ready?"

"I shall be in a moment. But don't wait. It is frightfully hot in here. I will finish my coffee and join you directly."

But his seat was scarcely vacated before the tea-saucers took possession of it.

"I say, how awfully funny!" was Miss Brown's characteristic salutation.

Sturdy bethought herself of no fitting response.

"You do seem to be having a good time!" She

17

glanced at the ringless finger. "Left the others at the foot of the hill, I suppose ? "

" Yes."

Poor Sturdy! Even in the excitement of the moment she suffered acutely for the lie.

" Well, all I can say is, you must have an amazingly accommodating chaperon. Mine is a regular old hawk. Won't let us speak to a soul, and expects botanizing and water-colour sketching to take the place of human intercourse."

Sturdy smiled feebly.

" You know you have improved tremendously. I didn't recognize you till my friend, Miss Carswell, remarked on the beauty of your teeth, and then I took a good look,—not that I noticed your teeth on the steamer."

Sturdy was conscious of a strong fellow-feeling with the wolf in *Red Ridinghood*, but she refraiued from quoting his precise words. "I think I must be going," she said, rising.

" Oh, don't be in such a hurry. I am longing to know how you met that fellow again. He isn't handsome, you know, but he is awfully aristocratic-looking. I thought the episode came to an end when he left you in the lurch at the docks."

Sturdy drew herself up instinctively. " I am afraid I don't understand you," she said, driven into serenity by the sheer force of her companion's impertinence.

" You are forgiving. I would have let him hear about it. He was so taken up with Madam and her baggage that he left you *plantée là*, and I noticed

that you were the very last passenger on board
to get a porter. Did you catch your train, by the
way ? "

"I shall miss it now if I stay here talking," said
Sturdy. "Good morning."

Her eyes and cheeks were very bright when she
joined Ned on the tower overlooking that wonderful sweep of country ; but she said nothing of the
interview that had just taken place. Why should
she ? It might annoy him, and make him regret
having brought her.

And indeed she soon forgot all about it herself as
they strolled through the woods to Bodenbach in the
glinting sunshine. The road was rough and stony,
and Ned's tall figure drooped in the drowsy afternoon warmth. There was something very tempting
to a weary man in the sight of that firm young
shoulder, and at last, almost unconsciously, he laid
his hand on it. Little by little she felt the weight
increase, but, as it grew heavy, her heart grew light ;
and so the strange couple walked on, regardless of
chance observers, scarcely conscious for the moment
that they were two and not one, for were they not
both, like the birds and the trees, only a part of the
summer afternoon ?

There were beds and to spare at Schöna that
night, and oh, the joy of seeing clean sheets and a
fair supply of cold water !

They resolved to " go to roost " immediately after
supper, but the night was so bright and still that
they wandered down to the Elbe once more. It was
hard to separate while that pleasant sense of intimacy

lasted, and all chance of reaction was warded off by the thought of Wednesday's parting.

Accidentally they discovered a wonderful echo ringing back from the heights across the river, and for a time they laughed and sang and jodelled like a couple of children. It was a pleasant hour to look back upon in after-life, though its details never would bear very accurate focussing. Every trifling event served to emphasize the harmony of their mood. Why try to express it in words that had been used so often before?

When they turned homewards a long silence fell on them, and Sturdy slowly gravitated back to her customary levels.

"Mr. Beresford," she began shyly, "do you re-member——?"

"Why don't you call me Ned?" he interrupted recklessly.

She shook her head. "It wouldn't do."

"Why not? We are all Adam's bairns." ·

"It doesn't fit in a bit with my conception of you."

"Ah! That's final. Well? Do I remem-ber——?"

"The lady with the little boy who crossed with us to Germany?"

"Your mind is running on Miss Brown, I see. Yes, I remember the lady."

"Have you seen her since?"

"I have. I called once or twice, but they did not remain long in Berlin. Why?"

"I have often wished I could see more of her. I never met anyone like her before."

"If you go to Cambridge, you will meet lots of nice people."

"*If!*"

"True. That question is settled. We are not going to reopen it."

"What a fortune it would be to a teacher to have a manner and presence like that! Do you mind telling me," she went on nervously, vaguely conscious that she was making a mistake, "whether my manner is just a degree—just a degree—better than Miss Brown's?"

"I decline to rise to that, Sturdy. And besides, Miss Brown left no very definite impression on my mind."

She sighed.

"I think you will find," he said rather deprecatingly—he was always ill at ease in the gown and bands of the preacher—"at least I imagine it is a fairly common experience—that as we grow older we see that we simply can't possess all the charms and virtues of other people; and when we once make up our minds to that, we find that we do possess them in a way. The things we appreciate are possessions that nobody can rob us of."

She did not answer immediately.

"Rather a bleak and negative sort of possession!"

"So it naturally seems to you now." And he murmured half to himself,

"'Think you, 'mid all this mighty sum
Of things forever speaking,
That nothing of itself will come,
But we must still be seeking?'"

"I know *that*," she cried with girlish eagerness. "Robertson quotes it."

"Robertson quotes it!" he repeated expressively, but he was in no mood to be hypercritical then.

"And I like Christina Rossetti better,—

> 'Does the road wind uphill all the way?
> Yes, to the very end.
> Will the day's journey take the whole long day?
> From morn to night, my friend.'"

"That is true too, and I can imagine you like it better. But the fact remains that we don't always learn most when we are trying hardest to learn. Certainly we don't grow most when we are trying hardest to grow."

Poor Sturdy! Her density at times was almost incredible. "I am sure that applies to my music," she said.

The subject of her music was not one that would naturally have suggested itself to him that lovely night, but he adapted himself to her mood.

"Then be content for a bit to listen to other people's music."

"Do you think I should give it up altogether?"

"*Gott bewahre!* Among my many follies I am thankful to think I don't include that dogmatising on other people's duties."

"I know; but I should so value a word of advice."

He shook his head. "Do the thing you want to do, my child."

"It is the moral force of her that will tell," he

said to himself, "but there is no need to draw her attention to that. It is the one thing she is not self-conscious about."

He laughed softly as he thought what a panoply she possessed in that moral force and moral ambition of hers. Assuredly there was no danger in her mood to-night.

XIV.

—that serene and blessed mood,
In which the affections gently lead us on,—
Until, the breath of this corporeal frame,
And even the motion of our human blood
Almost suspended, we are laid asleep
In body, and become a living soul ;
While with an eye made quiet by the power
Of harmony, and the deep power of joy,
We see into the life of things.—WORDSWORTH.

BUT it was next day—Tuesday in Whitsun-week—that they reached their high-water mark of physical enjoyment,—it was then that Sturdy entered, without knowing it, into Wordsworth's secret, and saw things eye to eye with her friend.

A heavy dew fell in the night, and then the sun rose royally as before, glowing down through an atmosphere rich in colour, and calling forth the subtle complex fragrance of all the scentless green things. The air was full of twitter and whirr and clear liquid notes; and through all one seemed to hear the very heart beat of the summer day.

The travellers set off leisurely with no very defi-

nite intent. It was not a day for maps and guide-
books. They crossed the ferry, and then took their
way through the glen that leads to the Prebischthor.

Oh, the glory of that morning!—the living harmony of golden greens, shimmering into silver where
the sun flashed off the leaves, and fading far away
into a rich blue haze! Sturdy did not speak, but
every now and then her breath came almost in a sob
of intense appreciation. When they reached the foot
of the hill, there was no talk of turning back, but
Ned laid his hand quite simply on her shoulder as
they began the climb. The sun soon became very
hot, but they were shaded by the fir-trees overhead,
and every few dozen yards they stopped to rest and
enjoy.

"What it must be to Sturdy!" Ned thought ever
and again as his eye revelled in all the wealth of life,
and the grandeur of the mighty walls of rock.

Then the path became so steep that it was impossible to walk abreast, but an occasional rude hand-
rail or flight of steps made the climb a comparatively
easy one.

But nothing on the way prepared them for the
beauty of the view from the summit. Shortly after
noon they emerged into the brilliant sunshine on the
top of the great natural arch. The outlook is always
an impressive one, but to-day the brilliant golden
atmosphere seemed to give a new value and defini-
tion to everything, and the air was full of the sounds
that measure the stillness of a summer noonday.
Even Ned admitted afterwards that he had rarely
felt so strongly the sense of an actual presence

round about him; and as for poor Sturdy—her first
almost irrepressible impulse was to fall down on her
knees,—she had never dreamt of anything like this
—but, fortunately for Ned, she remembered herself
in time.

"Oh," she cried, when at last she found voice,
"why do we preach to people? Why don't we just
bring them out and let them feel things?"

It was some time before he answered.

"I think," he said quietly, "it was you who only
yesterday were advising me to write."

"Was I?" She drew her hand across her brow
as if she were half dazed. "I suppose I was. I
don't know what I think or believe. My mind
seems all turned upside down. I feel almost as if
I had crossed the river of death."

He shivered. "I hope Jordan's flood may prove
as pleasant! Come."

They took a path through the woods which
brought them very gradually nearer earth again.
The air was full of the aromatic fragrance of pines,
and the thick carpet of needles crunched pleasantly
under their feet. Now and then they got a sunny
glimpse of the surrounding country away down
below, or the undulating way was varied by a deep
ravine, whose steep rocky sides were tapestried with
dark velvety mosses and sprays of delicate green;
and here and there tall firs and birches sprang from
the moist ground at the bottom, and stretched their
dainty heads to the light above the rocks.

By common consent the travellers turned aside,
and threw themselves on a mossy bank in the

dappled sunshine. Neither was in any mood for words, but of course it was Sturdy who at length broke the silence.

"Do you know," she said in a queer broken voice, "it has come to me what you meant last night about our possessing things outside of us. I feel to-day like a river that has joined the sea. All the *me* is slipping away, and yet—I feel the tide sweeping in, so still, so—*big*. It makes me smile at my own little ambitions and aims. I see now how one inherits the earth. . . . And it is so simple !—you have only to let yourself go."

She stopped,—her eyes bright with unshed tears. "Am I talking nonsense ? "

"On the contrary, my child : something nearer sense than I ever expected to hear from you."

Did her simile recall to his mind the river whose surroundings have inspired one of the noblest poems in the language ? Possibly ; for, a few minutes later, he began to repeat in a low level voice,—

> "Five years have passed, five summers, with the length
> Of five long winters ! and again I hear
> These waters, rolling from their mountain springs
> With a soft inland murmur——"

And, like an almost inaudible accompaniment, the wind rippled softly through the tree-tops, and the insects hummed on.

When he came to the last paragraph, Ned stopped short. Indeed he smiled to himself at the bare idea of going on. Those personal references to the "dearest Friend," the "dear, dear sister," struck him as purely ridiculous in the present connection. They were too nearly true, too "sentimental," too grotesquely appropriate to the situation.

So he stopped, and Sturdy thought the poem was at an end.

"How lovely!" she said dreamily. "Your voice and the poem are just like the throb one feels to-day in the sunshine."

Yes, no doubt it would have been ridiculous to go on to the end of the poem; but there came a day—— Yet why talk of it? Have we not all learned that in this world of partings there is sometimes but one step from the ridiculous to the sublime?

Having almost unwittingly come so far, they resolved to go on by the ordinary tourist route towards Schandau. At the top of the Great Winterberg there was an announcement of a "Pony to let," and Ned gladly availed himself of it. Of course he insisted that Sturdy should have her share of the luxury, but she succeeded in reducing this to a minimum on the true plea that the unwonted exercise tired her more than walking.

As they climbed the hill to the Kuhstall, they overtook Miss Brown's party, and the "tea-saucers" were brought into full requisition. Sturdy tried hard to keep out of their way, but of course in vain. As they passed, Miss Brown contrived to whisper in an expressive undertone,

"Well, I must say you have an *amazingly* accommodating chaperon!"

Then she turned to her companion in tutelage.

"Do you know, I believe that is a runaway couple."

The other looked sceptical. "Humph!" she said. "One would wish them a swifter steed!"

The incident was a very trifling one, yet it always seemed to Sturdy the beginning of the end. From that moment the shadow of the parting was upon them. The sky, too, began to cloud over; a sudden ominous sough of wind swept through the trees; and they were startled to hear the patter of rain on the leaves overhead.

At the first opportunity they hired a conveyance and drove on to Schandau.

Sturdy kept up gallantly. Intuitively she recognized that she must make no reference to the parting, and indeed she wanted Ned's last impression of her to be as bright as possible.

So they talked and laughed—a little too conscientiously perhaps, but to all appearance as gaily as though a lifetime of companionship lay before them.

And next morning he went with her to the steamer, and she started alone for Dresden in a blinding slant of rain.

XV.

"And now the time has come, and we must go hence."

IT was autumn, and Ned and Sturdy were on the North Sea once more. They had met but seldom since the parting in Saxon Switzerland, and it was very pleasant now to talk over the golden days, and all the experiences of the interval. Sturdy had much to tell of her music, her teaching, the books she had read, and the plays she had seen; and he listened and laughed with the old friendly interest and amusement.

"And do you still look forward with enthusiasm to your life-work?"

Her face clouded.

"Oh yes, but just at present the immediate future bulks too big for me to see beyond it. I do so dread going home."

He turned to her with a look of brotherly concern.

"Nothing wrong, I hope?"

"No, no. Nothing of that sort. I suppose it is difficult for you to imagine what an uncongenial home means."

He drew down his brows in simple disapproval.

"Oh, stow that, Sturdy!" he said good-humouredly.

Her face crimsoned.

"One doesn't expect *banal* conventionalities from you, little woman, and you must be aware that it is the fashion nowadays for young people to 'outgrow' their homes. The butcher's boy is sent to college, enters the ministry—'leaves all for the cross,' in fact!—and then finds that his father and mother are quite unable to enter into his delicate feelings and lofty aspirations. It is astonishing how little sense of humour some people have! And in ninety-nine cases out of a hundred the old folks at home are, not only more interesting, but also a dashed sight better form, than these crowing upstart bantams."

She did not answer.

"Offended?" he asked at length.

"No. You are—bracing."

"But it is true, isn't it?"

It was a minute or two before she answered.

"*So* true," she said meditatively. "I never thought of it quite in that way before. 'He *endured* as seeing Him who is invisible.' Of course our resignation must be the measure of the depth of our insight."

But, from Ned's point of view, this was going from bad to worse.

"If there is a word I detest," he said, exasperated, "it is resignation. *Resignation!*"

"I know you do. I am stupid at choosing my words. But you don't detest the thing I mean."

"Look here, Sturdy,—swear a bit, will you? There is no fun in being too good for this world."

She laughed. "There is less fun in missing one's opportunities."

He groaned and stretched himself wearily. "Do you know, you positively make my back ache? If you mean to go through life in this laborious fashion, sweeping up your opportunities, what will you be at fifty—thirty even? It is enough to make a man wish he might be there to see. I hope you are not missing that fine gleam through the mist?"

"It is lovely," she said, "and it is late. Good-night."

The season of fogs was not yet; but, without regard to recent precedent, the fog gathered denser and denser; and, from midnight on, the horn kept sounding with dreary iteration. Glass in hand, the captain spent the night on the bridge, and he appeared at breakfast in the morning, red-eyed and weary.

"I would rather you were all sick in your berths," he said, as he mechanically counted the full tale of passengers. "There is no danger in that."

"Why don't you put into some port?—or cast anchor?" asked a lady anxiously.

He smiled. "There are difficulties; and if we cast anchor every time there was a fog, there would soon be a rival company. One has to be careful what one says to ladies, but we don't always get a chance to be quite as cautious as we would like."

"But there is an invention by which you can stop instantly, isn't there?" asked an intelligent young man. "I saw a model of it at some exhibition."

The captain shrugged his shoulders. "If there had been a practical one, I would soon have heard of it," he said. "We can't see three-quarters of a mile through the fog just now; and, even though we reverse engines, we can't stop short in anything like that distance."

Even as he spoke the grunt of the horns rose in an anguished blast, there was a scuffle of feet overhead, the shriek of a whistle, the convulsive throb of reversed engines,—and the captain was up the companion-way before the passengers could look round.

Quick as light a glance passed between Ned and Sturdy, and they followed without delay.

The steamer quivered and throbbed like a live thing, the water all around was churned into foam, and high up, through the fog, loomed the prow of a mighty vessel.

Sturdy shivered. If the only chance of escape lay in scaling that slippery cliff——!

Instinctively Ned caught her trembling hand, and drew it within his arm.

" Frightened?" he asked, in an odd, tender voice, looking down at her ashen face.

" Horribly."

" Dear little lass!" He clasped the hand firmly in his great warm palm. " You make me feel that there are advantages after all in spending the best years of one's life with one foot in the grave."

She did not answer. At that moment it seemed as if she could almost have touched the approaching vessel with her hand.

" If you knew how I have wasted my life," she began rather hysterically;—" if you knew all I meant to do——!"

"Bless my soul, child, is it possible that you, who are just brimming over with moral enthusiasm, need to be told by an old pagan like me that we can't choose our work? And do you expect me to believe that you, who meant to do your duty so heroically as a teacher, will do it any less well if, · instead of all that grind, you have simply got— to die?"

Ah me, how often he had preached that doctrine to himself in the feverish watches of the night! But to her in her eager vitality it was a hard saying, just beyond her own moral grip, and consequently perhaps the grandest saying she had ever heard.

Pitifully she raised her face to his in search of strength—and their eyes met for the first time in a long, full look, without raillery, without reserve. I think perhaps there are some whole lives that contain less meaning than a look like that.

"Thank God!"

The exclamation came involuntarily from one of the passengers, and the two friends turned to see the great prow slowly, slowly receding.

Sturdy drew a deep breath.

"What a hero you are!" she said softly.

But even in a moment like that he could stand no sentiment.

"Custom, my dear, custom," he answered lightly. "If you had a tussle with Bony every six months or so, you would become used to the grimness of his visage."

Little by little, as the day wore on, the fog lifted, taking with it for the most part, as it rose, the momentary insight it had lent, and leaving the fogs of convention to settle down again.

But Sturdy's voice was still very shaky when at last her reflections took form—

"Will you forgive me," she said, "for all the times I have been conceited and 'superior.' I believe I *have* sometimes thought I was more—more moral than you. But it is the Valley of the Shadow that tries a man, and you have stood the test, and I have failed."

"Don't be ridiculous, dear," he answered affectionately. "I have told you already that has nothing to do with it. My philosophy is a more restful one than yours.

> 'This I know,—
> I should live the same life over if I had to live again,
> And the chances are I go—where most men go.'"

"Oh, don't," she cried.

"Does that shock you? It has comforted me many a time; and indeed I am only applying your own principles anent resignation. Whittier says almost the same thing—'*nur mit ein bischen andern Worten,*'—

> 'Suffice it if—my good and ill unreckoned,
> And both forgiven, through Thine abounding grace—
> I find myself by hands familiar beckoned
> Unto my fitting place.'

That will suit us both perhaps. . . . Do I hear the luncheon-bell? Joy!"

The voyage was a good deal lengthened by the
fog, but Sturdy awoke next morning to find the
level rays of the sun streaming in at her cabin
window, and she hurried on deck with all the speed
she could make.

Land was already in sight, and Ned was awaiting
her. The water lay a leaden expanse on every side,
but the white caps danced and sprang into the glow
of the rising sun. For a time they stood together in
silence.

" Sit down, Sturdy," said Ned at last. " I want
to speak to you. Do you dislike letter-writing? "

She turned to him with the light of the white
caps in her face.

" I should love to write to *you!* " she said.

He smiled. No, she never would learn to be like
other women!

" I was thinking," he said, " it would be very
kind if you would write—once a month or so.
Tell me about the books you are reading, the
music you are hearing ;—and I will do the same to
you."

" Oh, how kind of you to think of it ! "

" On the contrary, my child. It is the other
way about. You will soon judge differently of our
relative value. But there is one thing I want to
say——" He raised one leg slowly over the other,
and nervously tapped the sole of his boot with the
book he had been reading. " Some day—any day—
the man may come along, who—whose step will
make your heart beat fast, and all that sort of thing.
Well—when he comes—you will give me a hint,

won't you ?   He will be a fine fellow I've no doubt;
but—my letters won't be meant for him."

They were alone on deck, and she laughed aloud.

"As if I wouldn't rather have your letters than
any other man's love!"

He nodded with quiet philosophy.

"All right—you will keep faith, I know.   And
now, my child, will you tell the steward to bring up
your things, and I will see that the custom-house
officer passes them at once."

It seemed only a few seconds before he was putting her into her cab.   Who knows what she might
have been tempted to say at that last moment?—
but he gave her no chance.

"And as regards *colour*," he said lightly, as he
held out his hand, "you won't forget, will you ?
Shun the calorific end of the spectrum as you would
shun poison.   Nothing could be better than that
soft willow green, but you might try an old tapestry
blue if—— Good-bye! God-speed!"

XVI.

—when thy mind
Shall be a mansion for all lovely forms,
Thy memory be as a dwelling-place
For all sweet sounds and harmonies ; oh ! then,
If solitude or fear or pain or grief
Should be thy portion, with what healing thoughts
Of tender joy wilt thou remember me.—WORDSWORTH.

A FINE rain was falling steadily, and the smoke of tall chimneys hung heavily over the town, when Sturdy arrived at the familiar, grimy station.

The most casual observer could have told that the young woman on the platform was her sister ; and it was well perhaps that Ned was not there. Most things are cheapened when we see them in duplicate. The same hair, the same height, something of the same build, and yet what a difference after all !

" I was determined to come alone to meet you," said the sister as they unfurled their umbrellas. " I wanted to tell you the news myself. I was so afraid it wouldn't be settled before you came home. It has been hanging fire so long. But last night it all came right. Look ! "

She drew off a soiled yellow glove and displayed a diamond ring.

All the snob in Sturdy rose in fierce rebellion. Surely their family was impossible enough without the addition of a "genteel" brother-in-law. Then the thought of the butcher's boy who " left all for the cross " sent the blood to her cheeks.

"I am sure I wish you joy, dear," she said humbly. "It is Mr. Johnson, I suppose?"

"Yes. Did you guess from my letters that there was something in the wind?"

"No. It never crossed my mind."

"Oh, you're not half sharp! But of course I didn't want to say too much in case it should all be off again. You know he has father's business now; and, with his London experience, he means to make the old place sit up. He says poor father was too much of a poet to succeed in business."

"Thank God for that!"

"Oh, of course; I know. It is very nice—especially now that he is dead. And it was all his doing that you got your grand education. But there is mother waving her hand to you at the window. Poor mother, she is awfully pleased about this."

So it seemed, poor careworn woman! She embraced Sturdy with tears in her eyes; but, as a family event, the wanderer's return was evidently a matter of small importance compared with the diamond ring.

"Mr. Johnson was hoping to come in and see you to-night," she said, when Sturdy's unpacking was completed and they sat at tea; "but he was afraid he couldn't get back from Screwborough in time. He is so anxious to hear you play the violin."

Sturdy did not reply. It was needless to explain at this juncture that she had lost even the doubtful skill she had once possessed.

"You know he is desperately afraid of you," said the sister gleefully.

Sturdy's smile was rather a dreary one.

"I wonder why, unless there is something very unusual about a young woman who has learned her own ignorance."

"I shouldn't wonder if he thought you quite pretty," was the generous response. "Is that a German way of doing your hair? And I like your dress—though it's not what I call stylish. Don't you, mother?"

The mother assented doubtfully, and strove for a moment to suppress the conscientious remark that followed. "But it seems to me rather extravagant to wear a dress like that on a journey. I noticed a spot of tar or grease or something on it. No, not there; somewhere in the back folds. Stand up and I'll show you. See! You must get something from the chemist to-morrow that will take it out. I am afraid you have come home with very grand ideas."

Sturdy laughed pleasantly. With dogged tenacity she was keeping before her mind the picture of the butcher's boy.

"If I have," she said, "it is not for want of trying to make my ideas simple."

And then the conversation returned once more to the ebbs and flows of the courtship.

Bed-time came at last, and the two sisters took their candles to go up-stairs.

"I see the big house is let," said Sturdy casually.

"Yes, to the new manager of the works, Mr. Brown. By the way, his daughter met you in Germany."

"Ah!"

"She said I was to be sure and ask you all about your tour in Saxon Switzerland. You seemed to be having such a good time. I said you had told us very little about it in your letters."

"Yes."

So the deluge was at hand, was it? Very good. Let it come!

On the threshold of her attic room she stopped, and kissed her sister affectionately.

"Good-night," she said. "I am very tired. You shall tell me more to-morrow."

The room was as plainly furnished as a nun's cell; the one thing in it to please the eye was a photograph of *Lohengrins Abschied* on the wall by the bedside. It was one of the very few treasures which Sturdy had brought with her from Germany.

But she did not stop to look at this now. She put out her candle, and, throwing open the storm-window, stretched out her arms into the starless night.

"God," she moaned. "God,—God! *How* I thank Thee! Who was I that this should come to me? And now, whatever happens, I have had my day, and the light has entered into my life for ever."

And, many miles away, a man sat wearily in a luxurious room with his slippered feet on the rich tiles of the hearth. All around were books, and on the table a great bowl of roses was half concealed by the wealth of photographs and music just unpacked.

On the sofa opposite lounged a young girl in

dainty evening dress, her beautiful head supported by her hand, her face full of eager interest and of pathetic recoil from an awful foreboding.

"So you see, Edith," the man was saying, "the episode simply came to an end. One can scarcely conceive how it could have been otherwise. Love is one of the things that have no place in a life like mine ; and, as it happened, she was not that sort of a girl. I don't suppose her mother would welcome me in the capacity of Platonic friend, and I can't fancy you and Sybil receiving her here. I don't even know myself that I should care to have her."

A curious little smile rippled his flexible lip. He stopped and relighted the cigar that had gone out while he was talking. He drew a few whiffs rather nervously, and then continued very calmly, as if he were talking of someone else.

"I made my will the other day. I wanted to leave her enough money to go to Girton; and I should like her to have my books,—of course not anything you or Sybil especially care about—but Wordsworth certainly. And if some day she should turn out a famous woman,—upon my soul, it wouldn't surprise me ! That moral force and moral fibre are the next things to genius,—and you should care to make her acquaintance—I think you will find she hasn't forgotten the poor old hulk, whom she towed along—so gallantly—in the sunshine."

THE END.

APPLETONS' TOWN AND COUNTRY LIBRARY.

PUBLISHED SEMIMONTHLY.

185. *The Lost Stradivarius.* By J. MEADE FALKNER.
186. *The Wrong Man.* By DOROTHEA GERARD.
187. *In the Day of Adversity.* By J. BLOUNDELLE-BURTON.
188. *Mistress Dorothy Marvin.* By J. C. SNAITH.
189. *A Flash of Summer.* By Mrs. W. K. CLIFFORD.
190. *The Dancer in Yellow.* By W. E. NORRIS.
191. *The Chronicles of Martin Hewitt.* By ARTHUR MORRISON.
192. *A Winning Hazard.* By Mrs. ALEXANDER.
193. *The Picture of Las Cruces.* By CHRISTIAN REID.
194. *The Madonna of a Day.* By L. DOUGALL.
195. *The Riddle Ring.* By JUSTIN McCARTHY.
196. *A Humble Enterprise.* By ADA CAMBRIDGE.
197. *Dr. Nikola.* By GUY BOOTHBY.
198. *An Outcast of the Islands.* By JOSEPH CONRAD.
199. *The King's Revenge.* By CLAUDE BRAY.
200. *Denounced.* By J. BLOUNDELLE-BURTON.
201. *A Court Intrigue.* By BASIL THOMPSON.
202. *The Idol-Maker.* By ADELINE SERGEANT.
203. *The Intriguers.* By JOHN D. BARRY.
204. *Master Ardick, Buccaneer.* By F. H. COSTELLO.
205. *With Fortune Made.* By VICTOR CHERBULIEZ.

Each, 12mo, paper cover, 50 cents; cloth, $1.00.

GEORG EBERS'S ROMANCES.

*Each, 16mo, paper, 40 cents per volume; cloth, 75 cents.
Sets of 24 volumes, cloth, in box, $18.00.*

In the Blue Pike. A Romance of German Life in the early Sixteenth Century. Translated by MARY J. SAFFORD. 1 volume.

In the Fire of the Forge. A Romance of Old Nuremberg. Translated by MARY J. SAFFORD. 2 volumes.

Cleopatra. Translated by MARY J. SAFFORD. 2 volumes.

A Thorny Path. (PER ASPERA.) Translated by CLARA BELL. 2 volumes.

An Egyptian Princess. Translated by ELEANOR GROVE. 2 volumes.

Uarda. Translated by CLARA BELL. 2 volumes.

Homo Sum. Translated by CLARA BELL. 1 volume.

The Sisters. Translated by CLARA BELL. 1 volume.

A Question. Translated by MARY J. SAFFORD. 1 volume.

The Emperor. Translated by CLARA BELL. 2 volumes.

The Burgomaster's Wife. Translated by MARY J. SAFFORD. 1 volume.

A Word, only a Word. Translated by MARY J. SAFFORD. 1 volume.

Serapis. Translated by CLARA BELL. 1 volume.

The Bride of the Nile. Translated by CLARA BELL. 2 volumes.

Margery. (GRED.) Translated by CLARA BELL. 2 volumes.

Joshua. Translated by MARY J. SAFFORD. 1 volume.

The Elixir, and Other Tales. Translated by Mrs. EDWARD H. BELL. With Portrait of the Author. 1 volume.

"Georg Ebers writes stories of ancient times with the conscientiousness of a true investigator. His tales are so carefully told that large portions of them might be clipped or quoted by editors of guide-books and authors of histories intended to be popular."—*New York Herald.*

For sale by all booksellers; or sent by mail on receipt of price by the publishers,

D. APPLETON & CO., 72 Fifth Avenue, New York.

D. APPLETON & CO.'S PUBLICATIONS.

BY A. CONAN DOYLE.

RODNEY STONE. Illustrated. 12mo. Cloth, $1.50.

The Prince and Beau Brummel, the dandies of Brighton and the heroes of the prize ring, reappear in the pages of this stirring and fascinating romance. Every one knows the saneness and spirit of Dr. Doyle's work, and here he is at his best.

THE EXPLOITS OF BRIGADIER GERARD. A Romance of the Life of a Typical Napoleonic Soldier. Illustrated. 12mo. Cloth, $1.50.

" The brigadier is brave, resolute, amorous, loyal, chivalrous; never was a foe more ardent in battle, more clement in victory, or more ready at need. . . . Gallantry, humor, martial gayety, moving incident, make up a really delightful book."—*London Times.*

" May be set down without reservation as the most thoroughly enjoyable book that Dr. Doyle has ever published."—*Boston Beacon.*

THE STARK MUNRO LETTERS. Being a Series of Twelve Letters written by STARK MUNRO, M. B., to his friend and former fellow-student, Herbert Swanborough, of Lowell, Massachusetts, during the years 1881-1884. Illustrated. 12mo. Buckram, $1.50.

" Cullingworth, . . . a much more interesting creation than Sherlock Holmes, and I pray Dr. Doyle to give us more of him."—*Richard le Gallienne, in the London Star.*

" Every one who wants a hearty laugh must make acquaintance with Dr. James Cullingworth."—*Westminster Gazette.*

" Every one must read; for not to know Cullingworth should surely argue one's self to be unknown."—*Pall Mall Gazette.*

" One of the freshest figures to be met with in any recent fiction."—*London Daily News.*

" ' The Stark Munro Letters' is a bit of real literature. . . . Its reading will be an epoch-making event in many a life."—*Philadelphia Evening Telegraph.*

ROUND THE RED LAMP. Being Facts and Fancies of Medical Life. 12mo. Cloth, $1.50.

" Too much can not be said in praise of these strong productions, that, to read, keep one's heart leaping to the throat and the mind in a tumult of anticipation to the end. . . . No series of short stories in modern literature can approach them."—*Hartford Times.*

" If Dr. A. Conan Doyle had not already placed himself in the front rank of living English writers by ' The Refugees,' and other of his larger tories, he would surely do so by these fifteen short tales."—*New York Mail and Express.*

" A strikingly realistic and decidedly original contribution to modern literature."—*Boston Saturday Evening Gazette.*

New York: D. APPLETON & CO., 72 Fifth Avenue.

www.ingramcontent.com/pod-product-compliance
Lightning Source LLC
Chambersburg PA
CBHW021044030726

47496CB00006B/1678